A Candlelight Regency Special

CANDLELIGHT REGENCIES

THE ARROGANT ARISTOCRAT

Rebecca Ashley

A CANDLELIGHT REGENCY SPECIAL

Published by
Dell Publishing Co., Inc.
1 Dag Hammarskjold Plaza
New York, New York 10017

Dell ® TM 681510, Dell Publishing Co., Inc.

ISBN: 0–440–10292–8

Printed in the United States of America
First printing—January 1982

For my father

THE ARROGANT
ARISTOCRAT

CHAPTER 1

"Joanna, you cannot allow some chance-met stranger to procure you vouchers to Almacks!"

"Daphne, he's not a stranger," Joanna explained reasonably. "I talked to him for quite thirty minutes over ices at Gunthers."

"Worse and worse!" Daphne exclaimed as she regarded her pretty younger sister in dismay. "A lady does not allow herself to be engaged with a man in conversation for fully thirty minutes without being properly introduced."

"But we were properly introduced," Joanna said calmly. "He told me his name is Sir Robert Drayton, and I told him mine."

"But you weren't even chaperoned!"

"Of course I was. Cedric was right outside with the horses."

"I believe I shall just sit down for a minute," Daphne said weakly as she sank onto a worn rose settee in the shabby front parlor and looked reprovingly at the cheerful seventeen-year-old girl before her.

Joanna was the beauty of the two sisters, with her curling golden hair and large violet eyes. She had their mother's delicate features as well as her easy laugh and open manner. Daphne knew her own looks were not so striking, although she was admitted to be something of a beauty herself with her blond hair—more a pale yellow than Joanna's burnished gold—and the same violet eyes. Her features, too, were small like Joanna's, although she had a slightly firmer chin and her nose was more prominent than Joanna's tiny retroussé nose.

The problem was, Daphne concluded as she gazed at her younger sister, Joanna was simply *too* beautiful. Joanna also had an alarming penchant for making friends with everyone she met. That, unfortunately, included men.

And men, Daphne thought wryly, were always very eager to be a friend to her petite sister. Daphne sighed as she recalled the devil of a time she had had extricating her sister from the designing clutches of the village rake back home in Clovelly after Joanna had decided to be a friend to him and help him reform his ways. He had been very willing to become more closely acquainted with Joanna, but Daphne suspected the reformation of his morals did not enter anywhere into his motives. And Devonshire rakes, Daphne strongly suspected, didn't hold a candle to London rakes.

She took a deep breath and patted the place beside her on the settee. "Joanna, sit down, dear. Let me explain myself more clearly," she began pleasantly. "I am certain that Sir Robert is a charming person." She doubted the words even as she spoke them, but this was no time to cast slurs on the man and put Joanna in a taking defending him. She continued smoothly: "However, we have precious little money and we are not the kind of people who would be welcome at Almacks. Do you understand?"

"No," Joanna replied promptly, and pursued rapidly as Daphne heaved an audible sigh: "Papa *was* the younger son of an earl even if he was disinherited because he refused to marry the woman his father chose for him. So we are of a class to be included at Almacks."

"Joanna, I wish you will see it behooves us to use what little money we have to find ourselves situations as governesses or companions. After all, the good vicar has only given us the use of this house until the end of July, and that is just three more months. After that, it is already rented to someone, and we will have to be gone. But the cost of living here alone—food and what few other necessities we have had to buy—has been much greater than I had anticipated. It will take all of our money to live in London for the next few months. After that, we shall be wholly without funds. Therefore we must make the most of what money we have to try to locate genteel positions." Daphne had finished her logical explanation and now looked at Joanna. "Do you understand?"

"Of course I do," Joanna declared warmly.

"Good," Daphne said, and began to rise, congratulating herself on her ability to handle her sister.

"But you do not," Joanna objected. "I *told* Sir Robert that we have very little money, and I told him I didn't think we could rig ourselves out in any sort of style to go to Almacks. That's why I declined at first. But he told me—really, Daphne, he's the nicest man—that it wouldn't matter what I wore because he was certain I should shine in anything I chose, and if my sister looked anything like me, she would too. Naturally I told him that you are *very* beautiful, and he said, then it was settled and he would send his carriage around to us Wednesday next to take us to Almacks."

Daphne dropped back onto the settee and put her head in both hands, offering a silent plea for help from some quarter before trying again. "Do you mean to tell me, Joanna, that you told Sir Robert we barely had a feather to fly with, and he said it was of no consequence?"

"Yes," Joanna nodded excitedly. "In fact, he said he thought something could be arranged."

"I have little doubt," Daphne commented dryly, "that I know what sort of arrangements he had in mind."

"Yes. Well, I hope you do see now that he is really the very nicest of men, so it wouldn't be at all the thing to cry off from going to Almacks, when he is putting himself to so much trouble on our behalf." Joanna finished with a happy smile: "If that's all, Daphne, I believe I shall go upstairs now and select something suitable to wear. Perhaps I could sew some trim on my green muslin to cover the small stain on the bodice."

"Joanna," Daphne said with a rising note of impatience in her voice, "ladies wear the finest silks and velvets to Almacks. They do not wear patched muslins—which is yet another reason why we cannot go."

"We shall start a new trend," Joanna called gaily, dancing from the room.

"Yes," Daphne muttered to the empty room, "or Sir Robert Drayton will start a new trend by taking his intended mistress to Almacks."

She sighed and ran her hand restlessly over the fading rose velvet of the settee, her fingers worrying the nap back and forth. Life had become terribly complicated all of a sudden. When her father had died a little over a year ago, Daphne had felt quite competent to manage the small family home near Clovelly. Really, there had been precious little choice, since they had no other relatives to take them in. But that was a matter of no consequence, since life was a relatively uncomplicated affair in their little coastal community.

The neighbors all knew the Brown girls and knew that their father had been a respectable gentleman farmer. And their servants were trusted family friends. Why, even now Daphne thought of Cedric, their very improbable butler, as more of an uncle than a servant. And Rose, the cheerful, pink-cheeked housekeeper, was like an older sister to Daphne and Joanna.

The death of their father marked the beginning of the disasters that were to befall them. The crops also failed that year, and their one set of tenant farmers moved on, leaving the girls with an acreage they could not manage themselves. The payments of debts that had for some time been owing on the house could be delayed no longer. To settle those obligations, they had been forced to sell the property; precious little money had remained after that.

12

The kind vicar had attempted to help them find positions in a household in Devonshire, but in such remote communities few companions and governesses were needed, and certainly the good wives did not look to fill what vacancies there were with lovely young girls. In the end he had realized the futility of seeking employment for them in that shire and had given them a letter of introduction to take to an agency in London, where he allowed them the use of his house. It seemed the only way. The little household had removed to the great city to find acceptable positions. Rose and Cedric had insisted on accompanying Daphne and Joanna; they had been with the family for so long that they could not conceive of remaining behind. Once the girls found employment, Rose and Cedric would return to situations awaiting them in Clovelly.

"Miss Daphne"—the butler interrupted her thoughts—"would you be able to manage without me for an hour or so? I have some, er, ahem, business matters to attend to."

"Of course, Cedric." Then wickedly she added, "And, Cedric, I *do* hope your cock wins."

He looked guiltily horrified. "How did you kn—? That is, whatever makes you suppose that I would indulge in such a pastime?" he asked with a belated attempt at hauteur.

Daphne looked at the tall, thin man with a shock of white hair who stood before her in the doorway. She smiled ruefully at the sight of his discolored red livery, livery that he had insisted on dragging out of the attic in Devonshire and bringing to London with him. He had been a butler in London before, he had informed her majestically, and he would do them proud. The poor dear did seem to be trying awfully hard, always remembering to attach a "Miss" to their first names and pompously announcing what few callers they had as if he were announcing royalty.

"It's just a hunch, mind you," she said, suppressing her smile, "but one of my clues is that there are enough feathers strewn about the house to make a fair-sized mattress."

He shifted uncomfortably.

"Go and enjoy yourself, Cedric," she said with a good-natured laugh. She watched him leave, then rose and walked out to the narrow flight of steps that hugged the wall on one side of the little hall.

With one hand she held up her blue poplin gown as she slowly mounted the stairs, taking care not to trip on the two places where the carpet runner had been worn into a large frayed mass. With her other hand she felt along the wall, touching the wallpaper. It must have been beautiful when it was first applied some years ago, she thought. But now the pastoral scenes of frolicking shepherdesses and fluffy lambs were discolored with both age and large brown stains, which hinted the roof might leak when it rained.

Without intending to, Daphne found herself going to her room and looking at the meager selection of frocks in her wardrobe. She chose one she might be able to make presentable to wear to Almacks, then stopped in surprise as she realized fully what she was doing.

Well, she thought defensively, it *would* be nice to go to Almacks just once. Not, of course, that such an event was possible. It would be highly improper for Sir Robert to procure vouchers for them. Should he do so, it would be totally lacking in decorum to accept such invitations from a stranger to whom they had not been formally introduced.

Still . . . Her mind wandered off into a pleasant daydream in which she was in a large ballroom surrounded by men and women dressed in fashionable elegance. Thousands of winking candles in crystal chandeliers threw a soft glow across the room while musicians played a stately waltz.

14

She sighed. If things had been different and her father had not been disinherited, then dancing at Almacks would be one of the things she did in the course of her season, she reflected wistfully. Now it was forever beyond her reach, and only in her imagination would she ever visit those exclusive assembly rooms.

The fantasy was pleasant, for all that, she thought, holding a white cotton dress in front of her. She began to turn slowly about the small bedroom, dancing gracefully as she hummed softly and imagined herself in the arms of a tall, handsome man, who was murmuring pretty nothings into her ear and declaring that she must marry him. He was tilted, charming, and outrageously wealthy, he was also top over tail in love with her. She smiled to herself and continued to dance.

In a very different bedroom, not so very far away, another conversation was taking place. Two men, both of them dressed in the first stare of fashion, were sipping brandy and looking out the window at the well-dressed passersby in dignified St. James's Square.

One of the men—tall, dark-haired, with gray eyes in a handsome if almost craggy face—was speaking to his shorter, stouter companion. "Do you mean to tell me, Robert, that you have asked some unknown chit to go to Almacks," he demanded incredulously, "and had the audacity to tell her you could procure her vouchers?"

"I say, Mark, you don't understand in the least," Robert remonstrated. "This is no ordinary chit—she's a real beauty."

"So are my matched bays, but I'm not promising them vouchers to Almacks," the taller man snapped. "Although," he continued, "I daresay they should stand a better chance than some streetwalker you happened onto at Gunthers."

"She's a perfect lady!" Robert protested hotly.

15

"No doubt she is," his companion said dryly "Look here, Robert, why do you not give her a green gown and have done with it. There's no call to squire her about town drawing attention to your indiscretions."

Robert puffed up indignantly "See here, Mark, I'll not have you talking of the young lady in that offensive way My intentions toward her are perfectly honorable Besides, she wouldn't accept a *carte blanche;* she's not the type."

His companion gave a short laugh at Robert's final sentence, since it somewhat belied the honor of his intentions Taking another sip of brandy, he walked nonchalantly to a massive Chippendale wing chair upholstered in muslin and adorned with green crewelwork flowers. He dropped into the chair, then absently placed his glass on the floor, beside one exquisitely carved claw-and-ball leg. With some amusement he studied Robert, who was still standing near the arched window pulling restlessly at the green Venetian silk drapes.

At four and twenty Sir Robert Drayton seemed to fall in love a good deal, Mark thought, and always with the most honorable of intentions. Intentions that he usually maintained reverently for the first few days, after which he would begin to hunger for more tangible displays of affection than a mere touch of his beloved's hand or the honor of escorting her about Of course, Mark knew this chit would be no different from the rest of Robert's light-skirts. What confounded him was what maggot had gotten into the boy's head to tell such a whisker about being able to obtain vouchers to Almacks for her and her sister

He carelessly crossed one well-formed leg over the other and idly picked bits of lint off his expensive blue superfine coat "You can't get her vouchers, you know." Mark observed casually

Robert abruptly ceased abusing the curtains and crossed the room to sprawl dejectedly in a matching Chippendale chair. "That's the rub. *I* might have a bit of difficulty, but you, being the marquis of Stranham—now, that's altogether a different matter. You could get the vouchers easily, especially since you have such a way with the ladies. I don't think the patronesses would refuse *you,* so I thought perhaps—" He broke off and looked hopefully at the dark-haired man.

"No," Lord Stranham said calmly, and picked up his glass to take a slow sip of brandy.

"You don't even know what I'm going to ask," Robert objected.

"I have a damn good idea, and the answer is no! Good God, Robert, what do you take me for? I'm not going to get your bits of muslin vouchers to the most exclusive rooms in London. That's the most harebrained thing you've ever asked me to do."

"Would you ask your lady mother to get them? The duchess shouldn't have any problem."

"I was wrong," Lord Stranham said with firm conviction. *"That* is the most harebrained thing you have ever asked me to do and the answer is an emphatic, unequivocal *no!"*

"I'll give you time to think about it, before I accept your final answer," Robert offered largely. "In the meantime I shall try elsewhere."

"Excellent idea. You might ask that madman in Piccadilly who walks about with the placard proclaiming the world is coming to an end. You and he should deal extremely well together, since you're both a couple of downy birds."

"I might ask Prinny," Robert said in a sudden burst of inspiration.

"I am proven wrong again. That madman doesn't hold a candle to you. You're the downier bird by half," Lord Stranham pronounced with a shake of his head.

Robert changed tactics, looking slyly at Lord Stranham

17

before saying in a suggestive voice, "She's a dashed beautiful armful, and if her sister is anywhere nearly as beautiful, wellll—" He drew the implicating word out meaningfully.

Lord Stranham laughed good-naturedly. "You mean, you would introduce me to the sister if I'll do you this one small favor? Really, Robert, do you think I need you to arrange my romances for me? I may be getting a bit old compared to you, but I think at one and thirty I can still contrive to make my own arrangements." He set the empty glass on the thick Aubusson rug and uncrossed his legs.

"And now, Robert, I find that this talk is becoming a bit tedious, and I have an appointment at Whites. I beg you will excuse me. Would you care to come along?" he asked politely as he rose.

"No, I've got to talk to some *friends.*" Robert enunciated the last word carefully while glaring at Lord Stranham. "I'll have one of them obtain vouchers for me."

"I wish you luck." The marquis laughed as the dejected young man flung himself out the bedroom door. "I fancy you will need a good deal of it to execute this hen-witted scheme," he added to himself with an amused shake of his head.

CHAPTER 2

Daphne took the card Cedric solemnly presented to her, and looked at it in confusion. "I have never heard of Lady Morley," she murmured. "I cannot think why she should call on us."

"She appeared respectable," Cedric ventured, "so I took the liberty of seating her in the parlor."

"Of course," Daphne said, untying her apron and tossing it aside. Perhaps the dear vicar knew the lady and had written to her about their desire to find employment. She patted down her hair and smoothed the skirts of her lavender day dress before proceeding down the hall to the parlor.

Inside the room she found a tiny woman with pink-red hair seated on the rose settee. She was dressed in a startling green pelerine with matching hat. A pair of spectacles sat far down on her nose, and she peered through them intently as she looked about the room.

"Lady Morley," Daphne said quietly.

"Oh, my!" the old woman shrieked.

"I am sorry. I didn't mean to alarm you." Daphne walked toward her guest. "I am Daphne Brown."

Lady Morley peered nearsightedly at her, nodded, and settled back on the settee. "I am most pleased to make your acquaintance, my dear. I hope I do not intrude on you at an awkward moment, but I thought it best to come immediately."

"Immediately, Lady Morley?"

"Why, yes, with the vouchers. I daresay you knew they would be forthcoming, but it is always agreeable to have

19

these matters confirmed. So hard to get," she confided, leaning nearer and attempting to focus her eyes on Daphne.

"Vouchers?" she repeated in confusion.

"Yes. You and your sister have obtained tickets to Almacks. But did you ever doubt it, with your connections?" The older woman cackled cheerfully before beginning to search through the bright green recticule on the seat beside her, mumbling as she rummaged, "I have them here somewhere."

"Lady Morley, I fear there is some mistake. I cannot think why we should be invited to Almacks. We are connected with no one in the *ton*. We do not even have a sponsor and—"

"Here they are! No one to sponsor you? Why, child, don't be ridiculous. With relations and a background such as yours, of course you are invited. I understand you and your sister have but lately come to London, but that does not alter the fact of your parents' breeding. Indeed, you have vouchers. We do not forget our own."

Daphne wordlessly accepted the envelope Lady Morley pressed into her hand. Did this woman mean to say that the fact that their father had been disinherited no longer mattered, since he *had* been of the nobility? But why should she go to so much trouble on their behalf?

"Lady Morley, were you acquainted with my parents?"

The older woman squinted her eyes in thought. "Yes, I believe I was," she said uncertainly. "As I recollect, they were exceedingly amiable people. Do you have a dress to wear to the assembly rooms, dear?"

"Well, I—yes, I think so."

"I didn't mean to pry." Lady Morley looked around the room, appearing to see, in spite of her deficient vision, that it was not the home of a wealthy person. "But this house is a bit—"

"It needs a great many repairs," Daphne finished for her.

"Precisely. That is what I meant to say. I trust you do not own it?" she inquired tactfully.

"No, we only have it for a few months."

"I quite understand. It is so very hard to find suitable accommodations in London during the season, and one is often *forced* to take whatever is available. Although"—she looked around doubtfully—"I have never known anyone to take such lodgings as this."

"We had very little choice," Daphne said politely.

"Of course. Well, as I have said, one is often incommoded by the severe lack of housing. I shall look about to see if I might be able to help you obtain something better," she offered.

"I thank you, but that won't be necessary." Daphne could have added that these accommodations were the result of their lack of funds rather than the general shortage of lodgings, but she wisely did not. If Lady Morley had memories of her family from better times, then Daphne didn't wish to disillusion her by telling her how very hard were the days on which they had now fallen. Besides, she was obviously a very dear person to have gone to so much trouble to obtain vouchers for them to such exclusive rooms.

But really, they could not accept such a favor. After all, their purpose for being in London was to find situations. "Lady Morley, I kindly thank you for your interest in us, but, you see, our reason for coming to London is to—" She broke off tactfully. She didn't wish to say they had come to find employment. "We are here to meet people who can assist us in the future."

"You'll meet any number of people at Almacks—regular crush," Lady Morley observed, pushing herself out of her seat with difficulty.

Daphne started to protest further and then stopped. It

would be rude to decline the invitations. Besides, what could it hurt for her and Joanna to have one night to enjoy themselves as other young ladies did?

As her guest slowly stood Daphne came to a belated sense of her duties as a hostess. "Do stay for tea, Lady Morley."

"I regret I cannot. There is to be a whist party this evening and I wish to return home immediately to practice a few rubbers beforehand. So very nice to meet you. I shall come round in my carriage for you and your sister at eight on Wednesday next to take you to the assembly rooms."

"You're very kind, my lady. I am deeply sensible of the great honor you do my sister and me; we appreciate it more than I can tell you."

"Of course," the old woman mumbled as she groped her way to the door. "Charming to talk with you, my dear. I don't doubt you will be the toast of the season with such as your cousin to introduce you." She gave a final rueful glance around the room. "I shouldn't worry overmuch about the house. You have only to lie about your address should anyone ask you. Lying is completely acceptable, you know. Everyone does it. Once something more suitable is found, you can move and no harm done."

Daphne nodded agreeably and closed the door behind her visitor. She waited a suitable length of time before allowing a small chortle of elation to escape her. Almacks! It was as if the skies had opened up and showered a miracle down on her. She had never thought to meet anyone who would remember her father's position and look after her best interests because of him. A brief frown creased her brow as she recalled Lady Morley's words concerning a cousin. Her father, she thought, had no living relatives, and her grandfather had given the estate to charity rather than leaving it to a son who had incurred his displeasure. Daphne had no time to think on such matters now, however; she was far too excited. At twenty she was still young enough to relish the thought of going to a grand entertainment.

She forced herself to make a ladylike ascent up the steps, then proceeded down the short hall to Joanna's room; but now her eagerness to speak of their good fortune could no longer be stifled. "You will never conceive what has happened," she cried as she burst into the room.

"What?" her sister demanded, looking up from a letter she was writing.

"We have received vouchers to Almacks!"

Joanna accepted her words equably. "Sir Robert told me he would attend to the matter. Obviously he has."

"Sir Robert, pooh. We should certainly never go if *he* had arranged for them; that would be totally improper. But these have been brought by a respectable woman who remembers Papa. Was that not kind of her, to look after our welfare?"

"She mentioned nothing of Sir Robert?" Joanna asked, a deflated note in her voice.

"Don't be a goose! He has nothing to say to this. I told you, we could not accept the invitations if I thought he had. You must forget all about him, my dear. I'm persuaded he is nothing more than a Corinthian."

"But he *did* promise vouchers to Almacks and now they are come," Joanna insisted.

Daphne settled onto the small bed in the sparsely furnished room, smiling happily. "Yes, they are come. Only think how delightful it will be to be among such refined and elegant people. It was so very kind of Lady Morley."

"How did she discover we were in town?"

Daphne knit her brow in thought. "I don't really know, but she did say something about the *ton* not forgetting their own, so I daresay they have ways of knowing. Anyway, it does not signify. What is important is that just when I thought things were darkest, something good has happened to us."

"You had no success at the employment agency?" Joanna probed.

The older sister looked down at the homemade coverlet, studying it carefully. She had not told Joanna what the result of her interview had been; she had not wanted to worry her any more than was absolutely necessary. But the truth of the matter was that it had gone very badly. A sharp-eyed woman in a muddy-brown dress had asked Daphne some curt questions before folding her hands on the desk in front of her and saying darkly that *her* agency did not obtain situations for young ladies who had no practical experience. The look she had bestowed on Daphne seemed to say she did not think Daphne a proper young lady and she certainly was not in the way of dealing with less than respectable persons. Why, the woman had treated her like some sort of light-skirt who sought to find a job in a gentleman's home! It had been thoroughly humiliating.

"I do not think she had anything at present." Daphne evaded her sister's question, still regarding the coverlet. "No doubt she will notify me should something come available."

"Oh."

With a gesture of her hand that expressed defeat, Daphne said mournfully, "Perhaps I should have married Clarence Woodson when he asked me."

"He was a crude beast of a man!" Joanna replied spiritedly. "The only reason you gave any thought to marrying him at all was that you wanted to make certain I was provided for. I won't have you sacrificing yourself for my sake; we talked of this before we decided to come to London and look for positions. I know you have always been protective of me, but you must see that I shall have to look after myself now and make my own way in life. I should be looking for a situation now if you did not insist that I wait until you found one first."

24

"Of course, dear," Daphne murmured.

She only wished her younger sister were better equipped to do so. But with her trusting ways and innocent belief in everyone, Daphne was afraid Joanna would never be in a position to manage for herself. What Joanna needed was a husband who loved and respected her, one who would look after her. But the hope of her younger sister marrying such a man had died when they had lost the farm. Very few young men were in a financial way to marry without regard to money.

"Daphne, you are not attending me." Her sister's words brought her from her reverie. "What will you wear to Almacks?"

Putting aside the worrisome concern of what was to become of them, Daphne joined her sister in a lighthearted discussion of clothes. Later, she resolved, she would write to the vicar and see what further means of seeking employment he could suggest.

Over the next few days Joanna threw herself into making over her second-best white muslin. Daphne dragged her own pale blue chiffon from the wardrobe, trimmed the two wide flounces at the bottom with lace, and replaced the discolored blue sash with a new white satin one which tied just below her bosom to form a high Empire waist.

The afternoon of the assembly she and Joanna took turns doing each other's hair. Joanna's long golden locks were scooped up in a crown of little curls; stray tendrils framed her face. Daphne's long blond hair was caught back in a Grecian knot, her face also framed by curls. Surveying herself in the murky cheval glass, Daphne thought she looked quite nice.

Tonight she and Joanna would enjoy themselves. She had already posted her letter to the vicar, who would surely write them shortly with some excellent advice on how to obtain employment. All would soon be well, she prayed.

CHAPTER 3

Daphne's eyes wandered around the noisy, glittering room. They had been in London for two weeks, and although she had seen a few ladies of fashion riding in their smart perch phaetons down Bond Street or entering the shops of exclusive modistes, she had not yet beheld such a gathering as this! She was awed in spite of herself. Scores of beautiful women graced Almacks' small assembly rooms, dancing with a gay grace or sitting on straight-back chairs flirting with highly interested men. And their clothes! High-waisted gowns of Indian muslin and other diaphanous materials, cut in shockingly revealing styles, clearly displayed their manifold feminine charms.

Joanna, too, was noting the women's clothes as she and Daphne settled themselves in a corner of the room. She gazed at their clinging gowns with eyes open wide, then glanced down uncertainly at her own bosom demurely concealed in her girlish white frock. "Daphne," she whispered, "look at the women's dresses! Some of them are quite shocking!"

"Yes."

"Do you see that lady across the room who is wearing the yellow gown with no shoulders? The one leaning close to the fair-haired man? He seems to be—well, I don't know—almost leering!"

"He *is* leering," Daphne affirmed as she looked at the hopeful admirer of a well-endowed woman whose charms were perilously close to spilling forth from her gown.

Daphne turned her attention back to the crowded room. The men's dress, she noted, was quite as remarkable as the ladies'. Their light-colored inexpressibles were topped with darker-colored coats of blue, green, and black; and all wore highly starched milk-white cravats tied in intricate and varying patterns.

Two hours later the glamour of studying the clothes and people of the *ton* had paled, and Daphne was in a decidedly irritable mood. Lady Morley had arrived for them at the exact time she had said she would. Her tiny figure had been shrouded in a high-necked purple gown, and on her head she wore a huge purple turban; she had kept up a pleasant monologue in the carriage all the way to Almacks. Once inside the assembly rooms, she had motioned the girls to seats in the corner, murmured something about their relative arriving shortly, and then wandered off.

After an hour of sitting unnoticed by anyone, Daphne had made a search for the older woman. She had discovered Lady Morley in a card room, lost to all that was going forward around her as she fretted over a bad hand. At Daphne's appearance and gentle hint that she and Joanna were alone, Lady Morley had nodded absently before asking a fellow player if it was her turn.

"Lady Morley," Daphne had pursued, to the obvious annoyance of all at the card table, "Joanna and I are much in want of company."

"Certainly, my dear, certainly. I shall be there momentarily. Did I take that trick?"

Daphne had returned to the ballroom to await her chaperon's arrival. Now, an hour later and still without benefit of Lady Morley's company, Daphne's kind feelings were all but gone. Their companion, she thought, was rather eccentric. Surely it was not the common action of a woman of breeding to leave two girls alone in a huge ballroom where they were not known.

And they were not becoming any more known as the night progressed. Neither one of the girls had been approached by anyone since they had entered the room, and

28

Daphne knew quite well that this was not because of their undesirability, as she had seen a great many gentlemen casting longing looks in their direction. The reason no one had ventured over to speak with them was that it was not known who they were or with whom they were connected.

For a time Daphne had thought one particular gentleman *was* going to come over and speak with them. In fact, he had watched them so carefully that Daphne had become considerably annoyed by his boldness. Now, as she glanced at the tall dark-haired man in a green waistcoat and buff pantaloons, she noted with chagrin that he was still watching them.

Daphne had observed him giving her and Joanna several minutes' hard scrutiny when they had first arrived, and since then he strolled about the room, talking to a lady here or a group of gentlemen there, but always his eyes came back to them within the space of a few minutes. He was an exceedingly handsome man, Daphne had to admit, but his countenance held much of condescension and arrogance.

Daphne was aware that Joanna was not unduly perturbed by their lack of a chaperon. Instead, as she looked about the room her delicate face was a study of happy expectancy, and her violet eyes were shining with excitement. Daphne did not doubt that the hope of seeing Sir Robert Drayton was the cause of Joanna's high spirits.

"There is Sir Robert!" Joanna cried as she grabbed her sister's arm.

Daphne turned quickly toward the door to see a red-haired man of average stature. His rust coat was cut away at the waist and fell into long tails behind, revealing a slightly rounded stomach. But what immediately caught her attention was the mindless smile he was bestowing on all and sundry.

"A half-witted coxcomb," she whispered, but Joanna did not hear her. She was starting up from her chair when

Daphne caught her by the arm. "Sit down," she ordered tersely.

"But he has not seen us!"

"Joanna," she said firmly, "you will not make a cake of yourself by running across the room to him. If he means to speak to us, he will come over here."

The younger girl subsided back into the chair impatiently, her eyes wistfully following the red-haired man about the room as he nodded to acquaintances and bowed to ladies. Daphne's eyes followed him far more critically. From the cut of his tight-fitting coat and the pure white of his unmentionables as well as the lazy indifference he affected as he stopped occasionally to survey the room with his quizzing-glass, she judged him to be a tulip of the *ton*. And that, she thought with a sniff, was probably the best that could be said for him.

"Oh, look," Joanna breathed, "he's stopping to talk to that tall, handsome man."

Daphne was looking. The man Sir Robert paused to speak with was the same man who had been watching them all evening.

On the other side of the room, beneath the orchestra's balcony, Lord Stranham greeted Robert abruptly: "Where the hell have you been?"

"Unavoidably detained, couldn't be helped. Is she here?" he asked, looking anxiously around.

"They're here, all right," the marquis snarled.

"Where?"

"Over in the corner," Lord Stranham gave a slight jerk of his head in their direction.

"Why aren't they dancing?"

"You fool, they haven't been approached by the first person because no one here knows who they are."

"Where's Lady Morley? She was to make introductions for them," Robert said, looking around curiously.

"She is where she can generally be found—in the card room. I daresay she has forgotten the chits completely."

"Why didn't you go over to them?" Robert asked accusingly.

"That," Lord Stranham began ominously, "is a very interesting question. I should have done so, improper as it would have been, save that I happened across Lady Jersey earlier. She cooed and tapped her fan on my arm and asked the dashed oddest questions about my fair-haired relations. I didn't know what the hell she was talking about, and since I didn't know if you'd told those chits some equally rum story, I decided to wait until you arrived."

"Oh." Robert laughed nervously. "I can explain Sally's words."

"For your sake, I do hope so," Lord Stranham muttered as he directed a penetrating look at the younger man.

Robert looked slightly discomfited, then continued with dignity: "I told Lady Morley—she got the vouchers for me from Sally—that they were some distant relatives of yours lately returned from Ireland."

"I do hope," Lord Stranham said, "that you are enjoying your last few minutes of health."

"See here, Mark, I had to tell her something," he argued defensively, adding logically, "they don't just give vouchers to Almacks to anyone, you know."

"How positively lame-brained of me to have forgotten that," the marquis said with a menacing look at his companion.

Robert wisely retreated backwards a step and offered a weak smile. "I guess I did take a bit of advantage of your name, but I knew the patronesses wouldn't refuse the vouchers for any relatives of yours."

"Do you not think," Lord Stranham began irritably, "that it may have been a subject of some discussion to the

31

patronesses that I have not yet approached my dear cousins?"

"We can discuss that matter later," Robert temporized. "Right now the thing is to go over there and get them out of that infernal corner. By the by, what do you think of her?"

"I collect that by 'her' you are referring to the one in white with the straw-colored hair?"

"Gold," Robert corrected with a fond look toward Joanna.

"She's a beauty, I must admit. Her sister is damned comely too, although she's been casting looks about the room for the past hour that make me suspect she would very much like to murder the person who invited them here and then left them stranded. I shall, of course, cheerfully assist her in that endeavor."

"She doesn't know I saw to their tickets," Robert informed his friend. "Come along, Mark," he prompted impatiently. "Let us find Lady Morley to introduce them around. We can't leave them sitting there all evening."

"How remiss of me not to have thought of that," Lord Stranham said dryly as he and Robert skirted the dancers to the door and proceeded to the card room in search of the chaperon.

They found her looking highly indignant. "I am certain the ace was my card! Whatever do you mean that I played the nine, Mr. Breuner?"

"Lady Morley," Sir Robert interrupted her courteously, "would you do me the honor of allowing me to escort you back to the ballroom?"

"What? Oh, yes, I daresay I ought," she grumbled. "I am accomplishing precious little here, although I am persuaded I am not being properly credited for the cards I play. Are you certain, Mr. Breuner, that it was not my ace?"

Sir Robert helped her rise, then steered her to the ballroom. "So very kind of you to have brought the Brown girls with you," he said. "I trust my carriage was acceptable for your use?"

"Perfectly, I thank you. I do hope mine is mended soon. So dreadfully inconvenient to ride about in my curricle." As they approached Daphne and Joanna, Lady Morley stretched her hand out toward the two girls. "I know you are enjoying yourselves, my dears," she said brightly.

The two men bowed politely. Joanna smiled warmly up at Sir Robert while Daphne regarded first the baronet and then Lord Stranham far less amiably than did her sister.

Lady Morley made the introductions, and the proper remarks were exchanged before the older lady excused herself. "Lady Jersey beckons," she informed them gaily, "but I shall return shortly. I leave you in good hands," she told Daphne as she turned to leave.

"Miss Brown"—Sir Robert addressed himself to Joanna, unaware that Daphne was even there, let alone that she was favoring him with a very sour glare—"I am sorry I could not have been here sooner."

Joanna smiled sweetly, nearly bubbling with pleasure. "We have been vastly entertained by the glamour of the people present."

"I was unavoidably detained," he continued glibly, "but now we must make up for lost time. Will you do me the honor of this dance, or are you already engaged?"

Daphne's cheeks flamed furiously. How dare he make sport of her sister? Already engaged indeed! It was quite plain they were not, nor had they been anytime these two hours past.

But Joanna seemed to find nothing amiss in Sir Robert's question and accepted happily.

As she and the baronet swept off to dance, Lord Stranham offered his hand to Daphne. "I should be very honored if you would consent to stand up with me for this set."

"I am here as my sister's chaperon, so I cannot dance," she replied in clipped tones, and then turned her eyes to follow her sister about the floor. It was a duty that had been thrust on her, she considered waspishly. She had thought Lady Morley would play the role, but that was merely another instance where she had overestimated her ladyship.

"You are acting as your sister's chaperon?" He sounded slightly confused.

"Yes, my lord."

"I see," he said slowly. "Forgive me, it is just that you look so very young. Do you mind if I sit and talk with you?"

"As you wish, my lord," Daphne replied with a faint smile. She had no desire to be rude, but neither did she wish to be distracted from watching her sister and Sir Robert.

"Thank you." He seated himself in Joanna's chair. "You are new to London?" he began amiably.

"Yes." Her eyes never left the dancing couple as they threaded their way among the other dancers, past swirling draperies and well-cut coats.

As she sat stiffly beside him the marquis regarded her in dismay. Whatever had possessed Robert to get these two chits invited to Almacks? And in his name! This girl's gown was hopelessly démodé, and her pitiful attempts to improve it with snatches of cheap lace and a new ribbon were not at all successful. It was probably for the best, he decided, that no one had asked them to dance. At least that meant no one else had been close enough to see how tawdry their clothes were.

"Will you be staying in London long?" he asked as a point of information. He certainly hoped not; he didn't want these chits parading about while people thought they were related to him!

"No, my lord. We do not expect to remain longer than three months."

She sensed his relief. What difference did it make to him how long she stayed in London? she thought indignantly. Perhaps he did not think she was grand enough to attend functions where he was present; he appeared just that toplofty. Well, he might think himself a nonpareil, but she found him excessively haughty and disagreeable. But that was entirely what she would have expected of a friend of Sir Robert's.

CHAPTER 4

"How was Armacks?" asked Cedric, in a convivial mood as he seated himself in a sagging wing chair in the front parlor and looked at Daphne, who was seated across from him, on the settee.

She stared right back at him. His nose was slightly red and bulbous, as if he had been in a fight—or, more likely, had been imbibing.

"You've been drinking!" she accused.

"No!" he denied emphatically and with a suspicious haste.

"You have," she pressed, leaning forward and looking, or attempting to look, into his averted eyes.

"I 'aven't touched a drop. Not the first one!" he declared feelingly to the floor.

"Ced-ric." She drew his name out accusingly.

"Not a touch." He wavered under her steady gaze. "Well, maybe I did have just the very tiniest bit of a nip," he conceded.

She looked at him sternly. "You promised you wouldn't," she reminded him in a wounded voice.

"I didn't 'ave enough to 'urt anything, just a mug or two." Deciding it would definitely be to his best interest to change the subject, Cedric tried again. "Er, 'ow was Armacks?"

"The correct name is Almacks and it was terrible."

"I see," he said ponderously. "Then you and Miss Joanna did not enjoy yourselves?"

"Oh, Joanna enjoyed herself immensely. Once Lady Morley finally introduced us to some people, she was the

37

hit of the evening, or," she added dryly, "what was left of it. Joanna seems to have attracted one particular man."

"You don't like 'im?"

"Sir Robert Drayton is his name, and no, I do not. He had met Joanna at Gunthers and I fear she encouraged him in her charming and unaffected way. He must know that she is an innocent young girl and practically unprotected. It is possible he thinks her an easy mark. He may even mean to seek an alliance with her, and it would not be marriage. Men are very unscrupulous in London."

The butler paled. "I'll kill 'im!"

"No, you won't, Cedric," she reassured him, "because I shall demand that satisfaction myself if he ever so much as makes the first improper move toward her. Actually, I think I have made a good beginning to nipping the whole affair in the bud. He asked for permission to call and I told him I didn't know when we should be free to receive callers. My manner was a good deal less than inviting."

"You wouldn't be supposing Miss Joanna would be slipping out to see 'im?" asked the butler worriedly.

"Now, Cedric, you know Joanna would give herself away. There is scant way she could contrive to conceal from us any liaisons she might contemplate with Sir Robert."

"I'll watch 'er sharp just the same."

"Thank you, Cedric. Now, I have some matters to attend to. I received a note only this morning from the vicar in Clovelly. He has kindly included a letter from the squire's sister, Millie, who sends an introduction to her cousin Mrs. Winter. Mr. and Mrs. Winter live quite close to us, and Millie suggested we might be able to meet some people through them and thus find situations. I have sent a note inviting them to dinner next week and don't doubt they will accept." Daphne didn't tell her butler that there had been a strong hint in Millie's letter that her cousin was a snob. Reading between the lines, Daphne had detected a suggestion that it would be better not to tell Mrs. Winter immediately that they were looking for positions, or that lady might not introduce them to anyone. "I have a great many things to do to prepare for them." Daphne rose as she spoke, and moved toward the door.

"If you needs me, I shall, of course, be available," Cedric announced as he crossed his legs casually and leaned back in the chair, closing his eyes as he did so.

Daphne smiled as she walked to the crowded kitchen, where the cook and the housekeeper were engaged in a battle over whether to serve York ham or capon to the guests. When Daphne suggested roast beef, the two horrified women united under the banner of ham, loudly extolling its virtues and endeavoring to change her mind.

The cook, a plump young girl newly hired from the neighborhood, assured Daphne she was on very good terms with the butcher. He would, she declared with a saucy smile, reserve an excellent ham for them if she but asked him to.

"Well," Daphne said hesitantly, "if you're certain that is the proper thing to serve. I do so want to make a good impression."

"Oh, indeed it is," Rose assured her sagely, nodding her head so firmly her cap flew off.

"Very well, ham it is"—Daphne capitulated—"and I shall draw up the rest of the menu now. I also need to make a list of the cleaning to be done and the windows are all terribly dirty, and oh—" She broke off with a defeated gesture. "There's so very much to be done. I had no idea the house would be in such a sad state."

The two women murmured sympathetic words about the deplorable state of the house as they turned back to their tasks, the cook bending over the wide open brick hearth to stir something in a black kettle while Rose ducked around the hanging spoons, pans, and ladles that projected out from the wall as she lunged at something with a rolling pin.

"What are you doing, Rose?" Daphne asked curiously, stopping in the act of leaving the room.

"Mice."

"Merciful heavens!" Daphne exclaimed in dismay. "Mice! And you're killing them with the rolling pin!?"

"Not a bit of it. I haven't hit the first one," Rose demurred, "but I shall clean the rolling pin afterwards if I do."

Lord Stranham was also considering the question of food as he sat in the sunny breakfast parlor of his spacious Palladian mansion, looking out through the bow window to the clipped green hedges of the garden. He took another bite of toast and then applied himself to the sirloin, pausing in his meal to glance up casually as Robert dashed into the room and began pulling on his arm.

"Mark, you've got to come with me," the baronet declared breathlessly. "It's urgent!"

"Is the house afire?" the marquis asked with no sign of agitation.

"No, of course not," his guest replied with some exasperation.

"Then I think I do not have to leave, which is quite wonderful, as I deplore the thought of leaving such a sumptuous breakfast. Do have some buttered eggs," he invited cordially, holding the platter up for inspection.

The younger man waved them aside impatiently. "We must call on the Brown girls."

"Do you know, Robert, there are two things I have come to object to in your manner of late? One is your unenforceable penchant for ordering me about, and the second is your lamentable habit of acting as if 'the Brown girls' were a matter of the least concern to me."

"But don't you see?" Robert persisted. "If I don't call

on Miss Joanna immediately, one of those other bucks from last night may do so first."

"I collected from the elder Miss Brown's remarks to you that she and her sister would not be at home to any callers this morning, and I do believe I detected the strong hint that they would not be at home to you on any morning."

"No," Robert argued, shifting his weight in his agitation and blocking the marquis's view to the garden. "You don't understand in the least. I told Miss Joanna I would call this morning, so she'll be expecting me."

Lord Stranham looked at his friend levelly, took one bite of the buttered eggs, and wiped his mouth with a linen napkin. "It is my considered opinion, Robert, that you are a fool."

"Why do you say that?" demanded Robert, shocked.

"That miniature mother hen of a Miss Brown won't let you in the front door. From the looks she divided equally between us last night, she suspects that any interest you have in her sister's virtue takes the form of lusting after it."

"I told you," Robert explained long-sufferingly, "my intentions are honorable."

"Tell her," Lord Stranham suggested dryly.

"Well," the younger man pursued relentlessly, "at any rate, I think you should come with me, since they are sponsored at Almacks under your name."

Lord Stranham favored his guest with a withering look and finished the last bites of food on his plate. "I thank you for reminding me of that fact," he said in a voice that did not betoken gratitude. "I do hope you have the good sense not to take them there again or I shall not be responsible for your health."

"Now, Mark, don't put yourself in a taking. Anyone could see that Miss Joanna graced Almacks with a beauty

41

never before seen there. Did you not think she looked like a veritable angel?" he asked, a faraway look in his eyes.

The marquis sighed and gestured the younger man to seat himself in one of the elegant cherry Queen Anne chairs. "I remember once," he began conversationally, leaning back in his own splat-back chair and folding his hands across his chest, "when I was still in my salad days—not nearly as old as you are now—anyway, as I was saying, much the same situation presented itself to me as is happening to you. I fell in love, or thought I fell in love, with a butcher's daughter." He grinned in self-mocking humor. "As I recollect, I made quite a cake of myself over her. I actually do believe I would have married the chit if I had attained my majority, which fortunately I had not."

"What happened?"

"Ah, yes. Well, I arrived early one sunny morning, roses in hand, looking the perfect fool, I don't doubt— only to find another young nobleman departing. He had been more fortunate in his suit than I and had just passed the night in the arms of my beloved."

Robert leaped up from his chair and faced Lord Stranham squarely, arms flexed and hands clenched, evidently failing to see a moral parallel. "You are fair and far out if you think Miss Joanna Brown is at all like that!"

"I may be," Lord Stranham said calmly, "but I doubt it. The ladies quite obviously accepted invitations to a place where they did not belong. And worse, they took them from *you*—an unknown man. Lady Morley may have been duped by your story of their relationship with me, but they were not. They know they have no connections and still they accepted the vouchers. Robert, can you not see they are nothing more than adventuresses? Why, they are very probably looking for a man to set them up in keeping."

The baronet left the marquis's house very nearly in a state of shock, mechanically taking his shallow-crowned beaver hat and malacca cane from the butler and walking down the brick steps to the sidewalk with a very grim look on his face.

The marquis watched him go with a worried frown, but he was satisfied that his words had had some effect. Driving through Hyde Park later in the week he chanced upon Robert. The younger man was with a very pretty brunette —the daughter of a wealthy peer.

"I didn't go to Upper Wimpole Street to visit with our mutual acquaintances," Robert informed Lord Stranham, making a great show of casualness before the young lady seated beside him in the satin-lined barouche.

"Indeed?" Lord Stranham asked noncommittally.

"No, I took your advice."

"Excellent." Then, fearing Robert's elaborate offhandedness would arouse the young lady's suspicions about their subject, he turned back to his horses. "I bid you a good day," he said with a bow to the lady, and continued on, driving his own smart perch phaeton to an inch and nodding and smiling to friends and acquaintances as he did so.

He left the park a short time later and on his way back to St. James's Square stopped at Sam's Royal Library in Bond Street. As he was stepping into the bookshop he noticed with a curious glance that parked in front of the shop was a most unusually battered-looking landaulet manned by a groom with a slightly red nose. In fact, the man looked downright bosky.

He decided with a shrug that it was none of his concern if someone entrusted himself to a driver who was foxed. He entered the shop and began to look around. Once he had selected a book, he walked toward the shopkeeper, then waited impatiently for a slender woman to finish speaking with the shopkeeper. Beside her was a plump, rosy-cheeked girl.

"It's a nice book, ma'am, and worth every bit of the price."

"Yes, of course it is," a slightly musical and vaguely familiar feminine voice replied regretfully, "but I fear that's a bit more than I was prepared to pay."

The woman's face was averted, and all that he could see was her serviceable and worn black cloak and drab gray bonnet with an incongruous pink plume waving from it. Some wisps of pale blond hair peeped from beneath the hat.

"Thank you for your time," she said politely, and turned to leave.

Lord Stranham averted his head quickly as she moved toward him. He made a great employment of studying some books in the corner as the lady—Miss Brown—walked past him. Then he tarried until she had left the store, before presenting his own book for payment. As the shopkeeper figured the price he glanced out the many-paned wide front window to see Miss Brown and her maid stepping into the battered landaulet.

The groom, hastily slipping a flask back into his coat pocket, made a swat or two at the horses with the whip, missing each time. Then, in a fit of frustration, he stood up and cracked the whip sharply, hitting the horses squarely across their backs with such force they took off down the street at a gallop.

While the astonished shopkeeper watched, the marquis dropped book and notes unceremoniously onto the floor and rushed to the door. He pulled it open with a yank and looked down the street to where the careening landaulet was rounding a corner on three wheels. There were only two occupants in the vehicle now—the tall groom and the heavy woman. Miss Brown had obviously been thrown out.

He swept a worried gaze over the length of the street before his eyes came to rest on a spot not ten feet from

44

him. A very startled Miss Brown was rising from the middle of the road, her bonnet left behind on the cobblestone street. A stocky man was assisting her.

"Oh, miss," the man said anxiously in a coarse voice, "air ye all right? It wore a good thing that ye jumped when ye did. Were ye 'urt when ye fell?"

"No," Daphne replied, dusting herself off as she spoke.

"Do ye want me to get ye an 'ackney coach?"

"Thank you, no. My groom and maid will surely return for me."

Lord Stranham strolled to the middle of the road and stooped to pick up Daphne's hat. She looked up in surprise as he returned it to her, then took her arm to pull her gently out of the way of the traffic she was impeding.

"I shall see you home, Miss Brown," he offered gallantly.

"Oh, well, that's all right, then," the man declared, and left satisfied.

The grateful smile that had started across Daphne's delicate features when she first saw Lord Stranham had been erased almost immediately, replaced by a withdrawn, distrustful look. "Thank you, but I shall walk," she said proudly. Then continuing a little more uncertainly: "It's only in Upper Wimpole Street, so it's no distance at all." She and Joanna walked all the time in the country, she reassured herself to stifle the rising trepidation she felt.

"My dear Miss Brown," the marquis argued politely, "it is over a mile."

"That doesn't signify. I'm used to walking and I can go right up here to Oxford Road and then straight up Wimpole Street, which will lead me right to Upper Wimpole. There's no danger of my getting lost."

The slightly woebegone expression in her voice, as well as the route she had said she would take home, told the marquis quite clearly that she was not absolutely certain of the way back to her house. He smiled and said firmly,

"Nonsense, Miss Brown. You cannot be wandering the streets of London unescorted."

As he spoke she looked up to note the rather predatory looks of two young men lounging across the street. They were regarding her through quizzing-glasses, faint smiles on their bored faces. The marquis was right, she admitted. It was not safe for her to be unescorted. The question was, Would she be any safer with *him* than with any other man? On the other hand, Cedric and Rose had not returned and she could scarcely stand here all day.

Lord Stranham appeared to take her acceptance for granted, as he placed a proprietary arm on hers and steered her to his high perch phaeton.

She looked up at the vehicle in awe as he helped her in.

"Upper Wimpole Street, I collect you said, Miss Brown?" he asked courteously as he seated himself beside her and picked up the reins.

"Yes," she murmured, giving the number as they started off at a brisk pace. "They certainly move smartly, don't they?" she observed, marveling at the well-groomed matched bays before her.

"Not so quickly as your own were moving when they rounded that corner," he returned dryly.

She turned to look ahead, venturing a glance at the impeccably groomed man beside her and, in spite of her best efforts not to, feeling proud at the stares they were evoking as the splendid yellow phaeton passed people along the way.

"Miss Brown," he began hesitantly, "I hope you do not think it presumptuous of me, but—" He stopped and looked questioningly at her.

She stiffened. Was the man going to make her an improper offer while riding down the city street? She should not have come with him! She should have risked getting lost rather than put herself at his mercy.

He seemed to gather his courage and then proceeded

more positively: "As I have said, I hope you do not think it presumptuous of me, but I must tell you that as I was on my way into the shop . . ." He paused. "I scarcely know how to put this delicately enough for you."

"I beg you will not say it, my lord," she cried. She looked around in a panic. The vehicle was too high and going too fast to permit escape.

"I must. It is for your own benefit."

She gasped indignantly. The nerve of the man telling her that becoming involved in an improper relationship with him would be to her benefit!

"Your groom, Miss Brown, was foxed," he announced gravely.

She relaxed, greatly relieved. "Oh, yes," she admitted gaily.

He looked at her sharply. "You certainly do not seem overset by the knowledge that your groom drinks. Why do you not turn him off?" he demanded gruffly.

She met his look with one of resentment. "I do not think that need concern you, my lord," she replied haughtily.

"I realize, of course, that it is none of my affair, but—"

"Quite right, it is not your affair," she agreed readily, and turned her head to look straight ahead.

"I apologize. I meant no offense."

She nodded coolly and continued to stare forward. The silence lengthened as they rode on. Lord Stranham made another uncomfortable attempt at polite conversation.

"Did you enjoy your evening at Almacks Wednesday last?"

"Yes," she said shortly, the faintest edge to her voice.

"I do not doubt that you have been visited by several of the young men your sister met there?" he pursued.

She shot him a keen look. "We have not been visited by any young men, not even one who promised he would call," she snapped, and then could have bitten her tongue. Of course Sir Robert Drayton had not called. She had gone out of her way to make him feel unwelcome, but that didn't stop her from feeling resentful toward him for casting Joanna into a fit of the doldrums. Her sister had cried for a full three hours last Thursday evening when she had finally realized that Sir Drayton was not coming.

"I do beg your pardon for broaching the subject," he said caustically.

"You do not beg my pardon," she flashed, irritated by his tone. "No doubt you find it highly amusing that no one called."

"Have you no polite conversation?" he asked testily.

"I have conversation suitable to the occasion," she answered stiffly.

"I see," he returned brusquely as he pulled up in front of her house, then jumped down and came around to help her down.

Suddenly she was painfully aware of the inadequacies of the neighborhood. People were actually stopping to stare at the sight of such a magnificent equipage, drawn by such beautiful, powerful animals, pulled up in front of her humble house. The house, as if her clothes had not already borne her genteel poverty home to him, definitely showed their lack of funds.

He impassively reached up to put his hands on her waist to swing her down from the high phaeton. For an instant, while in his arms, she looked into his cold gray eyes. Then he set her on the cobbled street and removed his hands from her waist, stepping back.

She felt very ashamed of herself for her outburst and more than a little humbled by her obvious lack of funds. "That was very ill said of me, my lord," she murmured contritely, attempting a weak smile. "You have been most kind and I thank you for your help. Good day, my lord." She turned quickly and disappeared into the modest buff brick house.

Lord Stranham stood motionless for a minute, looking

after her. In the flash of that wavering smile and the undefined plea in her violet eyes, he had felt an uncomfortable and most unfamiliar lurch within himself. He walked thoughtfully back around to the driver's seat and sprang up into it, pausing to look at the house a final time before flicking the whip and driving back to the gracious luxury of St. James's Square.

CHAPTER 5

Lord Stranham alighted in front of the imposing house in Cavendish Square, walked up the steps to the large white door, and stepped inside when the footman opened it.

"How are you, Masters?" he greeted the servant.

"My teeth are paining me a bit, milord," the elderly footman admitted.

"Ghastly things, teeth," the marquis commiserated. "Where's Robert?"

The footman directed Lord Stranham into a sunny sitting room where he found the baronet lying on a chaise lounge and staring moodily out the front window. He was holding one bandaged arm carefully while he ate from a lap tray with his good arm. He was bruised about the face as well. The careful position his leg occupied—propped up in front of him with pillows—suggested it had also suffered some of the indignities to which the rest of his person had been subjected.

"Got your urgent note," the marquis greeted him cheerfully as he drew a small chair from across the room and placed it backwards by the chaise lounge, straddling it casually and folding his arms across the back. "What's amiss?"

"That," Robert said darkly, "should be perfectly obvious."

"Yes, I see you've had a bit of a dustup with someone, haven't you?" the marquis asked absently as he glanced about the buttercup-yellow room. Taking a fine Sévres snuffbox from his pocket and flicking it open, he began to dust snuff on the back of his wrist with great concentration.

"You don't seem unduly concerned," Robert noted with chagrin.

"Oh, don't mean to be rude. I'm terribly sorry that you're all laid up," Lord Stranham said with perfunctory courtesy. "Now, what was the meaning of this singularly dull-witted note you sent me requesting that I call on the sisters Brown?"

"It was not dull-witted," Robert argued sullenly before popping a large piece of brown bread into his mouth and swallowing it with a minimum of chewing.

Lord Stranham watched him in fascination. "Gad, Drayton! Don't you ever chew? It's the very devil for your stomach, bombarding it with large chunks like that."

Robert looked suitably annoyed at the reprimand. "When my mother dies, I shall give you her position of attending to my eating habits. In the meantime I don't know what you're doing here wasting time when I particularly asked you to call immediately on Miss Joanna."

"You are perfectly right," Lord Stranham agreed, rising as he spoke.

"You're going to call on her now?" Robert asked hopefully.

"No, I mean I don't know what I'm doing here wasting my time with you either, so I shall take my leave."

"Dash it all, Mark, will you stop making light of this very serious situation? *I* am laid up, as any fool can see."

"I must agree," Lord Stranham murmured, "though it means being branded a fool by one who should know his own kind."

"And while I have been lying here, I've been thinking about Miss Joanna. I made a mull of it, Mark. I did the wrong thing by not calling on her. And now, of course, I'm in no position to call on her, as I can scarcely arrive lying down."

"I don't know," the marquis observed thoughtfully. "A great many gentlemen of my acquaintance assume such a position immediately after calling on certain ladies."

"Mark," Robert warned sternly, "this is a very serious discussion."

"Of course," the marquis agreed unrepentantly.

"Now, the thing is, since I ain't able to go, I thought you might go and smooth the way for when I'm recovered enough to call on Miss Joanna myself."

"Would it be considered rag-mannered of me to ask exactly how you came to be so sedentary?"

"Got into a bit of a row with Tommy Atrium. He said some most improper things about Miss Joanna and my relations with her."

"I see."

"Yes. So now you must call on her."

"At the risk of sounding very stupid, may I inquire as to why it is suddenly necessary to visit the young lady?"

"Because," Robert explained impatiently, "I was wrong. The whole two days I've laid here I haven't thought of anything but the flower-blue color of Joanna's eyes and her petallike lips. I'm in love," he finished simply, and gazed off into the distance with a cherubic smile.

"How poetic," Lord Stranham commented dryly. "Her eyes, by the by, are violet like her sister's."

"That's not the point," Robert snapped irritably.

"Quite right. That is not the matter at hand. The point is that you intend to send me to do your courting to some ladies about whom you know next to nothing and into whose home you are not welcome?" Lord Stranham asked sarcastically.

Sarcasm was wasted on Robert, however, for he agreed readily, pleased that the marquis had finally grasped the assignment.

"I will not call on them," Lord Stranham said with stubborn finality.

"You won't?" Robert cried in a tone that indicated he didn't believe he could have heard correctly.

"Do be sensible, Robert."

"I have been sensible all of my life!"

"That is not altogether true, Drayton," the marquis contradicted mildly. "I recollect you told me once when you were at Eton, you and some of your fellows were laying in gunpowder to blow up the headmaster. That's hardly being reasonable, now is it?" he reasoned. "I further recall another instance where—"

"Mark," Robert interrupted plaintively, "you are not going to visit them?"

"That is correct. And if you will take my very good advice, which you have shown the great sense of having done so far, you will forget all about those chits and concentrate on recovering your health so that you may escort that very attractive and very well-dowered brunette I saw you with the other day."

"Well," Robert began again in injured accents, "if you won't call on Miss Joanna, then at the very least you can deliver a message to Tommy Atrium for me. It's a bit urgent, so you'll have to go right away. You'll find Tommy at the cockfights at—"

Lord Stranham rose abruptly, jammed his beaver hat on his head, and yanked up his York tan driving gloves and walking stick. "I will take my leave now, Robert. Your requests are becoming more addlepated by the minute."

"Wait," Robert protested loudly, "it's most important!"

"Then send your man," the marquis advised curtly.

"I can't; it has to do with a matter of honor."

"If it concerns a matter of honor, I fail to see how you or Tommy Atrium could possibly be involved."

Robert continued undaunted: "You see, I shall have to call him out for the odious things he said about Miss Joanna."

Lord Stranham checked at the door and whirled round,

a thunderstruck expression on his face. "Those blows about your face must have affected your brain," he pronounced with conviction. "Have you run mad, you young corker? You can't seriously be considering dueling over a chance-met chit?"

"I am!" Robert declared hotly. "And I need you to deliver the challenge to Tommy."

"At the cockpits, you say?" Lord Stranham asked with an air of resignation.

"Yes."

"I shall go there immediately."

"Thanks, Mark. I knew you'd be bang up to the mark!"

"A very poor choice of words," the marquis commented cynically, and left Robert to his cold lunch.

As he walked to the door his exasperation with his young friend gave a briskness to his step. He had no intention of delivering a challenge to Tommy Atrium. The two made a fine pair, he thought with a contemptuous snort—two reckless boys wanting to meet on Wimbledon Green over some silly chit. It was best to nip this affair in the bud, and the most effective way to do that was to extract some sort of hackneyed apology from Tommy for his words concerning the Brown girl, who incidentally, he paused to consider, was becoming a deal of trouble for a girl with no claim on anyone.

With a resigned air he stepped up into his phaeton. There was nothing to be done for it if he was to extricate Robert from this coil. Looking regretfully at his finely cut brown coat and flawless camel unmentionables, he touched the cravat his valet had labored over so meticulously this morning. Hardly the attire one wore to a cockfight, but there was little sense in going home to change, he decided as he turned the horses in the direction of St. Giles Rookery.

Half an hour later, as he pushed open the rough-hewn door and stepped inside the smoke-filled room, he wrinkled his nose in disgust. The scent of the smoke from clay pipes was the least offensive of the odors. The smell of bodies—none too clean to begin with and perspiring heavily in the stuffy heat of the low-ceilinged room—made for a pungently repulsive odor. He looked about at the closely packed spectators—burly tradesmen, street vendors, and butchers in blood-stained aprons, with an occasional wench scattered among the crowd. Seated on long low benches, they gazed raptly down into the pit where sounds of fighting cocks could be heard. Latecomers stood in the aisles and against the back walls.

Lord Stranham began to edge through the crowd, moving across the sawdust-covered floor to the thick of the action. In the front row he glimpsed a few sporting young bloods. Tommy Atrium would undoubtedly be among them, if he was here at all.

The marquis's passage through the crowd was greeted by loud and profane requests for him to remove his tall frame from the views he was blocking, interspersed with some rather demeaning references to his lineage. He continued placidly forward until he reached the rope around the pit. Directly across from him, on the other side of the pit, the dandies sat on a long bench. He looked down the row of bucks, his eyes traveling from one well-tailored young man to the next until he sighted Tommy. He began to circle the pit where the enraged cocks were fighting with noisy fierceness, their silver spurs clicking as they engaged in angry combat.

Midway to his quarry his progress was interrupted when a scuffle between two men broke out. He stopped and waited impatiently. It was rapidly developing into such a bawdy fight that the spectators were drawing their eager eyes from the bloody cocks to the men. Money began to change hands as bets were placed on the outcome.

Lord Stranham glanced casually at the fighters—two

white-haired old men. He tapped one well-polished Hessian boot in boredom. He had not wanted to come to this squalid place to begin with, he thought testily, and now to have to watch a fight between a couple of old men was tiresome in the extreme.

A cry went up from the crowd as a short fat man who had been taking ineffective swings at a tall thin man finally landed a punch. His opponent staggered backwards.

The tall man was a bit of a ridiculous figure, the marquis noted, dressed as he was in some sort of outmoded and outworn livery. His swings were even more ineffective than his partner's, and he was taking the worst end of the other man's fists when Lord Stranham felt a tug of recognition. The tall man had a slightly bulbous red nose. Where had he seen him before?

Wherever the marquis had seen the man before, it was obvious he was losing badly. Another loud cry escaped the assemblage as the thin man fell gracelessly to the floor, his hands flailing wildly as he landed on his back. His opponent stepped back several paces and gathered his forces, preparing to run forward to jump on the downed man's stomach while the spectators held their collective breath.

At that moment Lord Stranham realized the man on the floor was the Browns' servant. Moving swiftly, he reached the athlete, grabbed him in the act of running toward the thin man, and aborted his rib-cracking finale. While the crowd booed loudly, the marquis swung him around and shouted angrily, "Enough!"

The heavy man raised an arm to hit the dandy who held him well over a foot off the ground, but his punch was never completed. In fact, the next thing to land was the fat man, skidding unceremoniously on his face across the floor. The watchers made a hasty path for him as he overturned benches in his way before stopping with a sickening thud against the back wall.

The noise subsided, and all eyes turned to stare in awe

at the tall dark Corinthian who was standing in the center of a small cleared space.

"Anyone else who wishes to come to cuffs," he challenged defiantly, "can fight me."

A low grumble went through the group, followed by an almost visible mass step backwards as people moved away —a precautionary measure in case he should decide to fight someone who had not volunteered.

However, that was not Lord Stranham's inclination. He ignored the gathering and walked to the thin old man who was still lying on the floor waving his fists.

The marquis pulled him to his feet, and Cedric looked about dazedly. "Where is 'e?" he demanded ferociously. "I'll kill 'im!"

"I have disposed of him for the present," the marquis assured him. "I shall take you home now."

"Eh?"

"I said I'll take you home," he repeated louder, pulling the wild-eyed man toward the door as the crowd parted respectfully.

"Home?" Cedric repeated vaguely, then groaned and closed his eyes as realization dawned. "What will Miss Daphne say?"

Lord Stranham led the stumbling man out to the phaeton and helped him in. "A pretty sight we must make, my friend," he noted as he turned the horses toward Upper Wimpole Street.

In truth, he was not displeased to have the opportunity to call on Miss Daphne Brown. While he might not want Robert to consider anything so foolish as courting a member of that family, there were other alliances with females such as the Brown girls that could be very satisfying. And even though the marquis objected to their attendance at Almacks, a place where they clearly did not belong, that did not mean he was not sensible of the young ladies' charm—particularly the elder Miss Brown's.

Aside from the very delicate nature of her beauty and the allure of her graceful figure, he appreciated her as a woman who had something to say for herself. In the short time he had spoken with her at Almacks, he had come to realize that she had read a great deal. So many light-skirts had no conversation at all. Not that they need to have a great deal, he considered; such women were meant to give pleasure in other ways. Still, it might be a pleasant change to spend time with a chit of some understanding.

A faint smile crossed his handsome face as he considered just how enjoyable a liaison with Miss Daphne Brown could be. Returning her groom home would provide him the opportunity to insinuate himself into her good graces. Such sensitive matters as setting up a woman in keeping required some time, but he believed he could make a good beginning today. And he was not averse to spending time cultivating Daphne; it would, he thought, be time very well used.

Thus it was that the phaeton wended its way through the teeming, warrenlike slums of St. Giles, past the crowded narrow buildings, the bawling street vendors, and the numerous coffeehouses displaying signs with a woman's arm and hand holding a coffeepot—indicating that the particular establishment could provide the whole woman, as well as the usual coffeehouse offerings of food and drink.

A few of the residents of the rookery looked askance at the finely dressed gentleman with a most incongruous faint smile on his face as he supported a man slumping at his side.

CHAPTER 6

At that very minute in the run-down house in Upper Wimpole Street, Daphne was pacing fretfully from the kitchen to the front-parlor window to look out once again. Nothing was going well. The ham had had a decidedly rancid smell when the cook had uncovered it that morning, and a hasty substitution had had to be made after a good many recriminations from Rose against the cook's good friend the butcher. The cook had feelingly answered with some pithy comments, more maligning Rose's character than defending the butcher's.

While Daphne had been engaged in trying to separate the two women—each one armed with a heavy ladle while circling about the kitchen table and taking an occasional wild swat at the other—Joanna had rushed downstairs to see what the matter was, catching her pretty green gauze dress on a nail in the back hall and tearing a large rent in it. She was upstairs now hastily trying to mend the damage to her dress. To top it off, Daphne thought fretfully, Cedric had been gone most of the day. His presence had not been necessary until now, but Daphne particularly wished him to be there when the guests arrived. It would be most embarrassing if she were forced to greet their callers herself. It would be even more humiliating, she thought dispiritedly, if Cedric arrived roaring drunk after the guests had already come.

The Winters were due in half an hour and she had not even had time to dress yet. With the back of her hand she pushed back her small white mobcap before running flour-coated fingers over the front of her apron. The sound of a vehicle stopping outside alerted her instantly.

Pulling back the curtains, she looked out anxiously. "Oh, Lord, no!" she whispered.

Lord Stranham had pulled up in front of the house. A man was slumped beside him, doubtless Sir Robert Drayton. As she watched, the limp man suddenly came to life and began to fling his arms about ridiculously—as if he were fighting someone. From Sir Robert's actions, she could only assume he was drunk. The marquis must also be in his cups, or why else would he have come here? Why else indeed! What sort of women did the men think she and Joanna were? she wondered as a furious blush rose to her cheeks.

Closing the curtains with an angry jerk, she marched into the hall, standing stonily by the front door and waiting for the knocker to sound. When it did, she flung the door open so forcefully that Lord Stranham and his companion practically fell into the little hall.

She turned hostile eyes to the marquis. "What do you want?"

Lord Stranham looked completely taken aback, nearly losing the grip on the sagging man he was supporting by his side. Then, in a tone to match her own, he replied, "I have brought your groom home, Miss Brown."

Daphne's eyes widened in a mixture of surprise and horror as Cedric shrugged out of his lordship's grip and straightened himself with the remnants of his dignity. "I'm able to take m'self," he announced unsteadily.

"Whatever have you done to him?" Daphne demanded, rounding on Lord Stranham.

The marquis was undergoing a variety of emotions—this was not at all the welcome he had anticipated. His complaisant magnanimity gave way first to surprise and then to the more earthy emotion of anger. "I have not done anything to him," he said abruptly.

Cedric, still getting his bearings, looked about some-what wildly. "Where is 'e? Let me at 'im, I'll kill 'im!" He swung a fist so vehemently that the force of his own motion pulled him around in a half circle toward the marquis.

Lord Stranham put a hand out to stop him. As he did so, Daphne brought a small but very resolute hand up to his lordship's face and gave him a resounding smack.

"Don't you dare touch him!" she shouted. "Haven't you done enough harm already? Look at him! His mouth is bleeding and there's a fearsome cut above his eye."

The sound of all the excitement brought the cook and the housekeeper into the fray, both women loudly demanding explanations.

"I shall depart, Miss Brown. Servant," the marquis said with chilly aloofness, turning to go.

"Before you leave, I believe you owe us an apology," she said in a voice husky with emotion; her eyes blazed angrily up at him.

Lord Stranham swung back around to face her. "Do I indeed, Miss Brown?" he asked icily. "Then by all means you shall have one. I can truthfully say that I am heartily sorry for my actions today. I regret that I ventured to that hellhole cockpit. I further lament that I chanced upon your groom there. And I am most assuredly sorry I brought him here."

"He is our butler," Daphne corrected with frigid composure.

"I scarcely see what his position matters. The point is, I collect, that I have used him most unkindly, is that not so?" he asked with controlled fury.

"Yes, it is!"

"Then I take my leave." He swept her a very slight, very curt bow and stalked out to his phaeton, setting off at such a fast pace that mothers came flying out of their houses to retrieve their offspring.

Daphne watched him go, her breath coming so hard she

63

had to stand for some minutes in the hall trying to calm herself. When she finally did, Rose had already taken Cedric off to the kitchen to attend to his injuries.

Joanna came down the steps in her newly hemmed frock. "Daphne," she ventured timidly, seeing her sister standing white-faced and rigid by the open door, "shouldn't you be getting ready?"

"Yes," Daphne answered blankly, still looking down the street. She turned slowly toward Joanna, then gave a startled gasp. "Oh, yes! The guests will be here any minute." She hurried up the stairs as Joanna watched in confusion.

By the time Daphne descended the steps, the guests were just arriving. She took a deep breath and went forward to greet them, smiling.

Mrs. Winter, a reed-thin woman with raven hair, regarded Cedric suspiciously before surrendering her olive-green redingote to him. Daphne suppressed a laugh. Poor Cedric. He did have the look of a pirate about him with his head swathed in a red bandana and his face full of bruises now turning from purple to black.

But Daphne gave no indication there was anything the least bit exceptionable about her butler as she went forward with her hand extended. "Mr. and Mrs. Winter, I'm Daphne Brown. I'm so glad you could come. Do let us remove to the parlor," she directed courteously.

Mrs. Winter favored Cedric with one last distrustful look before following Daphne and her husband into the parlor, where they settled themselves into chairs and began to exchange commonplaces. It soon became evident to Daphne that Mrs. Winter was the only one of the two who had an opinion, or possibly the only one whose ideas mattered. At any rate, Mrs. Winter cast an appraising look about while her husband leaned back comfortably in the armchair and allowed his lids to creep downwards.

Joanna appeared a short time later, curtsying to Mrs.

Winter and the snoring Mr. Winter. The three women pursued polite conversation for several minutes before dinner was announced. Mrs. Winter roused her husband with a light hand on his shoulder and, Daphne noted with a suppressed giggle, a subtle kick. The foursome proceeded to the dining room.

After an opening course of fish, served by Rose, Cedric entered the room in a last-century black satin tricorne hat and a threadbare but highly adorned blue coat. He bore in a rather pathetic-looking baked chicken hunched in the center of a huge platter. The exaggerated pomp with which he presented it would have done credit to a roast suckling pig, complete with an apple in its mouth, offered to the inhabitants of Windsor Castle.

Mrs. Winter watched him in fascination before turning resolutely away and saying in a businesslike voice, "So you girls are new to London?"

"Yes, ma'am," Joanna answered politely.

"There are some most interesting things to see. First, of course, is the Tower . . ."

While Mrs. Winter began a detailed description of the Tower, Daphne allowed her mind to wander. She was still preoccupied with the scene that had taken place a short time ago in the front hall. Of course, she had suspected from the start that Sir Robert Drayton was a coxcomb. And since the haughty Lord Stranham was a friend of his, she could only assume he was cut from the same cloth. But she had almost hoped to have herself proven wrong. There was something so, well, almost appealing about Lord Stranham's gray eyes, and he had been most gentlemanly when he had escorted her home from the bookshop. But, no doubt, that had all been an act to put her off her guard. Besides, she reminded herself sternly, for a man of his birth to have ventured to such a low place as a cockpit told her a great deal about his true character. And then to have attacked poor Cedric—a man twice his own age—was inexcusable!

Daphne started as she felt a light tap on her arm. "I beg your pardon, I wasn't attending," she admitted as she turned a questioning gaze to her sister.

"Mrs. Winter was just saying how delightful it is to be invited out and served something other than ham," Joanna said tactfully.

"Indeed," Daphne murmured, and brought her attention back to the gathering. She looked down the little table to where a bowl of daffodils had been placed off center to cover a large rust-colored stain in the damask tablecloth. Were they making a good impression on the Winters? She must concentrate harder. After all, she and Joanna needed to have friends in London. It was the only way they could hope to obtain employment.

"We went to Almacks the other night," Joanna announced pleasantly.

There was a palpable pause. Mrs. Winter looked at her husband in obvious disbelief. These, her eyes seemed to say, were not the kind of girls who obtained vouchers to those exclusive assembly rooms.

Daphne groaned inwardly and berated herself for not thinking to warn her sister against mentioning *that* event. Now she felt compelled to offer the silenced little group some excuse that would show that Joanna was not lying while at the same time indicating that they were not, as Mrs. Winter had so correctly deduced, the type of ladies who received vouchers to Almacks.

Unfortunately, while she hesitated Joanna continued cheerfully: "It was quite lovely and we met some of the most charming people. Didn't we, Daphne?"

"Yes, Joanna"—she smiled weakly—"some most delightful people. But I'm certain our guests are bored with such talk." Judging from the look on Mrs. Winter's face as she leaned forward, she was anything but uninterested.

"I'm not bored," Mrs. Winter denied swiftly. "I should love to hear all about it."

Joanna continued happily, "Well, Lady Morley obtained the vouchers for us, but I'm persuaded it was at Sir Robert Drayton's request and—"

Mrs. Winter broke in with a sharp question: "Sir Robert Drayton? You know him?"

Even Mr. Winter took time out from the chicken he was attacking to look up with mild interest.

"Oh, but of course. I've had ices with him at Gunthers, and he stood up with me at Almacks and—"

Mrs. Winter interrupted again. A little of her surprise was fading from her face, to be replaced by the most avid curiosity. What was Sir Robert Drayton doing squiring a chit of no birth about the likes of the hallowed Almacks? With a very I'm-going-to-get-to-the-bottom-of-this look on her face, she pursued, interrupting once again, "Do you know any other noblemen?"

"Oh, yes," Joanna answered breezily at the same moment that Daphne gave an emphatic no. Joanna stopped in surprise to look at her sister. "Well, of course we do, Daphne," she contradicted gently. "Lord Stranham and —"

But this was altogether too much. Mrs. Winter was on her feet now, her chair pushed back and her hands gripping the table as she looked at Joanna in complete shock. "*You* know Lord Stranham?" she demanded in a tone indicating that that was tantamount to knowing one of the twelve apostles.

"Yes," Joanna admitted mildly. "He's very nice and quite handsome," she added helpfully.

"Handsome!" Mrs. Winter ejaculated. "I should think so! Every mama in polite society has been angling for him for the past ten seasons. Handsome, indeed!" she sniffed. "He's a nonpareil!"

But the mention of that particular peer's name had had

a disconcerting effect on Daphne. "If *that* is the sort of man that mothers wish their daughters to marry," she said, "then I take leave to say I find a complete lack of discrimination in the mothers of this city."

Mrs. Winter, still standing a little ridiculously by the table, suddenly recovered herself. She sat down sheepishly and placed her napkin back on her lap, straightening it with great concentration.

"Why so, dear?" she asked with careful indifference. A suspicion was forming in her mind that these girls might be telling the most outrageous rappers. An even more provocative thought was that they were telling the truth, and the gentlemen mentioned *had* displayed some interest in them. What kind of interest? What kind of girls were the Browns anyway? Fresh from the country and looking like two ripe peaches, they could just as easily be two very shrewd women looking for a man to set them up in keeping.

After all, all she knew about them was the letter from Millie, and even that could have been forged. She hadn't heard from her cousin in five years and, now that she came to think on it, she wasn't even certain that Millie still lived in Clovelly. Yes, there was something altogether questionable about the Brown girls, and *she* was not going to introduce two girls into her circle of friends who were anything less than proper.

Daphne, having a shrewd intuition of what was taking place in Mrs. Winter's mind, tried again: "I daresay it all sounds a bit odd, two girls up from the Devonshire coast meeting such illustrious members of the nobility, but"— improvising swiftly, she lied with a decided air, as there was really nothing for it now but to brazen it out—"Lady Morley was a very dear friend of my father's family, so she has shown concern for our welfare." That that good lady had all but disappeared from the face of the earth and was taking no further interest in them did not show in any way in Daphne's assured manner.

Mrs. Winter looked as if she were digesting this information as she sought to determine whether or not it could be true.

While she thought, Joanna sat quietly, watching Daphne with a thunderstruck expression.

"If you are friends with Lady Morley and Sir Robert Drayton, then you are surely acquainted with Lady Drayton?" Mrs. Winter asked craftily.

Daphne felt for all the world as if she were a small furry mouse being pursued by a stealthy and determined cat. The question was obviously of some importance to Mrs. Winter, and perhaps her decision to admit them into her circle of friends, or not to do so, hinged on her answer. No, she didn't know Lady Drayton, but she doubted if Mrs. Winter did either. And if a small lie was necessary to secure the older woman's good opinion, then Daphne would take the chance.

"Oh, yes," she said casually, and then glanced quickly at Joanna.

Actually there was no need to throw a warning look at her sister, as Joanna had just swallowed a large piece of chicken whole at the shock of hearing such an outrageous lie from her ever-honest elder sister. Fortunately for Daphne, the sputtering, back thumping, and sips of water accompanying that action kept Joanna out of the conversation for several minutes, as well as provided a distraction that gave Daphne time to think. By the time a very red-faced Joanna had recovered herself, she merely looked intently at her plate, afraid to interject anything into the talk.

"Tell me," Mrs. Winter pursued, "is Lady Drayton's hair the same color it always was, or has she gone white?"

A tricky question, Daphne had to admit. "Oh, it's still

red," she said nonchalantly. After all, her son's hair was red so wasn't it likely that hers was too?

Mrs. Winter nodded her head almost in admission of a thrust. The girl did know what color Lady Drayton's hair was, or else she had made a very wise choice. Possibly they were friends of Lady Drayton's. Unable to restrain herself, Mrs. Winter asked one more question: "And her figure? Has she kept it?"

Her son was stocky so . . . "I had rather imagined she was always a trifle fat. I collect the whole family runs to corpulent frames."

Yes, the girl was telling the truth. Lovely! She could use someone with influence with the *ton*. After all, she would be bringing her own dear Carlotta out in two years, and connections such as the Misses Brown had would be very helpful.

"Such a nice dinner," Mrs. Winter murmured politely.

CHAPTER 7

In St. James's Square the following morning the servants were making a wide circle around Lord Stranham. His lordship, the word was rapidly spreading throughout the household, was in a most disagreeable mood. That knowledge was at the very moment being whispered from one underfootman to another as they polished the brass sconces in the large formal parlor.

Upstairs, in the largest of the twenty bedrooms, Charles, the valet, was well aware of the marquis's state of mind and not a little curious as to the reason for it. He had seldom seen Lord Stranham looking so harsh.

"Dammit, Charles, what's the matter with you this morning?" Lord Stranham fired at the hapless man. "You can't tie any kind of cravat that far away from me."

It was true Charles had maintained quite a safe distance. In fact, his arms were stretching their length to tie the intricate folds of the mathematical, an elaborate creation of cravat on which he greatly prided himself.

Lord Stranham, noting his valet's anxiety, gave a short laugh. "Do I look a bit formidable this morning?" he asked in a rueful voice.

"A bit," Charles acknowledged hesitantly.

"I daresay I am something of an adder today. Well, don't fear, I shan't harm you. Although," he added wickedly, "I was held accountable for roughing up a groom—or no, I collect it was a butler—yesterday."

The marquis laughed heartily at the stricken look that passed over his valet's face. "Never mind." He spoke

71

soothingly. "Let me give you some advice, Charles," he said affably to the aging valet.

"Sir?"

"Don't ever let a pair of eyes, violet—well, any color, but especially violet—overset you." What had he been thinking to allow Miss Daphne Brown to cause him any ill humor? He was a marquis and she was a woman totally beneath him. Why, her house and clothes were evidence enough of that.

"Of course not, my lord," Charles agreed blankly, and stepped back from his completed task.

"Good," his lordship said, turning to leave. "Now I have some people to call on and shall be gone the whole day. You may have the day off, Charles."

"Thank you, my lord," his valet called wonderingly after him.

Lord Stranham proceeded cheerfully down the steps, seated himself in the airy breakfast parlor that overlooked the carefully trimmed garden, and ate a hearty breakfast of eggs, ham, and toast. Afterwards he called the cook up to the breakfast room.

That good woman arrived in a most apprehensive mood, received his compliments in a state of surprise, and left with the firm conviction that the way to a man's heart was, now as ever, through his stomach. Solely through her cooking she had succeeded in reversing the shockingly bad humor in which Lord Stranham had awakened.

In this new frame of mind, the marquis started off to Robert's house. No chit, he told himself, was going to put him out of countenance. Lud! It was the outside of enough that Miss Brown thought him capable of harming an aging servant. He had always behaved in a manner that befitted his high social position. It was annoying to be misunderstood and reprimanded by someone whose situation was not nearly so lofty as his own. It was even more irritating when that person was a woman he had intended to grant

72

the singular honor of being in his keeping. There were a great many opera dancers who would give more than a little for such a distinction.

He found Robert as he had yesterday, reclining on his chaise lounge in the buttercup-yellow sitting room and looking decidedly dejected.

"Oh, it's you," Robert greeted him cheerlessly.

"I say there, Robert, I am not the grim reaper," the marquis observed sunnily as he strolled over to a brown Hepplewhite chair and seated himself comfortably.

Unfortunately, that choice of metaphor had the effect of making Robert pale noticeably. "I-is Tommy going to m-meet me?" the baronet asked morosely.

"Got something stuck in your throat?" Lord Stranham asked with casual indifference.

"N-no."

"I thought you were rather stumbling over your words there," he observed as he studied the younger man. Sir Robert Drayton, he decided, looked like another man who had undergone a sleepless night. No doubt the young fool had had time to worry over the duel that he thought he was to engage in, and had rightly decided that the chit was not worth dying for.

Robert began again in a shaky voice: "Is he—" He broke off, unable to finish the sentence.

Lord Stranham finished it cheerfully for him: "Is he going to meet you?"

"Yes," Robert whispered.

"Oh, but of course." The marquis lied with jovial affability, stretching his legs out casually before him and looking at the hearth—of white marble veined with pink streaks—as if it were a source of great interest. Out of the corner of his eye he saw Robert's normally somewhat ruddy face blanch even further. "However," he continued wickedly, "he is not one for pistols."

"Oh?" Robert croaked.

"No," Lord Stranham pursued amiably, "not even swords. He prefers a more direct method. A bit of a cut-and-thrust person, old Tommy." He chuckled.

Robert groaned and put a hand to his head.

"Did you say something?" the marquis asked politely, pausing in the act of taking snuff from a blue enameled case to look curiously at Robert.

"No."

"Well then, where was I? Oh, yes, he prefers—are you attending?"

Robert was listening so hard he was about to fall out of his chaise lounge, his wrapped leg forgotten as he leaned forward to hear what method his execution would take. Whatever had he meant by saying he would meet Tommy? No doubt Tommy had meant no harm about Miss Joanna. London was full of girls, he thought wildly. Surely it didn't signify if one of the thousands was vaguely maligned by a few ill-chosen words.

Lord Stranham, satisfied that he had the younger man's full attention, said with a flourish of his hand, "Tommy wants to meet you with daggers! Is that not original! Fancies himself a bit of an expert and declares it is the only sport where you can look right into your opponent's eyes before you—" He broke off as Robert gasped. "Did you say something?"

"Daggers?" Robert whispered hoarsely. "And Tommy an expert! God, what an awful way to die!"

"Yes, daggers. Probably for the best, as I collect Angelo taught him fencing, so he'd pink you quick, I don't doubt. Since I was your chosen messenger to deliver the challenge, I took the liberty of telling Tommy that you should be pleased to meet him at the time and place he specifies. He did mumble something about forgetting the whole incident, but I told him most emphatically that you would not consider such an action. I further told him you should judge it an insult that he would think—"

"Yes!" Robert interrupted excitedly.

"What's that? You agree that it is an insult? Well, and that's just what I told him and—"

"No!"

Lord Stranham broke off, looking perplexed. "I say, cawker, what's amiss with you? First you can hardly get a sentence out and now you keep interrupting me yelling first yes and then no. What the devil are you trying to say?"

"Tell Tommy to forget it!" Robert shouted. "Now I come to think on it, I'm certain I misunderstood what he said about Miss Joanna."

"Well, of course," Lord Stranham said hesitantly, "if it was a misunderstanding, then perhaps it would be improper to meet him. I merely thought that, as your chosen messenger, I must uphold your honor and the dignity of your position."

"But I misunderstood Tommy. I'm certain of it!" Robert shouted.

"Look here, Robert, if you want satisfaction from the man, I say take it. Name your seconds, and you could meet him at Battersea and no one would be the wiser. Unfortunately, I could not be your second. I've never been much good with daggers," he explained apologetically, "but I daresay any number of others will offer their services." He continued wistfully, "I rather had a fancy to see how proficient Tommy is with his dagger. Of course I know he's quite a nonpareil at boxing—works out at Cribb's Parlor and Gentleman Jackson's and all. I say have a go at it. What's to lose, after all?" he added with a suppressed smile.

But Robert, with a joyous smile on his face, was not even attending the marquis's words. He was fiercely ringing a small hand bell by the chaise lounge. The butler entered dutifully.

"Pen and paper!" Robert commanded. "And be quick about it!"

"Are you writing a message to Tommy?" Lord Stranham asked in feigned confusion.

"Yes, I shall tell him that although I wanted the chance to meet him above all things, under the circumstances—misunderstanding and all—it wouldn't be proper."

"Of course," Lord Stranham murmured as he stood politely and watched the younger man pen a letter with a hand that shook with happiness. He folded the incoherent note and handed it to the marquis.

"It shall be in its proper place inside of two minutes," Lord Stranham observed as he took the letter.

"You can't get it there that fast."

"Oh, but of course I can." He walked out the door, leaving a limp, but extremely happy Robert. Striding down the steps to his curricle, he tossed the letter back to his tiger and directed shortly, "Burn this," before starting off at a brisk trot to call on the incomparable Lady Diedre, the young lady who would soon be offered the honor of being his wife.

A few minutes later he was shown into the well-appointed drawing room of the late duke of Needham's lavish neoclassical house. He waited patiently for Lady Diedre, surveying the room as he did so.

It was a large, square apartment with a profusion of furniture, fern stands, and bric-a-brac. The seats of the shield-back chairs were covered with delicate brocade in shades of pale blue and candy-pink. Lacquered tables painted a glossy black and adorned with oriental designs testified to the duchess's passion for the latest foreign craze.

"Lord Stranham," Lady Diedre greeted him as she came forward smiling, her hand outstretched. Her mother followed her.

As the marquis bowed over the younger woman's hand,

he looked up to catch a glimpse of her eyes. He had no idea what color they were, but he did not think they were violet. He observed with satisfaction that they were brown.

"Diedre, love," the duchess said as she saw the eligible young nobleman for whom she held such hopes looking intently into her daughter's eyes, "I must speak with the cook about the menu."

As he watched the duchess leave with a sly smile on her face, Lord Stranham realized she thought he was there to make a declaration. Of course he intended to marry her daughter, and had for some time, but there was certainly no need to rush into a proposal.

"Was there something particular you wished to ask me, my lord?" Lady Diedre asked with a dazzling smile that didn't quite mask her calculating look.

"Yes," he said, and watched her eyes light with triumph. "I have come to ask after your health." The gleam went out of her eyes, and she flashed a narrow look at him. He smiled blandly back at her, as if unaware something further had been expected of him.

"I go on well, my lord," she replied, and changed the subject: "Have you seen the *Gazette* today? Lady Darby is to wed Lord Cissell. I think Sir Charles had been on the point of offering for her, but, alas, he has waited too long. That is often the case, do you not agree, my lord? Gentlemen do not fix their interest quickly enough and the lady accepts someone else."

"Do they indeed?" he asked politely.

"Yes, I have frequently seen it happen. I was used to wonder why a man would not ask a lady to marry him once his mind was made up. Of course, some men *do* trifle with women," she noted with a penetrating look at the marquis that was quickly concealed beneath demurely lowered lashes.

He considered her in silence for a moment. Lady Diedre

77

would certainly be a shrew someday. Still, for all that, she was a beauty of the first water, and her rank was above question. He would doubtless spend little time with her after their marriage, at any rate; he intended to keep his bits of muslin. Lady Diedre would be the perfect mother for his children. After all, her father had been a duke, and her blood was some of the oldest and bluest in the realm. Then why did he not propose to her? The answer, he concluded, was that he did not mean to be manipulated into it. He would pay his addresses when the time suited him.

Smiling pleasantly, he noted cheerfully, "Lovely weather, is it not, my lady?"

"It is," she said shortly, but made no further attempt to force him into a declaration.

CHAPTER 8

While Lord Stranham was engaged in his conversation with Lady Diedre, a much more lively discussion was about to take place in Upper Wimpole Street.

Joanna was standing patiently at the foot of the steps in the hall, waiting for Daphne to come down. She and Daphne were going to Burlington Arcade to buy ribbons and possibly a new cashmere shawl. Visions of that article of apparel floated in Joanna's mind, and as she drew on her old black cloak she was deciding on a color when her sister joined her.

"I'm ready, Joanna," she announced as her sister pulled on her own sky-blue pelerine, and they started for the door. "Oh, one minute, dear. I haven't spoken with Cedric since he came home yesterday."

After dinner last evening Daphne had been so occupied with explaining to Joanna why she had told such monstrous untruths that she had not had a chance to see how Cedric was. She wanted to hear his whole story. It was just possible, she thought in a sudden burst of anger, that she would bring charges against Lord Stranham for attacking poor Cedric.

Responding to her summons, the butler entered the room a few moments later and stood looking dejectedly at the floor, very like a man who suspects his mistress is about to read him a severe lecture. He looked up in surprise, as Daphne began with gentle concern.

"How did it happen, Cedric?"

"Well, 'e said as 'ow my cock—that would be the one I was betting on, the large banty with the black comb—'ad

79

been given some brandy to get the fighting spirit up. I told 'im straight out like that I couldn't 'elp it if 'e bet on a cock that were 'alf dead and then 'e called me a name that I dare not repeat to you and I took 'ception to that and then 'e said some further things that was most unflattering to my person. And then I must have pushed 'im—not hard, you understand—and then 'e 'it me, so I plants him a facer and—" Cedric warmed to his subject, striking a clenched fist on his open palm as he spoke and squaring his scrawny shoulders.

"That will do, Cedric," Daphne interrupted. "The point is, I fear, that you did hit him first. I suppose he would think that justified his striking you back. Although, of course, it's unforgivable of him to have taken such unfair advantage of you."

"Well, he had all that weight on his side, being so terrible fat and all," Cedric admitted.

Daphne looked at the old man curiously. "Lord Stranham is not fat, Cedric."

"Well, no, of course 'e's not, but then that 'as nothing to say to the matter." Thinking the conversation was at an end, Cedric turned to leave.

Daphne stood frozen to the spot, a terrible suspicion forming in her mind. "Do you mean, Cedric," she whispered huskily to his retreating form, "that the marquis was *not* the man you were fighting with?"

He stopped and turned back in genuine surprise. "Of course not!" he replied in shocked tones.

"Oh," Daphne murmured faintly as she leaned against the wall, her head spinning.

Joanna entered the conversation for the first time. "Was the marquis at the cockfights?"

"Yes," Cedric replied.

"Was he with a red-haired man named Sir Robert Drayton, a bit stocky but excessively nice and—"

Daphne cut through her interrogation: "Do you mean,

Cedric—listen carefully—you were not fighting with the marquis?" She sought one final clarification.

"Of course not," Cedric reaffirmed disdainfully.

"Then why did he bring you home?"

The butler looked around the hallway before beginning uncomfortably: "I was getting a bit of the worst end of the fight. I would 'ave won in the end, of course, but Lord Stranham, 'e jumps in and pulls the other man off me and then brought me back 'ere. 'E's a cove fellow, your marquis."

Daphne ran her hand across her forehead as if trying to wipe away the memory of the words she had spoken to Lord Stranham. She had made a horrible fool of herself and, worse, had accused him of being a bully and a villain when in fact he had gone out of his way to help. What had he said before he left? Oh, yes, he had told her he was sorry he had ever come there.

She rallied to her own defense. What was the marquis doing at the cockfights in the first place? But her sense of fairness came to his side; after all, there was no reason why he should not frequent such low spots if he chose to, and that did not excuse her words to him.

"Are you ready, Daphne?" Joanna asked after a silence during which Daphne had stared at the floor with a stunned look on her face.

"Yes, yes," she murmured. "Come along, Cedric, we are ready to go."

As they walked out to the battered landaulet and Cedric took the reins, she rehearsed in her mind what she would say to Lord Stranham when she wrote to apologize. This was terribly mortifying, she thought, blushing red at the thought of the things she had said to him. And she had slapped him! Her face turned redder still.

"Do you think pink a good color for a shawl?" Joanna ventured the query after several worried looks at her sister.

"Pink?" Daphne repeated vaguely.

"Yes."

"Certainly, a very nice choice," Daphne agreed distantly. She was unaware that she even spoke. Her mind was occupied with the humiliation she felt at having made such hasty and terribly wrong charges against the marquis.

It developed that learning of her mistaken attack on Lord Stranham was not the worst of the fates that were to befall Daphne that day. When she and Joanna arrived back at the house after their shopping trip, Rose greeted them with the whispered knowledge that Mrs. Winter awaited them in the parlor.

Daphne entered—Joanna trailed behind—to find Mrs. Winter examining a small figurine on the fireplace. She put it down abruptly and turned to greet them.

"Good afternoon, Mrs. Winter, do sit down," Daphne said pleasantly. Perhaps her lie of last night had not been so very wrong if it was having such a beneficial effect. After all, if Mrs. Winter was calling on them so soon, it could only mean she wished to invite them somewhere. Splendid. They needed to go places where they could meet people and begin making discreet inquiries for situations.

"Good afternoon, girls," the older woman said brightly. "I have the most delicious *on dit*! Although," she noted cheerily, "I'm certain it won't be news to you."

"What is it?" Joanna asked.

"Well, my dears," she began, still standing in front of the fireplace and spreading her hands dramatically, "I have heard only this morning that Lady Drayton is giving a large ball on Friday. I wouldn't ask this of anyone else, but I feel that you are already such good friends of mine, as well as being friends of my dear, dear cousin Millie, so I think a favor between us would be like a gift to one of the family." She paused expectantly. "Don't you agree?"

"Yes," Joanna said automatically, although she appeared somewhat confused by the preamble.

Mrs. Winter seemed satisfied with this affirmative if perplexed reply, for she plunged ahead: "As I have said, your dear friend Lady Drayton is giving a ball, and since we are practically cousins, I thought perhaps—" She broke off with a hopeful look.

Daphne suddenly realized where the conversation was heading. "Do let me ring for tea!" she cried as she bustled over to the bell rope. "Joanna and I have only just returned from shopping. The Pantheon Bazaar was packed, just simply packed with people! You cannot conceive, my dear Mrs. Winter, how many people there were. And Burlington Arcade! Were there not a great many shoppers there, Joanna?" Daphne sought reinforcement to help turn the topic away from what she strongly suspected was to be a request for invitations to Lady Drayton's ball. Why, Daphne asked herself angrily, had she lied about knowing Lady Drayton?

Joanna was regarding her blankly. "I didn't think it was crowded, Daphne," she said quietly, "and I believe you interrupted Mrs. Winter."

Why was the girl always so polite? Couldn't she be nasty just once? "Did I interrupt?" she forced herself to ask sweetly.

"Yes, you did," Mrs. Winter agreed, not stopping to cavil over polite demurs. "As I was saying, I collect you have already been invited, and it would mean so much to me, a very great deal, if you could possibly arrange for John and me to receive invitations." She ended with an expectant smile, her arms still opened in an appeal.

Mrs. Winter looked more like a swooping bird of prey than a meek supplicant, Daphne thought as she regarded the thin woman in dark gray.

"You *are* going, aren't you?" she pressed with a quick look at the two girls.

Daphne still stood by the window, her hand arrested near the bell rope. "Of course." She lied with an effrontery brought on, in part, by Mrs. Winter's chameleonlike change from near relative to unfriendly interrogator.

"Well," their guest said in a mournful voice, changing roles once again—this time, to long-suffering friend—"if you go, do have a good time. I should wish that for you."

Daphne stood uncertainly, not sure what to say to the older woman. Rose entered the room and set the tea tray down on a gateleg table, and Joanna busied herself with the teacups to avoid looking at either party.

"I shall have to contrive to console myself with a small party of my own on that evening, I daresay," Mrs. Winter continued. "I had thought to wait until the following Friday. It would be such a wonderful opportunity for you girls to meet some of the many charming young men John and I know, but I suppose I shall go ahead and have it this Friday if I cannot look forward to the glamour of Lady Drayton's ball."

"Mrs. Winter, I very much fear that—" Daphne broke off, searching for the right words.

Their guest continued smoothly, "Of course if you *cannot* get the invitations . . ." Her voice trailed off and she shrugged, as if to say that *that* would tell her all she needed to know about the Brown girls.

Daphne froze at the tone of negligent contempt in the woman's voice. She did some rapid thinking. Hadn't Lady Morley procured vouchers to Almacks for Joanna and her in deference to their father's memory? And it was certain she knew Lady Drayton, since she knew Sir Robert Drayton. Surely Lady Morley could be prevailed upon to obtain invitations to the ball for them.

"Of course," Daphne said dulcetly, "there is no difficulty in securing tickets." She gave a deprecating little laugh at the absurdity of thinking she could not get them. "I was merely going to say I'm very much afraid we can't get them today. In truth, it may not be until tomorrow or the day after."

Mrs. Winter's face lit with joy. "My dear! Can you really?"

"Oh, of course," Daphne assured her with airy casualness.

Joanna, who had looked up from the tea tray in astonishment, turned hastily to look out the window. The teacup she held in her hand rattled as she affected great concentration on the urchins playing on the cobblestone street in front of the house.

Mrs. Winter moved across the room to Daphne and embraced her in an appreciative hug before floating to the door and turning to call back, "I cannot thank you enough!"

"Wouldn't you care to sit and have some tea?" Daphne asked with strained courtesy.

"No, I haven't time. I have so many preparations to make for the ball. Imagine! Wait until I tell that hoity-toity Mrs. Burns that *I'm* going to Lady Drayton's ball. She'll turn positively pea green with envy!"

"Mrs. Burns?" Daphne repeated.

"Oh, yes, she's a friend of mine."

"I am certain," Daphne said with well-concealed irony, "that there is absolutely nothing more heartwarming than making one's friends turn pea green with envy."

Mrs. Winter nodded agreement and swept gleefully from the room.

CHAPTER 9

Joanna turned slowly from the window and lowered the teacup back to the table. "You lied," she said to her sister accusingly. "We're not invited to Lady Drayton's ball and we can't get invitations for Mrs. Winter."

"Of course we can," Daphne said with a great deal more assurance than she felt.

"I don't understand it in the least," Joanna complained. "First you tell Mrs. Winter we are acquainted with people we do not know, and then you inform her we are invited to a ball where we are not invited, and now you promise you can get her invitations to that same ball."

Hearing it thus phrased, Daphne felt more than a tremor of remorse mixed with panic. What had she done?

But she continued bravely: "Let me explain it to you, Joanna, in the form of a parable. If someone had something you wanted, say a dog, and he told you you could have the dog if you would give him something in return, say a cat, then wouldn't you make every effort to get a cat for him to trade?"

Joanna's small face bore a quizzical look. "How can you stand there talking about animals when you have just told the most shameless rappers?"

Daphne sighed. "Jesus had such great success with parables," she murmured. With a firmer inflection in her voice she said, "We simply *must* get them. We are running very short of funds and I had little luck at the employment agency I visited yesterday. It has become apparent to me that no one is going to hire us except someone who knows us. And the only way we are going to meet people is to move about in society. Mrs. Winter could introduce us to a great many persons, so we must cultivate her friendship."

"Could we not apply to Lady Morley for aid?"

Daphne gave a regretful sigh. "I fear not. I tried to broach the subject gently by asking her how people go about finding situations, while I was sitting next to her at Almacks. She told me very sharply she did not concern herself with such lowering matters. That stopped me from applying to her. But she *can* get us an entrée to Lady Drayton's ball, and if that is what is necessary to satisfy Mrs. Winter, then I shall simply have to ascertain that we are invited."

Actually, for all her brave words, Daphne felt far from assured that they could procure invitations to Lady Drayton's ball. The practicality of fulfilling her pledge to Mrs. Winter loomed large; it seemed even more frightening when she considered that her note thanking Lady Morley for escorting them to Almacks had never been answered. In fact, they had heard nothing further from that woman. It was possible that they had receded to the fuzzy edges of Lady Morley's mind and they would never hear from her further, regardless of how great a friend the old lady might have been to their father.

Daphne must somehow bring them back to Lady Morley's attention, she realized. But how?

She pondered the problem all evening, allowing Joanna to beat her in chess for the first time since her younger sister, at the age of ten, had left off cheating. Daphne was much too occupied with the problem of how to acquire invitations, to pay much heed to the game. She came out of her reverie to hear Joanna prompting her to play.

"Daphne, it's your move. I have your king checked."

"Oh."

"I have an idea."

"About where to move my king?" Daphne asked indifferently.

"No."

"What is it?" she inquired absently as she brought her attention back to the carved wooden figures on the chessboard.

"Why do we not send a note around to Lady Morley's house saying I think I left a pair of gloves in her coach and asking if she would be so good as to look? That would give us an excuse for writing to her and perhaps remind her to call on us."

Daphne gave a happy cry, upsetting the chessboard as she rose from her chair and leaned across the small table to engulf Joanna in a hug. "That's an excellent idea! Why didn't I think of it?"

"Perhaps you were concentrating too hard on the game," Joanna suggested innocently.

The rest of the evening Daphne was entirely too excited to play chess. She paced the small parlor, turning over in her mind the proper note to send Lady Morley—one that would recall the Browns to her mind and induce her to call on them. Once Lady Morley was in their house, the matter of securing the invitations would be minor indeed. Daphne went off to bed humming happily and arose early in equally good spirits.

In the first light of the morning she pulled an aging dressing gown over her thin nightdress and padded over to the small desk in her room. Seating herself, she dipped the pen in the standish and proceeded, after a great many efforts, to write a letter that satisfied her. When she had written the last line, she folded the paper and hurried down the steps.

"Cedric! Cedric! I have a message for you to deliver immediately." She stopped in front of the old servant, who looked at her with faint surprise. "Listen and tell me what

89

you think of it," she ordered before clearing her throat to read:

" 'My dear Lady Morley, I should not trouble you except that I fear when you were kind enough to come round in your carriage for my sister and me Wednesday last, Joanna must have left her gloves within. How silly of her, but she does so need them. If it is not too much trouble, I should dearly appreciate your returning them to her. And I thank you once again for taking us to Almacks. It was ever so lovely and I can't think when I've had such a wonderful time. Respectfully yours and etc., Miss Daphne Brown.' "

She finished reading and looked up hopefully. "What do you think?"

"I believe ye should just buy a new pair of gloves," he answered honestly. "It seems a deal of trouble to go to. Now I think on it, I'm almost certain I saw several new pairs delivered last week."

"You don't understand in the least"—she laughed happily—"but that doesn't signify. What is important is that you give this note to Lady Morley's butler and tell him you will await a reply. Do you understand?"

"Yes, Miss Daphne," he replied wearily. He hated delivering messages, and today was the day the unbeaten gray was to fight the speckled cock.

"Oh, and Cedric," she called as he shuffled toward the door, "*do* come straight home."

"Of course," he returned frostily.

A quarter of an hour later he stood in the small, cluttered entryway of Lady Morley's house regarding a tiny woman in a bright orange dress.

"The maid tells me you are here about some gloves," she said, peering at him first through and then over her spectacles.

"That is correct, ma'am," Cedric replied at his most dignified. He hazarded a glance down at his blue uniform to see if something was amiss with it, she was staring at it in such disbelief.

"It was not my carriage we took to Almacks," she explained, "and I have no notion if anything was left in it. I was so excessively preoccupied at the time, you see, what with the cards all going against me and Mr. Breuner insisting I had not played the ace and . . . Gloves, you say?"

"Yes, ma'am."

"It was Sir Robert Drayton's carriage. You will have to inquire of him whether he found anything within the coach. I have written his direction down." She handed Cedric a piece of paper. "I am persuaded he can help you."

"Thank you." He accepted the paper and stepped outside. On the sidewalk, he lingered indecisively. Sir Robert Drayton was the man Miss Daphne had mentioned who might have improper designs on Miss Joanna. He really didn't want to call on such a man, but Miss Daphne had been most particular in her instructions that he retrieve the gloves. For a moment Cedric toyed with the idea of going to a shop and simply purchasing another pair, but he finally decided against that course of action—after all, the gray was fighting today and he didn't wish to spend all his betting money.

If the articles were so important, then he would continue on to Sir Robert's and try to discover what that man knew of them. A few minutes later he was in the foyer of the baronet's house, looking down at the black-and-white-lozenge floor as he waited for the butler to return with a reply to the letter he had handed him.

Behind the closed door to the dayroom Sir Robert was seated uncomfortably in an overstuffed chair with his healing leg stretched out on a footstool in front of him. He was gleefully rereading the message while his dignified butler stood stiffly by.

"The vixen!" Sir Robert chortled.

"I beg your pardon, sir?"

"Oh, nothing, nothing." Gloves indeed! That one won't fadge, he thought happily. It's transparent enough even for a slow-top like me. It was perfectly obvious that the note was a ploy to attract his attention. Oh, it was addressed to Lady Morley all right, but surely Joanna had known his carriage had conveyed them to Almacks. Doubtless Joanna had hoped Lady Morley would direct the note to him so she wouldn't look too coming. That was also why she had had her sister write the letter. Ah, she was a rare handful, that Joanna, he thought with a contented sigh.

Robert relaxed back in the chair and let his mind drift to the pleasure he had felt upon touching her slender waist while they stood up at Almacks. She had been like a tiny fairy, dancing with a grace and ease that was quite natural, if a bit untutored. And such a lovely face! Lord, but he would like to see her now.

Sir Robert came back to the present with a start. He couldn't see her. He'd look a perfect fool hobbling around on this blasted leg. And these dashed bruises on his face—they were fading quickly and would undoubtedly be gone in time for his mother's ball, but he couldn't face Miss Joanna until they were.

Now, there was a thought, he considered. Why not invite Joanna and her sister to his mother's party? That— he congratulated himself—was an excellent idea. Hadn't she mentioned how much she had enjoyed Almacks? And he could extend the invitation through Lady Morley, just as he had arranged for them to attend Almacks. Yes, he'd invite them. "Bring me pen and paper," he commanded the butler.

"Very good, sir." The servant went off in search of writing equipment and returned a few moments later to hand them to his excited master.

Sir Robert scribbled furiously, stopped, reread and crumpled up the first sheet. He tried again. No, it sounded wrong. He gave up on the third attempt. He couldn't find the right words. He'd wait to write later when he had Mark to tell him what to say. Now, there was a man who had a way with words, especially with the ladies.

"Inform him there is no message," Sir Robert directed the butler.

"Very good, sir." The servant started to leave and then turned back. "The messenger mentioned something about a pair of gloves. Should I look for them?"

"Don't be a fool, Giles," Robert admonished the man with a snort of laughter.

"Quite right, sir," the butler answered gravely.

Half an hour later, stopping only for the very tail end of an exceptionally good cockfight—after all, there was no need to rush back, since there was no message—Cedric arrived in Upper Wimpole Street. Daphne met him at the door.

"Was there any reply?" she asked breathlessly as he stepped inside the front hallway.

"No."

"Oh," she said with a sigh of defeat. "Well, that is that." Turning slowly, she started upstairs to her room. She might as well write immediately to Mrs. Winter confessing her lie, she thought morosely. Taking a piece of paper, she sat down at the small maple drop-leaf desk and dipped the quill pen in the standish.

"Dear Mrs. Winter," she began. She tore the sheet up and tried again. What could she say to the woman? That she had lied? Such a bald statement of facts was frightening. With little more than two months' money to live on, Daphne had desperately depended on a connection with Mrs. Winter to help her and Joanna in finding positions. The way things now appeared to be proceeding, they would be shunned by Mrs. Winter when she discovered they would not be able to introduce her to *ton* people. Daphne stared out the window past the ancient red curtains and tried to think of words to write.

Perhaps, she thought inspirationally, she could say that Lady Drayton was seriously ill and would be forced to cancel the ball. Her mind lingered on that appealing idea for a time, but she finally concluded that if Mrs. Winter knew about the party, she was bound to find out whether or not it actually took place. Possibly the idea of illness could be put to a better use. She and Joanna could fall sick with something dreadful and be unable to attend. And of course, if they couldn't go to Lady Drayton's ball, there would be no conceivable way they could take guests.

Daphne balled the paper up and threw it into the unlit hearth, pursuing her thought. The unfortunate possibility struck her: If she and Joanna were "sick," Mrs. Winter might go ahead and have her own soirée and they would not be able to attend it. What to do?

It was most confusing. Pushing back a lock of her tumbling blond curls, Daphne slid out of the chair and paced the room in indecision. She wouldn't write the letter to Mrs. Winter just yet. Something would happen to save her. It had to, she thought desperately. There was always the remote chance Lady Drayton's house would burn down. Daphne gave brief consideration to the wild idea of setting a torch to the house, then abandoned that thought. Surely there was a better means to her end.

CHAPTER 10

The following morning Lord Stranham walked inside Sam's Royal Library and checked in the doorway. Standing not two yards from him was Miss Daphne Brown. He gave her a curt nod and turned to depart.

"Pray do not leave, my lord," she said anxiously, and moved toward him. "I wish to speak with you. In fact, I had meant to write but have not yet done so."

He regarded her coldly. "Concerning what?" he asked unhelpfully.

Daphne faltered and glanced about the shop self-consciously before lowering her voice to just above a whisper. "My lord, I find that I owe you an apology. I have discovered I was grievously wrong in my accusations against you."

"I accept your apology," he said stiffly.

"I cannot conceive why we came to this poky little store when there are so many glorious millinery shops to be explored," a dark-haired woman complained as she approached Daphne. Seeing the marquis, she transformed her petulant expression into a dazzling smile. "Oh, my dear, I was not aware you were engaged in conversation. Do introduce me to your friend."

Mrs. Winter's eyes combed Lord Stranham in a glance, missing nothing of his green Bath coat, superb tan trousers, and mirror-shiny Hessians. And the casual air of command about him did nothing to diminish him in her eyes. He was obviously Quality. Her face lit in delight at the anticipation of meeting one such as him.

"Mrs. Winter," Daphne said tonelessly, "this is Lord Stranham. He is—"

"My dear, you need not tell me who he is! I am so very honored to make your acquaintance, my lord, I'm sure," she said, bowing deeply, as if he were royalty.

The marquis returned a polite bow. "I am most pleased to meet you, madam."

"We shall no doubt see you at Lady Drayton's ball," Mrs. Winter said happily, and then glanced about the shop to see if anyone she knew was present to witness the spectacular feat of her meeting the marquis of Stranham! Although she saw no one she recognized, she was not daunted; someone might chance by, she thought as she turned back to her quarry to pursue a conversation. She wanted to have a lengthy dialogue with his lordship to relate back to Mrs. Burns.

For his part, Lord Stranham was regarding the older woman in some confusion. Whatever did she mean she would see him at Lady Drayton's? From the corner of his eye he saw Daphne dart an apprehensive look up at him before she nervously pulled a crumpled handkerchief from her reticule and held it clenched in her hand.

"You will be there, won't you, my lord?" Mrs. Winter probed.

"Yes, I shall," he replied coolly, but he took leave to doubt that she would. Whoever this woman was, she was definitely not connected with society. Her unfashionable drab gray pelisse and gaudy hat made of feathers and flowers were evidence of that; besides, he had never heard of her. She must be some friend of Miss Brown's who hoped to insinuate herself in with people above her touch.

"I can hardly contain myself, I am so looking forward to the ball," Mrs. Winter confided cheerfully.

"Indeed," he said in unencouraging accents.

"Yes, and I—" She broke off with an exclamation of joy. "There is Mrs. Burns entering the shop across the street! Do excuse me, my lord, I must speak with her. She's such a *dear* friend." In a quick aside to Daphne, she murmured, "Do not allow him to leave on any account until I return with Mrs. Burns."

The older woman was gone before Daphne could reply, leaving her standing foolishly in front of the marquis. She unconsciously wrung her handkerchief while she silently berated herself for not having explained the whole of her falsehood to Mrs. Winter before they had left to go shopping. Daphne looked around in distraction for Rose and saw her two aisles over, glancing through a book. Her maid was not likely to come to her aid.

"Your sister is well, I trust?" the marquis asked distantly.

"Quite. She was too busy to come today."

"I collect you are to attend Lady Drayton's ball." Was that young fool Robert still pursuing Joanna Brown in spite of his advice?

"Well, I—" She took her bottom lip between her teeth and hesitated.

"I understand," he said coolly.

"Yes," she rejoined sadly, "you must comprehend quite well. I am certain it is obvious to you that I am not invited, and you can only wonder where Mrs. Winter conceived the idea that *she* was. My lord"—the words tumbled out in a rush—"I have done the most foolish thing. You see— no, you do not see at all," she said, looking at his harsh face, "but I shall try to explain it to you. When you brought Cedric home, I thought that you had misused him, and I was terribly angry."

"You made that fact abundantly clear to me at the time."

"Yes, I suppose I did," she allowed mournfully. "I mean I slapped you and shouted at you; that must have made you dreadfully angry?" she questioned timidly, looking up at him cautiously.

"I was not best pleased," he agreed stonily, his handsome face set in taut lines, his gray eyes granite hard.

"Oh," she said in dejection. "It's of no use."

"Pray do not distress yourself making explanations. After Lady Drayton's ball I shouldn't think it likely we shall see each other in any event, so you needn't worry about feeling uncomfortable with me."

Daphne raised large violet eyes to him; her voice also reflected her anguish. "We are not invited, nor is Mrs. Winter."

"I see," he murmured in complete bafflement.

"I daresay it all sounds a bit confusing," she noted as she made a great study of a row of leather-bound books behind him.

"So very vexing!" Mrs. Winter interrupted as she breezed back up to them. "Mrs. Burns had gone before I reached the shop. I am certain she would have wished to meet you, my lord." She bestowed a fawning smile on the marquis.

"I should have enjoyed the pleasure," he said mechanically. "I regret that I must be leaving now."

"So very soon?" Mrs. Winter asked in obvious disappointment.

"Yes. Servant, ladies." He bowed and turned to go.

"My lord," Mrs. Winter called after him, waving a handkerchief and stretching a hand out to stop him, "Miss Brown and her maid came in my carriage, but I shall not be ready to leave for some time. I must wait to speak with dear Mrs. Burns. Would you mind escorting them to their house?"

Daphne gave the older woman a look of dismay. "His lordship is *quite* busy, I am sure. If you must wait, then Rose and I shall remain with you."

"Nonsense, I am persuaded Lord Stranham would be delighted to see you home." She encouraged Daphne with a meaningful look. "Would you not, my lord?"

"Of course," he said with rigid courtesy.

"There, you see," she said triumphantly. "Do run along, my dear. Rose—where is that girl? Come here, your mistress is ready to leave." Mrs. Winter gave Daphne a sly wink as she pushed the maid toward her. "I shall stop by your house later to hear how you got on," she said brightly.

"I really don't think—" Daphne began with an uncomfortable look at the marquis, who took her arm as she spoke.

"Do not distress yourself. I shall be honored to see you home."

Wordlessly he assisted the two women outside and helped them up into his carriage. The groom set off through the crowded streets, his progress considerably impaired by the traffic, which was moving at a snail's pace.

Lord Stranham watched the slender girl seated across from him who alternated between looking out the window and staring down at her hands. She was obviously uncomfortable. He was roused to speak partly by curiosity and partly by a desire to relieve her of her discomposure. "Does something overset you, Miss Brown?"

"No, my lord," she replied with downcast eyes. After a moment's silence she added in a small voice, "I wish you will pay me the compliment of not repeating to Lady Drayton or her son anything Mrs. Winter said."

Looking out the window, Lord Stranham saw the rows of bow-fronted shops moving slowly past the carriage. "It promises to be a long trip to your house, Miss Brown. We shall have plenty of time, so you may as well tell me the whole of this masquerade."

She began in a hesitant voice: "I told Mrs. Winter that we knew Lady Drayton and that we could help her obtain a ticket to a ball her ladyship is giving." Having admitted her sin, Daphne hurried on without looking at him: "It was a terrible lie, and I am certain I shall burn for ever-so-long for telling it, but I was prepared to do that if it would bring us into Mrs. Winter's circle of friends."

"Did it?"

She continued, looking determinedly downward at the hands clenched and turning white on her lap: "Everything was going well until she appeared yesterday and demanded to be invited to Lady Drayton's party. I started to tell her that we weren't going, but she made it almost like a challenge, so I—well, I—"

"So, of course, you told her you were invited and you could obtain invitations for her as well," he finished for her. "Am I correct?"

"Yes," she admitted in despair, feeling totally disconsolate.

To her surprise, he threw back his head and laughed.

She looked at him in puzzlement, which gave way to resentment. "I don't see that it is at all funny," she said in a wounded voice.

"Tell me," he asked with a chuckle, "what did your sister think of these machinations?"

"She thought it was a horrible string of lies," Daphne admitted.

"It sounds as if she is the levelheaded one in the family," he commented mildly.

"It's true I am excessively dim-witted," she agreed contritely, "and, as I said, I daresay I shall burn for a very long time, which hardly seems fair, because I'm not going to derive any benefit from my lies in this world, so why should I be punished for them in the next?"

"I fear you will have to take that up with some higher authority than me," he commented with a smile.

Daphne dropped her eyes back to the floor. She had told him everything; he considered her very stupid, that much was apparent from his laughter. What else must he think her?

She would have blushed to know what Lord Stranham

was actually thinking at that moment. The little beauty before him, he reflected, seemed to have a way of embroiling herself in situations she could not handle. Well, she was not the only woman he knew who lied. A great many women did so for the exact same reason she had: to increase their consequence in someone else's eyes.

All in all, he thought, his happening onto her in the book shop had been a fortunate occurrence. He was glad for the chance to see Daphne and further his acquaintance with her. In the ordinary way of things he would never consider giving any chit a second chance once she had done something as unpardonable as slapping him. But in her case he found he was willing to make some exceptions. She had an appeal he had not encountered for some time.

What Daphne was angling for, he knew, was for him to offer to secure an entrée for her to Lady Drayton's. He did not approve of women in her position in life going to places where the company was obviously above their touch. No, he would not obtain invitations to Lady Drayton's home for her. In fact, he thought he and Miss Brown would go on much better if she had a clear understanding that he would be the undisputed master in any relationship they had. And right now, he intended to set the tone of that liaison by reading her a lecture on propriety.

"Miss Brown, permit me to say that such outrageous falsehoods as you have perpetrated rarely bring good results," he began firmly. He paused; in fact, he could not continue. Daphne's bottom lip began to quiver as she brought a dainty lace handkerchief to her eyes. It was not that he abhorred seeing a female cry; he had quite steeled himself against the tears of the weaker sex. It had stood him in good stead when refusing requests from his *chères amies* for expensive jewelry and clothes. But as he looked at Miss Brown he experienced the uncomfortable realization that he did not wish to cause her any pain. And worse, he did not want to do anything that would hurt the friendship he sought to establish with her.

"Miss Brown," he said with resignation in his voice, "I shall help you."

"W-what?"

"I shall ensure that you and . . ." He paused before adding distastefully, "Mrs. Winter go to the ball. I daresay Lady Drayton won't object. The more people she can crowd into her house, the more successful she accounts her parties."

Upon seeing the unaffected smile that spread across Daphne's face, lighting her eyes and curving her soft lips upward delightfully, Lord Stranham wondered why he had waited so long to offer his assistance. He had not known she could smile so enchantingly.

"Oh, thank you, my lord!" she cried, a stray tear from her earlier moment of anxiety running unchecked down one smooth peach-pink cheek.

He felt an urge to wipe it away but refrained. The sight of her maid, sitting on the seat beside her mistress and gazing at him reverently, recalled him to his senses. There would be time enough later—when he would be alone with Daphne—to feel the softness of her skin.

"Let me see," he said with careful casualness. "How many invitations do you need? One for you and one for your sister and Mrs. Winter—and I collect she is married and—"

"Four!" she interposed quickly.

"Thank you," he replied with a politeness that masked his amusement.

"I—I really do appreciate it, and I don't know how to thank you, my lord," she said shyly, blushing prettily as she averted her eyes.

The marquis was at that moment thinking of a delightful, if most improper, way in which she could express her gratitude. But he merely mused aloud, "Sir Robert has also been telling some rappers of late; I cannot think how I contrive to surround myself with people who tell such prodigious lies."

Daphne looked at him apprehensively and was relieved to see a slow smile spread across his face. "If I were you, Miss Brown, I should avoid the subject of relatives the evening of the party."

"Oh?"

"Yes," he replied. There was no need for her to know Robert had given out the lie that they were related to him.

"I will," she promised.

"And I shall exact one further command. You must agree to stand up with me at the ball."

"But as Joanna's chaperon, I cannot dance with you," she protested.

"On the contrary, I insist you do. You will be present as a friend of mine, and Lady Drayton will think it odd if I do not single you out for the honor."

She looked down at the floor of the carriage. "I am dreadfully sorry. It's terribly embarrassing to be thought connected, even if we are not."

"I am sorry you feel that way."

"I don't mean *us,* my lord! I mean *you,*" she declared in shocked accents.

"It is a good deal nicer to be thought related to two blond beauties than to the humpbacked, cross-eyed people who compose the bulk of my society," he observed urbanely.

"You're too kind," she murmured, feeling another shy blush creep into her cheeks as he looked at her with surprising intentness.

"I know," he agreed amiably. "And now," he said, turning the conversation, "how do you find London?"

"It is an admirable city, my lord." As the carriage edged slowly homeward Daphne chattered on happily about the weather—the clouds, the glorious day, the sun—and other

103

variations on the general theme of the weather. She was barely aware of her own words, she felt so relieved.

Lord Stranham didn't mind. He enjoyed hearing her talk and seeing her smile, her violet eyes glowing with excitement in her small face. Every once in a while she laughed, a light, tinkling laugh that made him look at her in fascination. He was glad the carriage moved slowly.

It pulled up in front of her house, and he alighted. She smiled conspiratorially as he reached up to help her down. "Thank you, my lord. So many girls would give their eyes for a chance to see such a glorious ball," she confided.

"That would rather defeat the purpose, wouldn't it?" he asked mildly, then bowed and walked around to take his seat before proceeding cheerfully on to the Draytons'.

CHAPTER 11

Lord Stranham was shown out to the garden, where the nearly recovered invalid and his mother were enjoying the sunshine.

Carefully ensconced in a wicker chair with a lap rug placed on his knees, Robert seemed to be in his element. His glowing complexion and the merry smile on his face indicated that he had reached the stage of invalidism where one is no longer afflicted with pains and aches and is, therefore, able to enjoy the attention showered on one by relatives and servants.

Robert extended his sunny smile to include Lord Stranham as the marquis walked down the path, past day lilies blooming soft pink and yellow and neatly cut beds of flowers giving forth tulips in the last glorious stages of bright yellows and reds. Beyond the beds of flowers, green hedges, which formed the main part of the garden, had been trimmed to careful bush shapes. Above the beauty of the garden was as cloudless a sky as ever graced England.

"Come to see me, have you?" Robert called to Lord Stranham with the innocent selfishness of the recently sick.

"No, I have come to see your mother," the marquis returned as he bowed over the hand of the lady seated on a stone bench beside Robert's wicker chaise. "You are as lovely as ever," he murmured to her.

The plump woman in the matronly rose dress with pink fichu collar smiled girlishly as she looked up at him shrewdly. "And you, Mark, are as flattering as ever. Can you not see that my hair is half white and I have gained a stone?" she asked archly.

"It only makes you more lovely," he remarked gallantly. "And your hair is an exquisite shade of heather-red."

"I was wrong, Stranham," she corrected herself. "You are *more* flattering than ever. But it won't fadge with me. I've known you since you were in short coats. No," she amended conscientiously, "I've known you since you were in leading strings, and I do believe you could turn a pretty compliment even then."

"I say the most charming things to you and you return with flippancy. Really, my lady," he admonished.

"Are you looking after my son?" she asked, abruptly changing the subject. She looked fondly at her only child.

"Every moment of the day," he assured her readily as he settled himself on a stone bench beside Lady Drayton. Nearby a statue of a cherub lent an idyllic air to the peaceful garden.

"Ah, then you must have been close at hand when he was attacked by that wild band of footpads," she pursued with a twinkle in her eye.

"I confess I was not."

The knowing look Lady Drayton bestowed on both her son and the marquis told Lord Stranham quite plainly that she did not believe for a minute that Robert had been set upon by robbers. She was a lady who was able usually to sort through a great amount of chaff and arrive at something very close to the truth. But she made no comment about her disbelief of her son's tale as she continued, "Your dear Mama requested me to deliver a message to you."

"And what does my lady mother say?" Lord Stranham asked pleasantly.

"She says she and your father are weary of hearing about your raking activities and wish you to marry and settle down to raise a large family of brats who will doubtless be no better than they should be, and will cause you the same amount of grief you have caused her and the duke." The speech was delivered with a seriousness that would have been more effective had Lady Drayton not ended on a peal of laughter.

"My lady mother is as delicate as ever in her messages. When next you see her, tell her that I shall attend her shortly at Castleway to give her a brief lesson on the ways a mother should address a son who is heir to a dukedom."

"Your mother would pay no heed to your lessons if you were the heir to the realm, and well you know it," Lady Drayton informed him, still laughing. "And as for attending her at Castleway, I would suggest that you do so because if you do not, she and the duke will descend on you here in the midst of your libertine activities and drag you to Saint George's by the ear with the first suitable maid to see you united in holy wedlock."

"Indeed," he said mildly. "What an exciting spectacle for the residents of Hanover Square. The sight of a man over six feet tall being dragged bodily through the streets by a woman a full head and shoulders shorter than he, should be most diverting."

Robert, appearing to feel that more was his due as the resident invalid, interrupted pettishly: "Are Mark's affairs the only thing we have to discuss?" He shifted his weight uncomfortably in the wicker lounge and looked accusingly at his guest.

"Of course not," his mother responded amiably. "You, Robert, could retell your very exciting tale of being assaulted by footpads. However," she cautioned, "I have noted that each time you regale me with that tale the settings are different." She directed a penetrating look at her son.

"You must have misheard me," he mumbled, suddenly finding great interest in the toes of his plump, bare foot.

He wriggled them nervously before making an interested study of the cherub statue.

Lady Drayton turned back to the marquis. "Will you be escorting a young lady to my ball?" she probed, returning once again to the subject of interest to her.

"I don't know, I could be," he replied evasively.

Lady Drayton seemed to take that answer for an affirmative. "Excellent. Your mother will be pleased to hear that. I do so dread having these affairs, but it is, I think, my duty to come to London at least once a year and make some showing to the *beau monde* that I still exist."

Lady Drayton, who loved her yearly trips to London above all things, and whose balls were always acclaimed the high point of each season, received with equanimity the assertions of both men that the Quality would be prostrate should she cease to exist.

"Well," she announced as she rose briskly, "I shall leave you two for the present. I need to put the house into some semblance of order for the ball."

"Lady Drayton," the marquis said, rising also, "might I have a word with you?"

"Not now, Mark," Robert interrupted irritably. "I have something of importance I need you to do for me. You can speak with my mother at some later time."

"Perhaps it would be better for you to call later," Lady Drayton agreed, "as I really have a number of things to attend to at present and poor Robbie is dreadfully in want of company."

"Of course, my lady." Lord Stranham acquiesced with a bow as Lady Drayton strolled down the brick path back toward the imposing white house. "Well, Robbie?" he asked, turning back to his friend.

"Robert," the baronet corrected sulkily.

"Very well—Robert, then. What is it you wish of me?"

"I need you to write a letter for me."

"Could it not wait until another time? What I particularly wished to speak with your mother about I could just as readily ask you; I need invitat—"

"Dash it, Mark," the younger man interjected darkly, "you're not attending me in the least. I need you to write a letter to Miss Joanna."

"Later." The marquis dismissed the request with a wave of his hand. "Now, as I was saying, I shall need you to obtain invitations to your mother's ball. Just write a letter inviting Mis—"

"Mark," Robert interrupted with a rising note of impatience in his voice, "you do not understand in the least, nor are you making any attempt to. I find your singular interest in your own affairs most offensive," he lectured sternly.

The marquis, who was rapidly developing a mutual feeling for Robert's request, nevertheless settled himself back on the bench. Fingering his nut-brown kid waistcoat, he listened impassively as Robert spoke.

"Now, I'm going to have my mother invite Miss Joanna and her sister to her ball," he began with a defiant look at Lord Stranham.

The marquis, surprised and gladdened by the announcement, opened his mouth to speak, but Robert forestalled him by continuing almost immediately: "I know you will not approve, but I am going to invite them anyway and I do not wish to hear your opinion on the subject."

"Very well," Lord Stranham said meekly.

"Now then," Robert continued in the same determined tone, "you must help me compose a note of apology. I'll send it with the invitations."

Robert picked up a hand bell beside his chaise lounge and rang it loudly. The butler appeared a moment later, wearing a harassed look that bespoke the hope his master's illness would not extend too much longer. He looked as if he were near to exhaustion at having to run to answer the bell.

"Pen and paper, Giles," Robert ordered.

The servant turned and walked dejectedly back to the house with the slumping steps of one who wished he had had the foresight to bring writing equipment with him, as well as every other item Sir Drayton could conceivably want.

Robert turned back to Lord Stranham. "Write something fancy," he instructed. "I'm not much hand at turning pretty phrases, but I thought it would be nice to begin by begging her forgiveness for not having called. Then you might mention that I am enclosing invitations to my mother's ball, and end with something witty and appealing."

Giles returned with the parchment, quill, and pot of ink. He placed them on a table beside Robert.

"Oh, Giles," Robert directed, "bring some port for Mark."

"Of course, my lord," the butler said impassively, and turned to make the garden-to-house-to-garden circuit once again.

"Now then," the baronet said, "I'll write and you tell me what to say."

"Really, Robert, it isn't necessary for you to write this note. You see, I happened onto Miss Brown and—"

"How's this?" Robert demanded. " 'My dear Miss Joanna Brown'—that way it is certain to go to the right Miss Brown. What should I say next?"

Lord Stranham sighed. He would have to let Robert have the satisfaction of writing a note.

The butler returned a moment later bearing glasses and a decanter on a tray. He set the silver tray down and began to pour chilled Madeira into each of the tall stemmed glasses. Beside the glasses was a delicate blue dish heaped with fluffy buttered biscuits.

"What are those?" Robert demanded with a repulsed look at the food.

"Biscuits, sir," Giles informed him solemnly.

"I *know* that," the invalid replied with dignity, "but why did you bring them?"

"I thought perhaps you would like to have them with your drink."

"Take them back immediately," Robert ordered curtly.

As the weary servant stooped to remove the offending morsels, Lord Stranham stopped him with an upturned palm. "Leave them, Giles, and give your notice immediately. I do not doubt that if this tyrant were in America, his slaves would revolt against his tyranny."

Robert looked suitably affronted. "I can't have those biscuits left here. I've done nothing but eat since I've been laid up."

"I rather think you have done several things besides eat in the course of your illness, Robert. In fact, I suspect one of them is to drive poor Giles past all endurance by having him run countless unnecessary errands."

"But I'll eat them if they're left," Robert objected again. "I have no power to stop myself."

"I shall break your arm if you so much as reach for one," Lord Stranham offered helpfully. "Now let's get on with this letter."

Robert transferred his attention back to the task at hand. As the marquis dictated rapidly, he scribbled furiously.

"My dear Miss Joanna," Lord Stranham began as he studied his well-manicured nails. "I regret that I have been unable to call upon you, but various pressing business concerns have kept me away from London for the better part of the week. I should like it above all things if you would consent to attend my mother's ball this Friday. I am enclosing four invitations for that purpose. Yours, Sir Robbie Drayton."

Writing a sentence and a half behind the marquis's words, Robert exclaimed gaily as he wrote, "I like the part about 'pressing business concerns.' It makes me sound very important."

"Yes," the marquis agreed dryly, "and she has no idea that your only employment is shouting at passing wenches from the bow window at Whites. Perhaps we should add a line about that," he suggested.

Robert, still writing hastily, was horrified to learn, upon a quick rereading, that he had actually signed his name "Sir Robbie Drayton." He furiously scratched it out to insert a more dignified "Robert" as befits the position of one who has important business interests.

"I shall deliver the four invitations to the ladies immediately."

"Four?" Robert asked uncertainly. "But there are only two girls. They would only need two invitations."

"My dear Robert, I am quite capable of adding," Lord Stranham explained lazily. "However, it would be churlish of you to invite only the Miss Browns, as they undoubtedly have a relative who acts as their chaperon and who will be expected to come." The authority with which the marquis delivered these words so impressed Robert that he nodded agreement, failing to recall that no such person had accompanied them to Almacks with Lady Morley.

"I shall stop for the tickets on my way out," the marquis said as he rose to leave.

"Wait!" Robert called in alarm. "You don't have my note."

The marquis turned to pick up the missive Robert held out for him. "I shall shortly deliver this into the very hands where it belongs," he assured his friend.

"Thank you," Robert said gratefully.

"Not at all," Lord Stranham demurred.

A few minutes later, having obtained the invitations from Lady Drayton, he swung up into his curricle and tossed the letter back to his tiger. "Burn this," he instructed as he tucked the invitations in a pocket inside his buckskin riding jacket and took up the reins.

CHAPTER 12

The following day Daphne found things were not going nearly so well as they had the day before. The simple matter of obtaining invitations to a society ball in a circle where they had no real connections seemed small today when compared with the problem she was now facing.

It was, in short, money. Seated at the maple drop-leaf desk in her bedroom, she was poring over the accounts. She was shocked to learn how much they had already spent in the month they had been in London. Daphne had made some very careful estimates before they removed from Devonshire, and she had thought she had a very good idea of the cost of food and lodging for the time they must live in London in order to find situations. Unfortunately, the price of food and clothes in the country did not at all compare to the cost of those same items in the city.

She pushed back her small white mobcab and added the row of figures again. To her dismay, they totaled the same number her first addition had yielded. She blew on the feather of her quill pen and studied the matter. What to do? she mused.

Cedric ambled to the open door of the room and stopped short on the threshold as he beheld the frown on Daphne's face. "Begging your pardon, Miss Daphne, but can I speak with you for a minute?"

"Of course, Cedric. About what?"

He began without preamble. "You're short of blunt, ain't you?"

"Yes," she sighed. "Dreadfully short. We have little

more than enough to live on for a month, and then I don't know what's to become of us."

"I was afeared of that. Costs money to live in London," he noted judiciously.

"Yes," she agreed wearily, and put the pen down. She looked dejectedly up into Cedric's face. His thin lips were pursed in thought.

"Well . . ." He paused uncertainly, then continued after a moment: "I might be able to help you."

Her face softened in a smile. "Nonsense, Cedric. *I* wouldn't think of taking your money."

"Oh," he pursued hastily, "that's just as well 'cause I ain't got none to offer you. But I got something better," he finished triumphantly.

"Better than money?" she asked in rueful amusement. "Dear me, I can't think what that could be."

"Cocks!"

"I beg your pardon, Cedric," Daphne said doubtfully. "Did you say 'cocks'?"

"Yes." He smiled happily, revealing a space where he had lost a lower tooth in his recent fight.

"I don't think the neighbors would approve of us keeping chickens, Cedric. Although it would be just the thing," she continued thoughtfully, "because we could have fresh eggs every morning. However, there's no place for them, so I'm afraid it won't serve." She shook her head and turned her attention back to the row of figures.

He looked at her with pitying patience. "Not chickens —cocks, fighting cocks."

"Oh, no. Really, Cedric! We can't be holding cockfights here! Whatever would the neighbors say to that?"

Cedric tried again with admirable forbearance. "I'm suggesting, Miss Daphne, that you *bet* on the cocks."

"What?" she gasped.

He pursued hastily. "I know that you ain't the betting sort of lady in the ordinary way of things. 'Owsomever, I

116

'ave a foolproof system worked out for winning money at the pit."

"But, Cedric, were I to even consider anything so outlandish, you have only just said you have no money, so *you* cannot be winning very much," she pointed out reasonably.

"I don't have any money right *now,* because it's 'nvested," Cedric related with dignity. "But after this afternoon's fight I'll be rich," he predicted modestly.

"You will?" she asked, interested in spite of herself. She leaned back in the ladder-backed chair and regarded the elderly servant.

"Yep. Like I told you, I got me a system."

"But I can't bet on those poor mistreated birds," Daphne argued forlornly, more to herself than to Cedric.

"Well," he countered, "they's going to fight whether you bet on them or not, so why not make some money?"

That was a reasonable argument, she had to admit, but the idea of betting on fowl seemed terribly lowering. A second voice spoke within her. Was it lowering to try to win some money? it asked sarcastically. It was hardly elevating to cling to the last shreds of respectability while the whole household went down like a sinking ship, swamped by the price of beans, bacon, and bread.

Heartened by the sight of his mistress weighing the possibilities, Cedric added further encouragement: "The secret is," he whispered, "to play two blacks, then a gray, and then a red."

Daphne looked skeptical. "Are you certain?"

"Of course I am," he declared, affronted. "It's the signtific way of betting."

"Well . . ." She bit her lower lip as she thought. "I daresay it wouldn't hurt to bet just a very little money, and then if I win, I might bet more." She was desperate enough to try almost anything.

Cedric gave an exasperated sigh and ran a scarecrow

117

hand through his white hair. "You can't do it that way; it won't work, Miss Daphne. Lady Luck won't be with you, and if she ain't, the cocks can feel it. They can feel 'er in their blood."

"Really?" Daphne conceded to herself that she knew very little about fowl. But Cedric attended the fights regularly, and he undoubtedly understood much more than she did.

"Course," he reaffirmed staunchly.

"Well." She vacillated; it was totally preposterous, but they needed money badly.

Joanna joined them, moving through the door past the butler. She looked curiously from Daphne to Cedric before seating herself on a reed-bottom chair near her sister. "What are you two whispering about?" she demanded.

Daphne hesitated. She disliked having her younger sister worried about money matters.

Cedric, however, felt no such compunction, for he explained readily, "You're almost out of blunt, and me and Miss Daphne is going to wager 'alf of what you 'ave left on the cocks this afternoon."

"Famous!" Joanna exclaimed gleefully.

"Then you think I ought to?" Daphne asked doubtfully.

"Of course! We could double our money!"

At that encouraging statement, Daphne nodded decisively. "Very well, we shall place a bet."

Her decision made, Daphne counted out half of their remaining funds into Cedric's palm while Joanna looked on with approval. The butler clutched the money tightly in his hand, smiled cheerfully, and turned to leave, promising to return shortly with the riches he was about to win.

Daphne and Joanna followed him out into the hall and down the stairs where he took his lucky tricorne off a peg and set it on his snowy hair at a rakish angle. He left grinning boyishly.

118

"Our luck has really changed," Joanna enthused after he was gone. "Only conceive how many exciting events are taking place. Not only have we been invited to the Draytons' ball, but we are going to win money and be sinfully rich. We shall buy all sorts of new clothes and drive a fine perch phaeton and move to the largest house in Saint James's Square."

"Well," her more earthbound sister pointed out, "perhaps we shall not be terribly rich immediately. But it would be excessively nice to be able to live without constantly worrying about what is to become of us."

"Do you think we could have new gowns for the ball with the money Cedric wins? We have only a day to have the dresses made, but the cook has a dear friend who is a seamstress and she would be happy to oblige us."

"The butcher with the rancid meat was also the cook's friend," Daphne reminded Joanna.

"Yes, but that all worked out quite well because Mrs. Winter didn't like ham anyway," the younger girl pointed out with a sunny smile.

"Well," Daphne declared with a stifled giggle, "I suppose if the seamstress couldn't sew well, the gentlemen present would be just as pleased by our absence of clothes as Mrs. Winter was with the absence of ham."

"Shocking!" Joanna chided as she joined Daphne in merry laughter. In high good humor they mounted the narrow flight of steps to the second floor.

Five minutes later, back in her room, Daphne was still smiling happily as she seated herself in front of the small oval mirror and pulled the lace-edged mobcab off her hair, letting it fall freely to her shoulders. She scooped the shiny yellow locks up in her hands and held them atop her head, trying her hair in various styles.

It was important that she look nice tomorrow night because— Why was it important? she asked herself, as she realized she was preparing to go to a great deal of trouble to attend a ball where she would know only a handful of the people present. It could very well turn out to be another evening such as she had spent at Almacks. But it wouldn't, she thought with a satisfied smile. This would not be at all like Almacks, for she had not danced there, and at Lady Drayton's ball she would be dancing with Lord Stranham. Yes, she definitely wanted to look well.

Her mind wandered to the approaching ball as she stared dreamily at her reflection in the glass. She would have to wear something very appealing, something in a dark shade of violet, which always set her eyes off to their best advantage. Perhaps, she would have the dressmaker cut it with a little bit lower scoop across her bosom than she usually allowed herself. She looked down at her breasts, well concealed beneath the gray cotton day dress. She didn't, she admitted regretfully, have the full, curvaceous swell that gentlemen seemed to find so attractive. But then, she was not exactly flat either.

As she recollected, Joanna had once spoken enviously of her figure when the then fourteen-year-old girl had been in love with the neighbor's groom. Joanna was lamenting the fact that he seemed to be attracted only to ladies with much more fully developed bosoms than Joanna's own board-flat chest. Ah, young love, Daphne thought with an amused shake of her head.

Love. The word repeated itself in her mind. What would falling in love be like? She silently put the question to the girl in the mirror. Without bidding, visions of Lord Stranham crowded into her mind. She saw him smiling as he had yesterday—with that same alert look in his gray eyes that he had had as he watched her babble witlessly. It was as if he had been unaware of what she said, but wished merely to look at her. What would it be like to be loved by him?

She brought herself up short in the act of imagining the pretty phrases the marquis might murmur into her ear if he had a violent affection for her. This daydreaming was pointless and childish, she reproved herself. Lord Stranham would no more fall in love with her than he would fly. After all, he had seen her house and clothes, and such matters must combine to make him think she was unworthy of him. Even if he *were* to conceive a *tendre* for her, it was not likely he would offer her more than *carte blanche.*

Shamelessly she found herself following *that* train of thought with a not displeased curiosity.

She blushed scarlet and stood up hastily. It was the water. The squire's wife in Clovelly had warned her against drinking London water. She had told Daphne it made simple country girls have the most unmaidenly thoughts and caused the downfall of more than one innocent girl. Daphne would definitely not drink any more of it. Shocking, the things she had been contemplating! What would Lord Stranham have thought if he could have read such scandalous ideas in her gently bred mind?

CHAPTER 13

Lord Stranham, had Daphne but known it, was at that very moment indulging in thoughts not so very different from her own, and without her sense of guilt. In fact, he was smiling pleasantly to himself as he recalled the graceful feminine curves revealed beneath the dowdy gown Daphne had worn to Almacks.

He leaned back in the Windsor chair at Watiers. The club had been organized at the prince regent's request by his own chef because of complaints by Prinny's friends about the monotony of the food in their own clubs. Watiers served its purpose well, for the food, Lord Stranham decided with a brisk pat of his flat stomach, was delicious. He had lost himself in a first course of Scotch collops, those savory slices of veal fried in butter and served with mushrooms, and had followed it with a cranberry twist, lemon possets, wine sours, and quinces.

Yes, the food had been excellent. But now his mind wandered to something even more delectable. Daphne Brown was a pretty piece, although not at all in his usual style. He had always courted biddable society chits or kept bits of muslin whose primary concerns were to please him and coax from him what presents they could. And he had been generous with his gifts of jewels and gowns. No woman under his protection ever appeared in public in rags such as Daphne Brown wore. What temptations lie hidden beneath those clothes, he speculated with a lazy smile as he tilted back in the carved chair and looked about the opulent dining room.

He had a very lovely little opera singer over in Mayfair

who would be glad for his company anytime, he knew, but somehow that prospect did not stir any feelings within him. He found himself instead returning to the picture of a delicate sculpted face with lustrous violet eyes and creamy satin skin.

Several hours later he alighted from his carriage and made his way up the steps to the Drayton house, caught in the traffic of other arriving carriages and swamped by the sea of peasants who had come to eagerly watch the nobility.

No wonder he always came late, he thought with a grimace as he felt someone step on his foot and brush against the leg of his pantaloons—which had been the creaseless pride of his valet when he had left his own house a quarter of an hour ago. His charcoal gray coat, tailored by Weston and accounted by that same valet to be a masterpiece of craftsmanship, was at that very moment being fingered by the reverent if grimy hands of an enthralled bawd who looked up at him adoringly.

He shook himself out of her grasp and attained the steep marble steps that led up to the classic Georgian home. He could hear the faint strains of music from within, and through the wide windows he could see the large, well-lit ballroom. Couples were moving about in graceful pairs on the dance floor, almost floating beneath the crystal chandeliers.

"Good evening, my lord," a feminine voice said just behind him.

Turning, Lord Stranham saw Lady Diedre and her mother ascending the steps.

"It is a lovely evening," he returned cordially. "This promises to be a very successful ball, judging from the size of the crowd."

Their conversation was interrupted by a small cry from Lady Diedre, who shrieked as she began to pitch forward.

The marquis caught her quickly and set her aright. "Are you hurt, my lady?" he asked.

"No," she said with a smile that was remarkably composed for one who had lately been in danger of falling. "I fear you think me a perfect ninny-hammer, my lord, but I am wearing a new pair of satin slippers. I am persuaded they will be the death of me; they're very like walking on glass."

"Permit me to assist you," he offered gallantly, taking her slender arm firmly in his sinewy one. She leaned close to him and fluttered long lashes up at him as he led her up the remaining steps. Her mother dropped discreetly behind and smiled fondly at the pair.

Lord Stranham was still holding on to Lady Diedre as they made their way through the receiving line. When they reached the end of it, she smiled warmly up into his face. "Thank you, my lord," she murmured, leaning toward him as she spoke. "You are most kind."

"Do not repeat such words, my lady. I shouldn't want it to get about," he replied lightly. He bowed courteously and disengaged his arm.

Lord Stranham walked away from Lady Diedre, a faint smile still playing on his lips. That, he thought, was a very obvious ploy. The chit must desperately want him to make a declaration, to go to such extremes as to pitch herself into his arms.

Across the room, sitting on a green satin Louis XIV chair and staring unhappily at the marquis, Daphne could still observe the smile on his lordship's face. But then, she reminded herself, he had a right to escort another young lady to a ball if he wished to. He had, after all, done all that she could possibly expect of him by obtaining her invitations for the ball. She had no reason to feel disheartened that he had arrived with a very beautiful dark-haired lady. Having logically explained these facts to herself,

Daphne settled back into her chair and proceeded to feel considerably disheartened.

Looking forlornly about the crowded room, Daphne restlessly smoothed the folds of her silk gown. She had been as excited as a schoolroom miss only a few minutes earlier, waiting in eager anticipation of Lord Stranham's arrival. Her gown, which she had skilfully made over the past week—since Cedric had not yet won any money—fulfilled her every expectation, and she was anxious to see the marquis's expression when he first caught sight of her in her pure violet silk with its temptingly rounded neckline. The dress revealed the rise of her bust above the high-fitting waist and then swept to the ground in loose swirling folds to end in a demitrain in the back. A nosegay of real violets was secured at her white throat on a velvet ribbon; more violets were threaded in the curls pinned atop her head. Yes, she had felt quite smart when she had arrived. Now she only felt melancholy.

Mrs. Winter, sitting beside her and keeping up a steady commentary about the clothes, manners, and looks of the wealthy nobility assembled before them, didn't notice that her remarks went unanswered.

Mr. Winter, having learned the direction of the refreshment room immediately upon their arrival, had proceeded there to cheer himself. He had been gone for over an hour, and Daphne rather suspected he had refreshed himself under the table by now.

Beside Mrs. Winter, Joanna tapped her foot impatiently as she awaited Sir Robert Drayton's release from the receiving line. He had been very warm in his greetings to her, complimenting her extravagantly on her yellow satin gown and saying how well she looked with the little bunch of primroses in her hair. Joanna smiled at the remembrance of his compliments. Several young men had approached and requested a dance, but she had politely refused them all, preferring to be free for Sir Robert when he arrived.

Daphne had also refused invitations to stand up with young men. She too awaited a particular partner. She continued to await him as she looked about the room with an exaggeratedly casual interest, hoping the marquis—his head towered slightly above the other gentlemen's heads —was unaware that her eyes were never off of him for long. She watched him now as he bowed to a group of dowagers with a graceful polish.

Then he continued through the crowd. Daphne noted every detail of his clothing, down to his carefully tied snowy cravat. She saw him pause to chat with some young ladies, then smile and move on. He approached a group of older gentlemen who were engaged in a serious discussion, and joined their talk as he nonchalantly held a wineglass, sipping from it now and again.

With a small sigh Daphne continued to watch the marquis. It was a large room, crowded with people, but not so large that he would not soon make his way around to her. He would, she knew, shortly be bowing over her hand. Even now, she observed, he was leaving the group of gentlemen and proceeding on toward her. He was almost to her chair, and she smiled in anticipation of the tingle she would feel when he picked up her small hand in his large one and bowed over it.

Daphne hastily turned to Mrs. Winter to initiate a conversation. She certainly didn't want to be caught sitting quietly as if she were waiting for the marquis to reach her!

"Is this not a lovely ball?" she asked her companion with an overbright smile and a burst of nervous enthusiasm.

"Indeed," the older woman agreed without taking her eyes from the crowd. "I do believe that's Lord Ponsonby over by the high arched window, and only a minute ago I spied Georgiana, the lovely duchess of Devonshire. And is that *him?*" Mrs. Winter demanded with a gasp. She flicked open her fan, two broken sticks clattering as she passed it swiftly in front of her face before answering her own question. "It's Wellington himself! Wait until I tell Mrs. Burns! Only conceive of her astonishment at learning of the noble and illustrious guests who swarmed about me."

Joanna interrupted with a happy exclamation. "Here *he* comes!"

"Wellington is coming over here?" Mrs. Winter breathed in hoarse disbelief as she patted her raven hair and flicked a quick glance over her rusty-black gown.

But Joanna, conscious of only one *he* in the world, did not hear Mrs. Winter. "Good evening, sir," she greeted Sir Robert warmly.

"Good evening. You look like a daffodil doe, Miss Brown." Robert greeted her with a trifle more warmth than a true Corinthian should allow himself. Suddenly conscious of his sin, he continued in a more formal and flowery manner, but the happy expression on his plump face betrayed his interest: "I recollect telling you earlier that you are quite enchanting in that yellow dress. The only flaw in the whole of your appearance is that your golden hair puts the garden primroses to shame. Their beauty cannot hope to rival yours."

Joanna blushed in pleased confusion and looked down at the tiny yellow slippers peeping from beneath her gown. "Thank you," she murmured shyly.

Daphne, aware that Joanna had forgotten there was anyone else in the room except Sir Robert, interrupted the smiling couple smoothly: "Good evening, Sir Robert. It is a lovely ball. Mrs. Winter and I were only just saying how much we were enjoying ourselves."

"Ahh, but you should be dancing," he replied. His eyes never left her younger sister's face, and Daphne knew he addressed the words to Joanna.

"I fear I cannot accept your kind offer to dance, Sir Robert," Daphne replied playfully with a suppressed smile. "I am here as Joanna's chaperon."

"I'm not," Mrs. Winter interposed, "and I should love to stand up with you." Putting her words into action, she stood up briskly and took Sir Robert's hand, drawing the surprised man to the center of the floor.

Daphne looked from the couple to Joanna. Her younger sister's face reflected acute disappointment. "Don't put yourself into a fret, dear," she advised kindly. "You can dance with him after this set."

"Of course," Joanna replied mournfully, her eyes never leaving Sir Robert.

Turning her attention back to her own prospective partner, Daphne noted in surprise that Lord Stranham was no longer in sight. She swept her eyes about the room until they alighted on the marquis's tall form. In his arms was the beautiful brunette with whom he had entered the room. He was smiling down into his partner's face; his smile was returned with an enraptured one from the lady. Daphne felt a pang of dismay to note how well that pleasant expression set on the lady's china-doll countenance.

She looked quickly away, but almost immediately her eyes strayed back to the couple. The woman, Daphne remarked in dejection, was dressed to perfection in a low-cut red brocade gown. Its square neck accented her full bosom before giving way, below an Empire waist, to clinging folds—all in all, an alluring display of her slender figure.

"Good evening, my dear," a voice intruded into Daphne's thoughts. She looked up into the plump face of an older, feminine version of Sir Robert.

"Lady Drayton," Daphne greeted her hostess with a pleasant nod.

"I am sorry I have been unable to speak with you, but I was engaged in the receiving line until just now." Lady

129

Drayton sat down on the chair beside Daphne and continued placidly: "I am given to understand you are connected with me."

Daphne could frame no reply. What had the marquis told her to obtain the invitations? She felt like a small child caught with her hand in the forbidden cookie jar, but the amiability with which Lady Drayton's words had been spoken did not imply censure or accusation. Rather they held the hint of a shared and amusing secret.

The older woman appeared unoffended by Daphne's failure to reply; she merely continued in the same pleasant voice: "I further understand you are related to Lord Stranham. We must have a pleasant coze and unravel the complexities of our relationship."

"Lady Drayton," she began sheepishly, looking uncertainly at the shiny oak parquet floor rather than at the lady seated beside her, "I fear I have told some shocking lies." There was little point in trying to deceive her hostess. Apparently she already knew a great deal. Taking a deep breath, Daphne looked apprehensively at the ruddy-cheeked woman beside her.

To her relief and surprise, Lady Drayton gave a chortle and lightly tapped Daphne's clasped hands with an ivory fan. "My dear, if you have told some untruths, it is no more than my son has done. In point of fact, he embroiled himself in quite a deep mire trying to give me a garbled version of Lord Stranham's family lineage that would encompass the Browns of Devonshire. I collect that it was his dim-witted idea to introduce you and your sister at Almacks as the marquis's cousins. No matter," she said with a gay, dismissive wave of her hand. "Ah, I spy my wayward son approaching now. You must stand up with him, and the two of you can put your heads together and invent something to tell the rest of the *ton* about your family ties. You really must concoct a story and stay with it. I've already told fully ten different versions of who you

130

are, and I simply cannot continue to lie about the two most fascinating girls in the room." She finished with a disarming laugh as Sir Robert approached.

He stopped in front of his mother. Mrs. Winter was still clinging to his arm and casting flirtatious looks up into his eyes in a manner that made him appear intolerably uncomfortable. She gave him a final sugary smile before dropping onto the seat beside Lady Drayton.

"Robert," his mother directed in a peremptory voice, "take Miss Brown out to the dance floor."

The baronet, seeing Daphne presented to him, looked wistfully toward Joanna, whose startled violet eyes and slightly parted lips reflected her further disappointment. His expression begged for understanding as he obeyed his parent's command and stiffly offered his arm to Daphne.

She cast one final look at her disconsolate younger sister before surrendering herself to Sir Robert for the set. She danced wordlessly while her mind struggled to accept the shocking knowledge that Lady Drayton had imparted. She had gone to Almacks under Sir Robert's offices! The thought was humiliating. She was made none the less miserable when she saw the marquis settled in a cozy corner of the room speaking to the beautiful brunette.

CHAPTER 14

Lord Stranham spent some very pleasant moments with Lady Diedre; at least it appeared so to Daphne as she watched the couple from her green satin chair with a growing sense of annoyance, not to say wrath. Every time smiles were exchanged, she bit her lip and felt a warm lump expand in her throat. The lady was very beautiful and doubtless a wealthy peeress. Certainly she would not have attached to her any such blemish as a disinherited father. And the doors of Almacks were assuredly wide open to her. Daphne wondered if the marquis knew under whose sponsorship they had gone to Almacks. He and Sir Robert were good friends, so it was almost certain he did. What must he think of her? She swallowed heavily; her pride was not going down easily.

Over the next thirty minutes she experienced much humiliation. It was not a pretty fact to accept that their inclusion in society had come not from Lady Morley but from Sir Robert Drayton. When they left this evening, Daphne resolved, she would never have any further association with that man, or allow her sister to. He had been most unscrupulous in the way he had pursued Joanna.

When she looked up half an hour later, Lord Stranham was bowing to her and smiling warmly. "I believe you promised me a dance, Miss Brown," he reminded her as he stretched out a hand to help her rise.

She ignored his hand. "Did I?" she asked with careful languidness. "I don't recall."

The marquis looked nonplussed at this chilly reception. His dark eyebrows lifted slightly in surprise.

As he stood looking down at Daphne, Mrs. Winter stood swiftly and explained, "Miss Brown is chaperoning her sister and is unable to dance, but I should be happy to stand up with you."

Lord Stranham's surprise at such an improper action was not betrayed by even the barest flicker of his impassive countenance. He merely bowed to the older woman standing eagerly before him. "The pleasure would be mine," he declared gallantly. Without a backward glance at Daphne, he led Mrs. Winter off to the cotillion that was forming and politely indulged her most unusual request that they stay as close as possible to the duke of Wellington throughout the dance. When the set had concluded, he led her back to her seat.

"And now, Miss Brown, you must do me the honor of standing up with me." The marquis spoke with a very firm note in his voice as he stretched an imperious hand toward her.

Daphne stood regally, then put the tips of her fingers on his arm, and they walked wordlessly out onto the floor. The first strains of the music sounded. It was, to her surprise, a waltz.

Lord Stranham hesitated. He knew that Daphne had not been approved by the patronesses of Almacks to waltz in public, and it was a severe social sin to flaunt that law. On the other hand, he thought recklessly, Daphne was not being presented into society, so it could scarcely make any difference if she did not conform to the proprieties for young girls being presented. His decision made, he placed a practiced arm about her waist and began to move across the floor.

Daphne followed as best she could. Although her dancing was passable, it was not nearly so good as her partner's. Discomfited, she struggled to match his steps while at the same time attempting to hold herself aloof from

134

him. The effort to do both showed in her face, and her normally serene countenance betrayed a look of distress.

The marquis noted her expression as he executed the steps of the dance with enviable style. "Are you enjoying yourself?" he asked devilishly, making a smooth turn.

"Yes," she replied curtly, her eyes focused directly on his shoulder as she spoke.

"Excellent," he murmured low to her ear, "for I should sorely dislike seeing your face were you not enjoying yourself. Even now, in the height of your enjoyment, you appear a bit agitated, not to say harassed."

"I am concentrating on my steps," she declared briskly.

He slowed his pace and pulled her closer against his wide chest. "Don't," he advised. "Let me lead."

"I am sorry my dancing displeases you," she said stonily.

"I did not say that it did, Miss Brown."

"No, but you thought it," she countered, her vanity considerably wounded.

"Forgive me," he said with no repentance reflected in his voice. "I feel a churlish dog for causing you discomfort."

"Your feelings do you credit, my lord," she responded tartly. Daphne regretted the words the moment she spoke them. She had no reason to insult him. After all, she couldn't hold him responsible for Sir Robert's actions.

To her surprise, he responded with a low chuckle, and she glanced up to see him looking at her with appreciation. "You are in rare form tonight, are you not, Miss Brown? One would never know I had done you the least favor."

This ungentle reminder that he had gone to some trouble in order that she might attend the ball brought Daphne back to full realization of whom she was addressing. "Oh, my lord," she began contritely, "that was very ill said of me. I cannot think why I should behave in such an odious

135

fashion. No doubt you think me dreadfully rag-mannered and I quite see that you should. Do forgive me."

His smile deepened as she made her little speech, and Daphne felt herself flush as he continued to smile down at her. Although he made no reply to her apology, she could see his gray eyes measuring her.

She bristled. "I have begged pardon for my ill-chosen words, my lord. I think you should make some answer."

"That is very much more in the way of it," he observed with satisfaction. "Playing the meek, repentant woman is not one of your better acts, but I like to see you attempt it. It's so—what is the word?—out of character."

She sniffed. "At least *I* have character to be out of, my lord."

"Touché," he laughed.

The marquis's unshakable good humor was having the disconcerting effect of annoying Daphne. She considered with resentment that her words were a source of diversion to him. No doubt, she fumed, the words of a green country girl were not nearly so clever or witty as those of the dark-haired society lady who had so occupied his time. "I am glad my speech does not overset you," she said sharply.

He shrugged carelessly. "I am rarely influenced by other people's opinions of me. In this case it is obvious you took me in instant dislike, so I cannot think I could ever redeem myself in your eyes."

"I did not take you in immediate aversion," she countered.

"Perhaps I was wrong," he admitted. "You might have reserved judgment for the first thirty seconds." He was aware that his words were becoming cold and short. But he was fast losing patience. The chit wanted only to argue. He had just spent above a quarter of an hour exchanging boring commonplaces with Lady Diedre while her mother looked on hopefully. He had extricated himself as politely as possible, but his temper had been somewhat ragged. To engage now in verbal combat with this fiery little beauty with whom he had such hopes for a happy liaison was altogether too much.

As the set ended, Lord Stranham led Daphne back to where Mrs. Winter was seated, and left her after sketching a curt bow.

Daphne excused herself from her companion. "I believe I shall just take a breath of fresh air." She felt in great need of it as she skirted the crowd to the open French doors leading out onto a wide stone balcony. Her cheeks were high with color from her altercation with Lord Stranham, and her pulse was beating fast as she stepped out onto the terrace. It was lit with the light emanating from the long windows; a sliver of moon added a romantic backdrop. But Daphne could not fully appreciate the beauty of the setting as she walked the length of the balcony before stopping to lean on the stone ledge outside the glow of the light. In the dimness she cupped her chin in her hands and studied the darkened garden below.

She had had the dance with the marquis, which she had been so looking forward to, and she had certainly made a cake of herself. She had not meant to exchange harsh words with him, but somehow she could not refrain from doing so. Of course, she reminded herself, he had probably thought no more of her words or indeed her after the set had ended. He had merely been fulfilling his promise to stand up with her. Such a thought was as lowering as the knowledge of how they had arrived at Almacks.

With a sigh Daphne turned to leave and then halted. From her dark retreat she could see the marquis strolling out onto the terrace with a slender woman beside him. He held the lady's hand companionably as they walked to the balustrade not ten feet from her and stopped. She could hear their words as they began to speak.

"I do hope the night air revives you," the marquis said with a touch of amusement.

"Don't be a fool," the lady parried. "I am not in want of air, and well you know it. In honor of my confession I believe you should give me the particulars of who the blond-haired chit was that you stood up with."

"My dear mother," Lord Stranham said silkily, "may I tell you how lovely it is to see you and how desolated I am that father was unable to accompany you?"

"No, you may not," she retorted shortly. "What you may tell me is who the girl was."

He complied: "Her name is Miss Brown."

"I am aware of that," she sniffed. "Do you take me for such a peagoose that I was not able to learn the chit's name? What I wish to discover is what she is to *you.*"

"She is Miss Brown to me also," he replied promptly, "and I think to all who know her. It is a habit in London to have only one name, although I did know a gentleman once who was fleeing from the runners and was forced to assume the name of Mr. Smith."

"Mark," the lady interrupted impatiently, "you are deliberately provoking me. Where did you meet the child?"

The marquis countered her question with one of his own: "Why have you taken such a singular interest in her?"

"Because she is one of two chits you have danced with tonight, and I mean to discover if she is to be my future daughter. Where did you meet her?" she repeated.

"At Almacks."

"Indeed." Her voice reflected surprise. "I had never heard of the Browns of Devonshire. What are their connections?"

Daphne shrank further back into the shadows and listened guiltily. She disliked eavesdropping on someone else's conversation; she particularly disliked it, since she was the subject of the discussion. But there was scant chance of her escaping now, for her way back into the ballroom was blocked by the marquis and his mother.

"I do not know her connections," Lord Stranham replied, then added unrepressively, "but I do know her sister was acquainted with Sir Drayton before she attended Almacks, so doubtless they have numerous social ties. I am further aware that one member of their household is interested in the arts of animal husbandry."

"Animal husbandry?" the duchess repeated uncertainly.

"Yes, he seemed to know the fine points of stock. I met him at a sporting event when I was there to deliver a message."

"I am not altogether certain I understand what you are speaking of," her grace said in a voice laden with suspicion.

Lord Stranham laughed easily, then he elucidated: "I met him at a cockfight."

"How shocking!"

"Not at all, my lady mother. I was there on an errand from a baronet, and the message I was to deliver was to Lord Atrium's son. I am persuaded it was one of the more elevating assemblies I have attended of late."

"I can think of nothing more lowering than to frequent a cockfight." She shuddered.

"Not a bit of it. In the course of affairs I was able to rescue a groom and deliver him safely home to his grateful mistress."

"I do not care about such unenlightened pursuits," she sniffed. "I am interested only in remarks pertinent to Miss Brown."

"I beg your pardon for straying from the subject," he said recalcitrantly.

"Now then," she continued briskly, "I consider it is time you leg-shackle yourself to some chit, set up a nursery, and proceed to be a proper husband. As yet you have not seen fit to gratify that wish." There was a pregnant pause for the marquis to explain himself. When he did not, the duchess continued: "However, since you have failed to do so and since you are now displaying an interest in another girl besides Lady Diedre, I can only conclude that she is the one you intend to wed."

"*You* are showing an interest in Miss Brown," the marquis said calmly. "I assure you that I have no thought whatever of marrying her. My wife shall someday be a duchess, and I am fully aware of the honor due that position. I shall marry, when I do wed, someone who has the breeding and social graces to fill the title to perfection."

"Sir Robert seems intrigued by the younger Miss Brown. Certainly they cannot fall so far short of being worthy of a high position. And if you are in love—"

"I am *not* in love," the marquis corrected placidly. "As I have said, I am a member of the nobility and will someday be a duke. I would not demean myself or my title by marrying beneath myself. That is all I wish to say on the subject. Allow me to escort you back inside."

Daphne waited breathlessly for them to leave before unclenching the fist she had placed over her mouth to stifle a gasp. Moving stiffly, she walked back to the French doors, where her courage almost faltered. What if Lord Stranham saw her reenter the ballroom and realized she had listened to the whole of his conversation? But there was nothing for it now; she would have to return to the assembly and act as if nothing had happened. Praying the evening would come to a quick end, Daphne continued woodenly back into the crowded room, crossed to a satin chair, and sank into it.

She had little time to collect herself before Mrs. Winter appeared wreathed in smiles and escorting a small woman with graying hair. The lady's face was still pretty, although Daphne judged her to be over fifty, and she was dressed well in a three-quarter length overdress of dark green brocade embroidered with tiny rose flowers. Under the brocade was a light green slip of purest gossamer silk accented by a huge diamond, which hung about her slender neck. Her matching earrings were also large diamonds.

"I am delighted," Mrs. Winter began with an unrestrained smile, "to introduce the duchess of Cochmeer. Your grace," she continued, "this is Miss Daphne Brown. Her grace most particularly wished to meet you," Mrs. Winter explained to the younger woman.

Daphne looked at the richly dressed woman in confusion. Why should the duchess wish to meet her? But the minute Lady Cochmeer began to speak, Daphne understood. She recognized her cultured voice as the same one she had heard only minutes earlier on the balcony.

"I am given to understand you are friends of the Draytons," Lady Cochmeer said.

Mrs. Winter intervened before Daphne could frame a reply. Her delight at having something to say to a real duchess apparently overcame her awe of her grace. "Of course she is, and she is also my close friend. Aren't you, dear?" Mrs. Winter appealed to her.

"Daphne," the duchess repeated her name slowly. "Wasn't she a goddess in Greek mythology?" Her eyes lit in a slow smile. "Ah, yes, as I recall she was a nymph who attracted the love of Apollo and was pursued by him." Her grace's eyes strayed from a blushing Daphne to the tall, athletic figure of her son across the room before she laughed lightly and turned back to the women. "This should prove most interesting."

"Oh, indeed," Mrs. Winter agreed readily. "It is one of the most interesting balls I have ever attended, and I am most anxious to regale my good friend Mrs. Burns with wondrous tales of the excitement."

While Mrs. Winter pursued a monologue on the pleasures of the party Joanna returned from the arms of her latest partner, smiling and chatting happily. At the same moment, Mr. Winter swayed up to the little crowd and loudly demanded directions to the nearest chamber pot. Daphne prayed the evening would end soon.

CHAPTER 15

"Only conceive," Mrs. Winter enthused. "I have been to the most elegant of events! Wait until I tell Mrs. Burns the wonderful people I have met. You must assure her it is true if she should ask you," she ordered.

"Of course," Joanna murmured happily.

In her corner of the Winters' dilapidated coach Daphne was not as enthusiastic. She too was pondering the events of the evening but with far less joy than the other two women.

"And Wellington! Did I tell you about what he said concerning me? Such a rare honor to be noticed by such a great man."

Daphne could have told Mrs. Winter that she had indeed related Wellington's words, no less than three times, but she held her tongue and said nothing.

"I heard him ask, quite distinctly, mind you, 'Who is that woman in the black gown? She seems to be everywhere I go tonight.' Imagine! He took note of me. Why, he was even aware of what I was wearing. Was that not a singular honor? Mrs. Burns shall certainly hear of this."

Daphne didn't doubt that she would. For an instant she felt almost sorry for the often-mentioned Mrs. Burns, then she turned her thoughts back to her own problem. How could she persuade Joanna to think no more of Sir Robert Drayton? When the coach rumbled past a streetlight, the brief illumination revealed Joanna still smiling dreamily. Daphne foresaw problems convincing her sister that anything about the baronet was less than perfect. She had never seen Joanna so taken with a man.

The vehicle stopped with a lurch, and Mrs. Winter awoke her snoring husband. "Do see the girls to the door, my dear," she said in the same sweet voice she had addressed to everyone that evening.

He grumbled his assent while his wife continued, "I shall of course call on you tomorrow to tell you the remainder of the interesting events that occurred to me at the ball. I must write dear, wonderful Millie and tell her how greatly I am enjoying your companionship; I cannot think when I have met a lovelier pair of young ladies," she rhapsodized.

"You are too kind," Daphne murmured as Mr. Winter helped her alight.

"It is *you* who are excessively pleasant. Wellington!"

Mr. Winter saw them to the door, and Daphne entered the house with weary steps. Beside her, Joanna danced inside to be greeted by Rose and helped out of her pelerine.

"My dear," Daphne said as she followed her sister up the narrow staircase, "I am aware it is quite late, but I would have a word with you." It was better to tell Joanna immediately that nothing further could come of her friendship with Sir Robert. After all, she didn't wish her younger sister to spend any more time investing the baronet with noble qualities.

"Of course," she replied, stepping into her room. Daphne assisted Joanna in removing her gown. As her fingers worked down the row of tiny pearl buttons, she said, "I have discovered tonight I was wrong in thinking Lady Morley arranged for our attendance at Almacks. She had no friendship with Papa. I doubt she had ever heard of him. The truth is that Lady Morley secured the invitations because Sir Robert requested her to."

"I knew he had," Joanna cried with pleasure.

"That is scarcely something over which you should be elated," Daphne reproved sternly. "Do you not see that it was extremely improper for us to accept the vouchers under such circumstances? We went at a gentleman's invitation! And an unknown and not entirely trustworthy man at that."

"Not trustworthy! Whatever do you mean? He is the very nicest of men. He complimented me countless times on my dress and appearance and—"

"That makes him a polished, perhaps an accomplished, flatterer, but it does not follow that his motives were above reproach." Daphne quelled her sister's arguments. "And further, the very fact that we took the tickets makes us look like adventuresses, especially if Sir Robert does not know the false impression under which we accepted. I really thought it was in Papa's name that we were invited." Daphne fretted. She undid the last button and paced to the window to look out at the dark sky.

"But he has made no untoward advances. Daphne, he is the most perfectly mannered man I have ever met. How could such a person be designing?"

"My dear, you must recall we have little experience with men who have been about in the world. I think it would be necessary for such a man to be pleasantly conversable in order to deceive innocent maidens. He would have to be able to convey the impression that nothing further is expected from a lady than the pleasure of her company in the most proper of circumstances. But sooner or later he doubtless means to become more—" She hesitated, then continued delicately, "—more marked in his attentions. A great many girls, I am persuaded, have been ruined by such a man."

"Ruined!" Joanna repeated in dismay. "You do not understand in the least. He has the highest respect for me and he would never attempt me. How can you think such a thing?"

Looking at the woebegone expression on her younger sister's face, Daphne softened. It was obvious Joanna really did care for Sir Robert. It was equally necessary that those illusions be shattered. But surely she needn't destroy all of them at once. Tomorrow she and Joanna could talk at greater length. By then the younger girl would have had some time to adjust herself to the things Daphne had suggested.

"Very well, my dear, he may not mean to compromise you. Let us speak no more of it now. In the morning, when we have both had time to review the facts, we shall talk again. But I warn you, it will be much better for you if you can contrive to put him from your mind."

"I shall never forget him," Joanna said fervently. "Even if I am never allowed to see him again, I shall remember him as long as I live."

With those discouraging words ringing in her ears, Daphne trudged off to bed. She tried to put the troublesome Sir Robert from her mind, and also to dispel thoughts of Lord Stranham; but sleep did not come easily that night.

The following day Daphne's spirits were no better and Joanna's were undiminished. The two girls lingered over chocolate in the tiny breakfast room, but neither of them spoke as they sat submerged in their private thoughts.

Daphne recalled the words she had overheard Lord Stranham speak to his mother on the balcony, blushing as she did so. He considered her totally beneath him! Well, she simply didn't care, she told herself as she buttered her toast with vicious little stabs at the bread. But, for all that, it was humiliating to have heard such statements. In Clovelly she and Joanna had always been treated with respect and deference. Certainly no one had ever said such lowering things about her there. After all, their father had been of the nobility.

In London, however, it was obviously quite a different matter. Here no one knew anything of her father and, worse, probably did not care. She rallied herself with the thought that although he had been cut off from his inheritance, he had been a fine man nevertheless—in fact, a much better person than the haughty marquis would ever be; so Lord Stranham needn't speak of her as if she were a rag seller's daughter. And as for his saying he would not marry beneath himself, she would not have him if he was the last, the very last, man living.

"Sir Robert looked so handsome last evening in his wine-red coat and wonderfully elegant cravat." Joanna broke the silence with a sigh and a faraway look in her eyes. "Did you not find him so? And Lord Stranham also looked well. I saw that he did you the singular honor of standing up with you."

"I noted nothing out of the ordinary way in either man's appearance," Daphne countered brusquely.

"Oh, indeed you could not have been attending very closely. Sir Robert looked excessively nice, as did the marquis," she added scrupulously. "He and the lovely Lady Diedre made a most agreeable couple. It is said that they are to marry."

"I wish them joy of each other," Daphne snapped, "although I think she is making a match she will regret."

"How can you say such a thing? She was the envy of every woman at the ball. Why, the marquis is quite rich and very handsome. And his breeding and manners are above reproach."

"Indeed." Rising abruptly, she said in clipped accents, "I shall be in the parlor figuring the accounts should you need me."

Daphne had not been employed in this occupation for more than half an hour before it became painfully plain to her that their funds were almost entirely gone. At most they had enough to live on for only three more weeks. The money she had given Cedric with such high hopes had cut deeply into their small treasury. How could she have done such a foolish thing? She regretted that bitterly.

Although Cedric said they had not yet lost the money,

147

Daphne considered it as good as gone. The fight it had been bet on had not taken place, the butler had reported, but the money had been placed and there was no way to retrieve it, even though she had begged him to try. She and Joanna desperately needed it.

Her forlorn thoughts were interrupted when Cedric appeared in the doorway, clutching his lucky tricorne and looking about uncomfortably.

"Yes?" Daphne prompted when he did not speak.

"Miss Daphne, it's about the blunt. Well, I placed the bet and—" The servant stopped and stared sadly at the floor. She regarded him for a full minute, then tears began to flow slowly down her cheeks as she realized her last hope had been dashed. Cedric had lost the money, and there was no further prospect that their pitiful remaining funds would be embellished. It had been a faint hope, but she had not known how prayerfully she had clung to it.

"Oh, Cedric," she cried as she buried her face in her hands. "What are we to do?"

There was a pause before the servant spoke. "Miss Daphne, I ain't lost. I only came to tell you the cocks fight today. I feel near to certain you will win," he added.

She raised her head and looked at him in disbelief. "You really think we will?" she asked breathlessly.

He nodded.

"If only we could," she said wistfully as she wiped a stray tear from her cheek. "I'm so very desperate; I am having no luck at all finding situations, and I don't know what will become of Joanna and me if we lose."

"I'm sure ye'll win," he declared, and turned to leave.

Daphne was so enraptured by the new hope she had been given that she failed to note the look of despair on her butler's face.

CHAPTER 16

"Robert showed a particular interest in the younger Miss Brown," Lady Cochmeer noted as she poured tea from a fine Limoges teapot and passed a china cup to her guest, Lady Drayton.

"Robert is of an age where he displays a deal of interest in a great many girls," she said, laughing.

"Of course," the duchess said mildly, leaning back in an Egyptian-style chair in her well-appointed gold saloon. "Young men are often like that. Still, she was a very charming girl, and I do not recollect him ever showing such a marked preference for any other young lady as he did for Miss Joanna Brown last evening. Would it overset you if he were to develop a real affection for her?"

Lady Drayton considered that question carefully before setting down her teacup and remarking, "She was a very prettily behaved young lady and seemed honest in her interest in Robert. I detected nothing of affectation or deception in her manners. As for where I hope my son to marry, I do not scruple to own I have spoiled him shamefully. I would never demand he seek to please me by marrying a society chit if his heart was not engaged. Nor would I ever attempt to stop an alliance with a young lady who might not have the advantages of great wealth if she truly loved my son. However," she ended, "I think Miss Joanna Brown may merely have captured his notice for a short while. I only hope he does not trifle with such an obviously unsophisticated child."

"I see," Lady Cochmeer replied thoughtfully.

"Of course," her guest continued, "Robert has already

inherited his father's title and will never be anything more than a baronet. That is a very respectable title, but even I am not so dull-witted as to think it compares to the dukedom which your son will inherit. I collect you are worried Mark might form an attachment for the elder Miss Brown?"

"I am concerned about where my son decides to marry," her grace began slowly, "but that is not to say Miss Daphne Brown would be unacceptable to me. On the contrary, she also seemed a very ladylike and unassuming young person. I should wish to know more about her before I can truly judge her."

Indeed, Lady Cochmeer would like to know a *great* deal more about the slender blond-haired girl she had seen Mark studying unobtrusively more than once in the course of the evening. He would someday be a duke, and she would not like him to ruin his life by marrying someone totally unsuitable. On the other hand, the woman he showed signs of offering for was a calculating piece who would never give the first thought to Mark's happiness. Indeed, Lady Diedre, the duchess strongly suspected, only wanted the title he could offer her; her personal feelings were unattached.

"At any rate," she continued with a smile, "there is scarcely any reason for me to be thinking of Miss Daphne Brown as a future daughter. She is a girl who has appeared from nowhere, and all I know of her is that she stood up with Mark for one dance."

"Aside from Lady Diedre, she was the only woman he danced with," Lady Drayton pointed out.

"Yes, she was," her grace murmured with a shrug. But her show of indifference did not alter the fact that she really was intrigued; she believed she would further her acquaintance with the Browns. "Have you heard the latest *on dit* about Lady Cowper?" she asked, smoothly turning 'the conversation into other channels and letting the matter of Miss Daphne Brown drop for the present.

But the following day her elegant blue carriage with a large gold crest on the side pulled up in front of the modest house in Upper Wimpole Street. Lady Cochmeer alighted and walked toward the building.

From the parlor window a surprised Daphne saw the regal-looking woman dressed in a stylish mauve walking dress and white turban descend from the grand vehicle and start toward her house.

"Whoever can that be?" she wondered aloud as she dropped the curtain and hastily straightened her tangerine day dress and fluffed the pillows on the settee. A moment later Cedric showed Lady Cochmeer into the parlor.

"Her grace, the duchess of Cochmeer," he said pompously, and then bowed himself out of the room with an excess of flourishes.

"So very good to see you," Daphne said, flustered. "Do sit down, I shall ring for tea."

"That's very kind of you, my dear, I'm sure. I shan't stay long, but I would like a cup."

Daphne crossed the room and pulled the bell rope, ordering tea when Rose appeared. Why in the world was the duchess here?

Daphne glanced regretfully around at the shabby parlor, but her grace seemed to notice nothing amiss as she settled herself in the wing chair and began pleasantly, "I trust you and your sister enjoyed yourselves the other night at Lady Drayton's ball?"

"Very much indeed," Daphne replied with enthusiasm as she returned to seat herself across from Lady Cochmeer.

Her grace looked around the room and lowered her eyes to the floor, pursuing slowly: "I may as well be perfectly honest with you, Miss Brown. I have come to pry."

"We have very little to hide," Daphne said with simple honesty.

"I apprehend you are pressed for funds?"

"We are, your grace."

"I see. Then may I be so bold as to ask how it comes that you and your sister attended not only Almacks but Lady Drayton's ball as well? Are you looking to find husbands in a class above your own?" she asked baldly.

"Oh, no! You must not think that."

"What should I believe?" she pressed.

Daphne chafed uncomfortably. "We have come to London to look for positions. Lady Morley obtained invitations to Almacks for us, and I accepted them under the mistaken notion that she secured them because she remembered our father. In all probability we ought not to have gone even under those circumstances, but there was something very appealing about the thought of being in such glamorous surroundings. The reasons we came to be at Lady Drayton's ball are a bit more complicated." She paused as Rose entered the room and set the tea tray down. Daphne busied herself pouring, glad for some use for her hands.

"You came to London to find positions?" Her grace's astonishment at this knowledge was evident. "How very peculiar."

"I daresay it is," Daphne admitted ruefully, "but after Papa died, we had no money and no relatives to help us, and we could find no employment in Devonshire. The kind vicar gave me a letter of introduction and loaned us the use of his house, and we repaired here to seek acceptable situations through a respectable agency. Unfortunately, we are having very little success doing so." As she spoke she recalled her latest attempt and how unencouraging it had been.

"I am not surprised," Lady Cochmeer said with a hint of a smile. "My dear, you and your sister are far too comely for any woman to hire you to work in her household."

"But what else are we to do?"

The duchess fixed Daphne with a firm gaze. "Young ladies in want of funds frequently marry," she said crisply. "Why did you not do so?"

Daphne dropped her eyes to the hands she held clasped in her lap. "I did have an offer, but I could not like the man and I did not wish to marry solely for money."

"You rejected the advances of a perfectly acceptable man?" her grace demanded sharply.

"Yes," she murmured.

"That was very foolish," the duchess chided.

"I don't doubt it was," Daphne agreed. "But at the time I did not think finding employment would be so difficult. London is such a very large town, I was certain any number of people would hire us."

Her grace took another sip of tea and looked around the room again. The girl was obviously very green if she thought she could simply walk into an agency and obtain a position. No one would take her without references, especially as a governess or companion. It was unlikely they would even accept her as a chambermaid without someone to recommend her.

"Anyway," Daphne continued unhappily, "that is really all there is to know of us. If we have deceived anyone, I am truly sorry. But I can vouch for my family's respectability even if my sister and I are now reduced to making our own way in the world."

"I recall you said Lady Morley knew your parents. Did they work for her?" Lady Cochmeer asked with interest. It would be highly irregular to take girls to Almacks under such circumstances, but Lady Morley was a peculiar person.

"Certainly not!" Daphne denied proudly, and then instantly added, "I beg your pardon, your grace, I did not mean to offend you. My father, you see, was Lord Geoffrey Arnold's younger son. He was disinherited for marrying my mother."

Her guest regarded her with new interest. This was news indeed. "You are Quality. Now I think on it I remember something of the event. I collect there was another son as well. Surely it is his obligation to help you in your hour of distress."

"I never met my uncle; he died before my grandfather, and the estate was then given to charity."

"Your grandfather was a stubborn man if memory serves me. He would not have forgiven a son once he cut him off."

"I should not have wished him to," Daphne said with dignity. "If he would not accept Mama, then I am certain I would not have liked him anyway."

"I see you have a bit of his stubbornness in you also," the older woman said with a light laugh. "I must own I am all amazement at your circumstances."

Daphne sat silently for a moment, gathering her courage. "Then perhaps you would be so kind as to assist us, Lady Cochmeer."

The friendliness of a moment ago was instantly gone, replaced by a suspicious look. "In what way?"

"Well, I—" Daphne fumbled for the words. "Is it possible you could tell some of your acquaintances about us—people who might be needing someone to fill positions in their households?"

The duchess relaxed in her chair. At least Miss Brown was not begging for charity. On the other hand, she did not wish to be advertising the fact abroad that the Browns were reduced to poverty if there was the least chance Mark had an interest in the child. "I shall think on the matter. If I were to assist you, it would take a few days, even weeks, to locate situations such as you seek. Those positions do not come vacant often and there are *two* of you," she admonished.

Daphne's face lit in excitement. It was as close as they had come to obtaining employment in the month they had been in London. "You are very kind," she whispered.

"In the meantime," her ladyship continued sternly, "I think it would be to your advantage to use what connections you have in the neighborhood to find husbands for yourselves. Such a solution is not to be overlooked."

"I should like for my younger sister to marry," Daphne admitted. "But I do not wish her to be forced to. Still, there can be nothing wrong with meeting young men while we await word from you."

"I insist you do so," Lady Cochmeer lectured. "I am persuaded Mrs. Winter could aid you." When Daphne nodded obedience, she continued, "And what of my son? Tell me your thoughts concerning him."

"My thoughts, your grace?" Daphne asked doubtfully, picking up her spoon and concentrating on stirring her tea.

"Certainly. He showed an interest in you the other night at the Draytons' ball, and I have it on good authority he also spoke with you at Almacks. Do you seek to entrap him into marriage?" she asked bluntly.

Daphne's eyes widened. "Your son considers me completely beneath himself, my lady. There is not the least need to worry that he would ever show a serious inclination toward me."

"But how do you feel about him?" she pursued.

Daphne hesitated. This *was* the marquis's mother she was speaking to, and a woman who was going to do them a great favor; it would not do to say anything unkind about her only son. "He is a very amiable person, I am sure. I like him well enough, but I would never hope to marry such as he."

With a nod the duchess took her leave. She had determined to her satisfaction that Miss Daphne Brown was not wholly indifferent to Mark. She had also discovered that even though the Browns' circumstances were very bad at present, they were still Quality. Therefore a marriage with either of the girls could not be termed a *mésalliance*. Finally, and most pleasing of all, she had assured herself that if Daphne Brown married her son, she would be in love with him and she would have his happiness at heart.

CHAPTER 17

"You won!" Joanna cried for the third time, clapping her hands together gleefully.

"I said I did," Cedric replied testily.

"Oh, that is by everything wonderful!" Joanna exclaimed, and subjected Cedric to yet another impulsive hug. He extricated himself with affronted dignity before extracting a leather purse from a pocket inside his threadbare blue coat.

Daphne too thought Cedric's winning was wonderful. She smiled with delight as she put both hands out to receive the coins. She had not dared to hope they would actually win money at the cockfights. But they had! Now he was pouring great wealth into her hands. Two thousand pounds! They were rich! She and Joanna could live comfortably forever!

"Only think what this money will buy!" she cried as she grabbed Joanna's hand, and together they rushed upstairs.

Cedric *was* thinking of what the money could buy. He slumped dejectedly into the creaking wing chair in the front parlor to sort out the coil he was in. What was to be done now? He had borrowed two thousand pounds, and he had not the least notion where he could obtain the funds to pay back the moneylender.

It had all seemed so simple at the start. Miss Daphne had been pressed for blunt, so he had naturally offered to help her. Didn't he have the perfect system worked out? Who would have thought the banty would let him down like that? He sighed, pushed himself up from the chair, and started for the door.

He had until Friday—two whole days—to recover the money and pay the cent per center back. Surely he would think of some way to make two thousand pounds in two days.

Unfortunately, as Cedric tramped the streets no solution presented itself. An hour later he turned his steps slowly back to the house. By tomorrow he would certainly have thought of some way to obtain the money. In the meantime he'd just have a bit of a nip to clear his head and help him think better.

By the time Cedric emerged from the bawdy gin shop some hours later, he was swaying dangerously. As he walked he sang in a loud, off-key voice a ballad not fit for delicate ears. He had not solved his problems, but he had effectively managed to forget them. It took him a considerable time to navigate his way home through the darkened streets. Once there, he crawled into his narrow bed and slept with childlike abandon, waking early the next morning to find he had a splitting headache as well as a nagging feeling that all was not well, and there was something he should be concerned about.

Just what it was he needed to worry about appeared a few minutes later in the form of a fat man with oily black hair, who waddled nonchalantly into Cedric's downstairs bedroom. He looked around the small room with interest.

"Got m' money?" he demanded without preamble.

"Your money?" Cedric repeated vaguely.

The man shook his head in disbelief. "How soon they forgets," he lamented. "The five monkeys ye borried from me."

"Oh." Cedric felt a sickening sinking in his stomach as he remembered the source of his anxiety. But five monkeys? That was two thousand and five hundred pounds and he had borrowed only two thousand.

"It were only four monkeys," Cedric corrected.

"That's all you borried," the man allowed as he sat

down on the foot of the bed, "but I gots to make some sort of profit, interest and all, you know," he offered apologetically. "You can't expect me to loan money for nothing," he pointed out logically.

"Well, I dunno," Cedric began uncertainly. "Making promises is rather hard, and I can't say for sure as I'll have the money tomorrow."

"Oh," the fat man contradicted jovially, "making promises is easy; it's keeping them that's hard. But don't worry," he advised. "If you can't pay, I can always take the house for payment."

"But it ain't mine," Cedric protested with a rising sense of alarm.

"The money ain't yourn either," the man reminded him practically.

"That's blackmail, is what it is. Blackmail, plain and simple."

The greasy man casually reached across and took Cedric's rumpled nightcap from his head. Twisting it on a stubby index finger, he spoke reflectively: "Blackmail is neither plain nor simple. I rather pride myself that it is an art, and I am an artist. Yes,"—he looked around with approval—"this is a nice little house you got here, and I could get my money back out of it."

"I got until tomorrow," Cedric reminded him hoarsely. In a panic he ran his hand nervously through his white hair, noting with a spectator's interest that his hand was shaking.

"Sure you do," the man consoled, rising as he spoke, "but the interest goes up another five hundred pounds tomorrow. If you want the bargain rate, you best pay today."

With that discouraging piece of advice he took his leave, walking through the kitchen. Cedric followed him protesting, "But—but—"

"You know where to find me," the man observed cheerfully, then picked up an apple from a basket and began to crunch it noisily as he waddled out the door, leaving it ajar.

"Oh, God," Cedric moaned, tripping against a table and falling slightly forward as he looked hopelessly after his caller. He turned and walked slowly back to his room. His head was aching something fierce, and he couldn't think what was to be done and— "Youch!"

A moment later Rose came rushing into the room, her long dark hair flying as she ran. Still pulling her robe on, she arrived breathlessly in the hall—and found Cedric performing a wild dance. She stared at him in disbelief.

"My foot!" he yelled, hopping on one leg and flailing his long arms. "Something's bit it!"

"Stand still," she commanded loudly as Cedric whirled madly past her, shrieking.

"I can't bear for you to touch it!"

"He's caught in a mousetrap!" the cook cried as she arrived in the hall. In the excitement she allowed a bag of groceries from the morning's shopping expedition to slip from her hands. Potatoes and onions rolled across the floor, and she swooped after them, adding further to the confusion. But as Cedric danced past her, she abandoned them for him.

The two women chased the screaming man into the front parlor, trapped him a corner, and succeeded in removing the trap from his bare toe. By that time Cedric was in no mood to be crossed. With that inauspicious beginning to the day, Cedric retired to his room to sulk while gingerly rubbing his toe and planning how to obtain two thousand and five hundred pounds within the day.

In the succeeding half hour he mentally reviewed his list of acquaintances and was forced to conclude regretfully that among them they didn't have the price of a bottle of gin. If only he knew someone wealthy, he thought. But the only rich person he had ever met, he concluded morosely, was Lord Stranham. It seemed unlikely that that gentle-man would loan him anything.

Then he rallied. Hadn't Lord Stranham taken his part in a fight? And hadn't the marquis brought Cedric home from the cockfight? At least he and the marquis were friends after a fashion. And what were friends for if not to do each other favors? Of course Lord Stranham would help him, he decided firmly—would, in fact, be anxious to. How had he been so addlepated as to have overlooked the marquis in the first place?

Half an hour later, his worn blue coat brushed and his hair combed down as neatly as the unruly white locks permitted, he started for the marquis's house. True, he had not taken the time to shave, but then a two-day growth of white beard hardly showed except as the fuzzi-est stubble, so he did not consider that a problem. When he reached Lord Stranham's house, he knocked on the door with authority.

The door was opened by the marquis's butler, a starched and liveried wonder who stood looking at his fellow butler in faint surprise. "Servants go to the back door," he announced impassively.

"I'm 'ere to see your master," Cedric informed him proudly. He would have entered the large front foyer had his way not been barred. "Stand aside, my good man," he directed with a flourish of his tricorne.

"His lordship is not at home," the butler replied with a condescending look at Cedric's lucky tricorne.

"I'll wait," he answered, and once again attempted to gain entry. His path was still firmly blocked.

"He won't be back today."

"I'll wait 'til tomorrow," Cedric offered.

"I think not," the butler returned in a chilly tone, and started to shut the door.

Cedric kicked at the closing door and then let out a blood-curdling scream. "Oh, my toe. It's broke sure!"

The startled butler looked uncertainly at the thin old man hopping about on the wide top step and cursing lustily.

Above them a window opened. "What the hell's going on down there?" Lord Stranham demanded as he thrust his head out the opening.

"Nothing whatever, my lord," his man answered hastily. "This person has the wrong house."

"I do not," Cedric denied wrathfully. He turned his flushed face up to the marquis. "I needs to see you urgent."

"Is that you, Cedric?" Lord Stranham asked in surprise.

"Course it's me," Cedric returned with offended dignity. "Your man won't admit me."

"Show him in, Bosley," the marquis ordered with a grin. "I'll be down in a moment."

Bosley stood back haughtily as Cedric limped into the foyer and favored his fellow butler with a malevolent stare. "You ain't fit to be employed 'ere," he growled as Lord Stranham sauntered down the stairs, tying a long forest-green velvet robe.

"You'll have to excuse Bosley, Cedric. He isn't used to such early morning callers, and I fear his manners may have been a bit churlish." The marquis laughed. "Isn't that right, Bosley?"

"Quite right, your lordship," the butler said with a decided lack of graciousness.

"I'll show our guest to the drawing room. See to the tea," Lord Stranham directed his servant.

"Very good, sir," Bosley said frigidly, and left.

"I fear I have sunk myself beneath reproach with poor Bosley," Lord Stranham chuckled as he led the way across the wide foyer to a set of double French doors. They entered a large square room richly appointed with carved Chippendale chairs, a thick red oriental rug, and red

162

swags and drapes. The marquis led the way to chairs by the massive walnut mantel. They seated themselves as he continued, "Bosley's the fourth of his family to serve as our family's butler. I hope he doesn't give notice."

" 'E lacks polish," Cedric criticized sullenly.

"Perhaps a bit," Lord Stranham agreed blandly as his impeccable butler entered the room with a silver tray and set it on the tea table in front of the fireplace.

Cedric shifted in the rose damask chair. As he gazed about the large drawing room his heart began to fail him. Lord Stranham was rich. That was evident from the gracious furnishings in the large room. Only wealthy people had curtains that dipped in such carefully arranged curves. The marquis—it suddenly dawned on Cedric— was not a man who was accustomed to receiving visits from other people's butlers requesting money.

But if Lord Stranham was not used to receiving visits from servants, he gave no indication of it as Bosley poured tea for Cedric and handed him a delicate Delft cup. "I realize it's a bit early for tea. I didn't think to ask you if you would prefer to have breakfast."

"I don't want nothin' to eat," Cedric muttered uncomfortably. He looked about again, noting the lush rug on the floor and making a careful study of its intricate oriental pattern. How could he ask the marquis for money? Lord, he barely knew the man!

His host waited tactfully as Cedric drank his tea and looked nervously about the room. He was curious to learn what had brought the man here. Did Cedric bring a message from his mistress? The marquis found himself oddly expectant.

"Well," Cedric said, finishing his tea with a noisy gulp before wiping his shirtsleeve across his mouth and rising to leave. "I best be off."

"Was there perchance something you wished to ask me?" the marquis asked casually.

"Oh, no!" Cedric denied hastily.

"I see. You were merely in the neighborhood and thought to stop in to pay a morning call?" Lord Stranham probed with an amused smile.

"Well, I, er—that is—"

"Sit down, Cedric." If he was leaving without stating his business, then he could not have been sent by Daphne; but Lord Stranham still meant to learn what had brought him here.

Cedric dutifully sank back into the chair.

"Are you in need of assistance?"

"Yes," Cedric admitted with a shamefaced candor.

"I see. Does it involve money?" Lord Stranham pursued.

"How did you know?" Cedric demanded incredulously.

"I thought if you were calling on me, you must need something which none of your other acquaintances could provide you with. I fancy that what I have and your other friends lack is money." He raised a dark brow questioningly.

"Yes, your lordship," Cedric admitted.

"Ah, good. We're making progress. How much?"

"Two thousand and five hundred pounds today."

"Today?"

"Three thousand tomorrow," Cedric explained.

"Dear me. You should have paid six days ago when the balance would have been zero."

"No, my lord, you see—"

"Never mind," the marquis interrupted with an upflung hand. It was not his habit to supply funds to servants—especially other people's—but he felt indulgent toward Miss Brown's butler. Cedric might be of service to him later should he wish to send any discreet messages to that lady. He rose and walked from the room, returning with a handful of gold coins, which he stretched out toward the servant. "Take what you need."

Overwhelmed at the ease with which his plan had succeeded, Cedric began to talk. "It's not for me, you understand. It's for the girls."

Lord Stranham's fingers curled over the coins. "Miss Brown sent you here to obtain money from me?" he asked in a harsh voice. It was all very well for him to supply money to women he had in keeping, but Daphne Brown was not yet one of those lucky few, and he disliked finding her so presumptuous.

"Oh, no, she don't know I'm 'ere. I came cause the girls is short of blunt. They weren't so bad off until they gambled at the cockfights and it wasn't a good day for the banty. You know cocks has their good days and their bad days, so when they lost the first time, there weren't nothing for it but to bet again," Cedric explained disjointedly as he looked hopefully at the marquis's closed fist.

Lord Stranham's gray eyes were riveted on Cedric. "Do you mean that Miss Brown and her sister attend the cockfights and place bets?" he demanded incredulously.

"Oh, no, your lordship! They wouldn't ever!"

"Then what the hell do you mean?" the marquis demanded.

Cedric's words spilled out, gaining coherence as he went along: "Well, they were running out of the ready and you could tell that Miss Daphne was worried, so I offered to 'elp. I told 'er if she gave 'alf of 'er money, I could win more for 'er. She didn't want to at first, but she didn't 'ave much choice with the bills coming in and all, so she says she'd try it once. Well, I lost the first time. Course I couldn't tell her that; so I bet again with my own money. And kept betting. Only I was losing every time, and pretty soon I had lost so much I seen I wasn't never going to win it all back, so I went to a moneylender and borried two thousand, only now—"

Lord Stranham concluded for him: "Only now, the lender wants back far more than you borrowed."

"Yes," Cedric agreed forlornly.

"I see," Lord Stranham said briskly. "In that case I shan't give you any money."

He raised dismayed eyebrows to look at the marquis. "You won't?"

"Certainly not. I shall attend to the moneylender myself. I fancy I can make a better deal with him, as well as keep him from hounding you for more money."

"You can?" Cedric asked reverently.

The marquis nodded confidently. "I trust I can persuade him with my logic. Should that fail, I shall exercise some of the skill I acquired at Gentleman Jackson's Boxing Salon, where I was accounted to be very handy with my fives."

"Thank you, sir. I don't know when I'll be able to pay you back, but I can give you a bit every week and—"

"Never mind," his host interrupted as he pressed a handful of coins into Cedric's bony hand. "If you need more money for the ladies, you will apply directly to me. In the meantime I will continue to supply you with funds to be given to Miss Brown. Tell her you won it at the cockfights."

"You're powerful generous, milord."

"I know," he replied softly. He had reason to be. He expected a satisfying return on his investment.

Cedric walked from the room in a cloud of happiness, even favoring the frosty butler with a kindly look as he limped back out into the street, considerably more lighthearted than he had been when he had entered the house.

Lord Stranham watched him from the wide bay window, a small smile lifting the corners of his mouth.

CHAPTER 18

Daphne leaned back in the gilt chair and once again regretted the impulse that had led her to invite Mrs. Winter along with her and Joanna on their trip to the dressmaker's. She had been carried away on the crest of her excitement when Cedric had presented her with two thousand more pounds he had won. She did not even recall having given him the money to bet! In her excitement she and Joanna had started on their way to Burlington Arcade to purchase some devastatingly saucy hats and had chanced upon Mrs. Winter, and regrettably Daphne had invited her to join them.

Now they were at the dressmaker's, and Mrs. Winter was embroiled in a heated dispute with the French modiste over that lady's prices. "I wish to help these girls select some suitable gowns," Mrs. Winter told the tiny dark-haired Françoise pompously. "It is obvious to me from the amount you have quoted that you have misunderstood my question. I did not ask the cost of purchasing the shop. I asked the price of a velvet gown with rhinestone bodice."

"Oui, and it will be three hundred and fifty guineas," the dressmaker repeated firmly.

Mrs. Winter turned back to Daphne and spoke as if the dressmaker were not present. "She has misheard me," she explained in long suffering accents. "She thinks I said diamonds instead of rhinestones, else she would never have named such an outrageous price."

"Yes, rhinestones," the shopkeeper echoed, nodding

her dark head in agreement. "As I have said, that will be—".

"I am aware of what you have said it will be," Mrs. Winter interrupted, "but I naturally assumed you named that sum only in jest."

Françoise, who had not the look of a jester about her, appealed to the two young ladies, who were shifting uncomfortably in their gilt chairs.

"Is it too much?" she demanded of them. "I, who struggle day and night with these same fingers to earn a meager living." She held her hands out for inspection and wriggled her fingers. "You would seek to cheat me?"

Daphne bit her lower lip in confusion. It had, she thought, been a shockingly high price for a gown. Why, the cost of all the items she had in her wardrobe did not amount to what this woman was asking for one dress. But, she decided recklessly, it was of no consequence. Had she not this very morning won a large amount of money? Yes, for once she and Joanna would have the finest.

Daphne stood up and looked about the small shop airily. "I do thank you for your interest, Mrs. Winter, but the money is unimportant." She noted with satisfaction the awestruck expression with which Mrs. Winter received this news, then she addressed herself again to Françoise: "We shall take the gowns as well as the other dresses we have selected from the fashion plates. When can you have them sent round to the house?"

"Friday," the woman answered promptly.

"Good." Daphne motioned Joanna to rise. "Now we have several other shops to visit."

Mrs. Winter, casting a final head-to-foot glance at the triumphant dressmaker, followed them out. "That woman," Mrs. Winter declared as they stepped outside the shop, "held people up on the high toby before entering this profession. And her occupation as a highway robber is standing her in good stead in her current line of business.

168

I further believe—" She broke off to smile dulcetly at a young man approaching them. "Why, Mr. Morne," she greeted him as he stopped and bowed. "What a surprise to see you here."

The attractive young man who had halted in front of them was of average height. A crown of brownish-red hair curled riotously about his pleasant face. Daphne noted with approval that he had warm brown eyes, a Roman nose, and an agreeable smile.

"It's good to see you, Mrs. Winter," he greeted her politely.

"Do let me introduce my dear little friends," Mrs. Winter said proudly. "This is Miss Daphne Brown and her sister, Joanna." She motioned to each girl in turn.

"Ah, so these are the beautiful Brown sisters of whom I have heard so much. All that I have heard has been high praise of their beauty, but none of the praise, I am persuaded, has done them justice."

"You are most kind, sir," Daphne murmured with a shy and pleased smile.

"Mr. Morne," Mrs. Winter informed them, "is a chemist and very successful."

"Indeed," Joanna said with a nice smile.

Good, Daphne thought smugly. They had finally met a suitable young man who would banish once and for all the thought of Sir Drayton from Joanna's mind. This man, while by no means wearing the extravagant clothes of the men they had met at Lady Drayton's ball, was dressed well in a knee-length redingote of brown frieze and close-fitting breeches of biscuit-colored whipcord.

"I should be honored if you would permit me to call at your house," Mr. Morne said courteously, addressing himself to Daphne.

"Of course, we should be flattered to have you visit," she replied encouragingly, and added a bright smile as a further inducement.

He swept another bow. "I shall call as soon as possible. Now I regret that I must depart. Good day, ladies."

The three women stood watching after him as he strode away.

"He's quite a catch," Mrs. Winter enthused as soon as he was out of earshot. "You could do a deal worse than to set your cap for him, my dear," she advised Daphne.

"Not I," she demurred. "But I fancy he would be a suitable husband for Joanna. Did you like him?" she asked her sister.

"Yes, I found him quite gentlemanly," the younger girl replied vaguely.

Not terribly encouraging, Daphne admitted, but it would serve for the present. After all, now that they had money, it would be a good idea to take Lady Cochmeer's advice and find a nice man for Joanna. Although her sister was less than delighted about Mr. Morne, if he became a frequent caller at their house, Joanna must soon see the manifold sterling qualities Daphne was certain he possessed.

As she and Joanna bid farewell to Mrs. Winter and set off back to Upper Wimpole Street, Daphne was in fine spirits. The fog was finally lifting, revealing a day of azure-blue skies and white puffs of clouds. Everything was new, Daphne thought contentedly as she and Joanna bounced along on the landaulet seat beside Cedric. New clothes, a new man for Joanna, and who knew what would come next?

Unfortunately for Daphne's soaring spirits, what appeared next turned out to be Sir Robert Drayton, who arrived shortly after they returned home. As Rose showed him into the parlor Daphne noted with annoyance that he was carrying a huge bunch of red flowers and uttering a stream of pretty compliments.

She was considerably vexed to see the baronet. It had been two weeks since his mother's ball, and she had just began to hope Joanna was putting him from her mind. Did Sir Robert know the circumstances under which they had attended his mother's party? Undoubtedly he did. Lord Stranham, she thought waspishly, had probably made short work of regaling Sir Robert with the joke of how he had come to obtain the invitations for her and the Winters.

At that thought Daphne flushed and glared at the hapless young man who was innocently engaged in conversation with a smiling Joanna. He leaned forward out of the worn wing chair and regarded her sister with a worshipful gaze.

"Tea?" Daphne asked in a harsh, grating voice, interrupting the pair.

They both looked up in surprise.

"Oh," Joanna said sweetly, "how kind of you to think of it. I quite forgot my manners. Sir Robert was telling me the most amusing story about Lord Stranham and what he said about us after the ball the other even—"

"I'll see to the tea," Daphne snapped, and stalked from the room, leaving behind a confused Joanna and a wary Sir Robert.

She had no desire to stay to hear what Lord Stranham had said about them. Undoubtedly it had been something cynical and amusing about their rustic manners and lack of polish. Well, she didn't care. Fuming, she pushed open the door to the kitchen, then began to stack stale biscuits on a chipped dish as Rose and the housekeeper watched in surprise.

"I've baked some fresh crumpets," the housekeeper volunteered while Daphne busied herself with the teacups.

"These will do nicely," Daphne said with a wry smile. "They're as stale as Sir Drayton's compliments."

The two women exchanged glances as she returned to the parlor with some lukewarm tea and the hard biscuits. She set the tarnished silver tray in front of Sir Robert and smiled warmly. "Do have some refreshments."

171

Smiling politely, he dutifully picked up a biscuit and crunched noisily on the dry food. He gave Daphne another wan smile and made great work of picking crumbs off his lap while she seated herself across from him and then watched him with a fixed stare.

Joanna continued to chatter gaily, but Sir Robert contributed less and less to the discussion. He was obviously unnerved by Daphne's steady gaze and her total silence. He took his leave shortly.

Watching him go, Daphne felt the slightest pangs of guilt. She experienced even stronger regret when Joanna returned from showing their visitor to the door and began to enumerate his endless virtues. As Joanna spoke, Daphne's mind wandered. Could it be that Sir Robert really did like her sister and had nothing dishonorable on his mind? Still, she reminded herself, he had met Joanna under improper circumstances, and sending them tickets to Almacks had been even more lacking in decorum. No, she couldn't think his motives for calling on her sister were entirely above suspicion. Daphne could only hope Mr. Morne would soon remove all thought of Sir Robert from Joanna's young and impressionable mind. Although the chemist had called only once, she was not discouraged; he had been very marked in his attentions to both of them while he was there. Surely he would call again.

In the meantime there were preparations to be made for the Winters' upcoming rout. That should give Joanna somewhere to focus her attention. Even now the dressmaker was sewing them new gowns and pelisses. The money Cedric was winning so steadily had freed Daphne from financial worries and allowed her to turn her thoughts in the direction Lady Cochmeer had suggested— that of making a suitable match for Joanna. For an instant the irregular method from which they were deriving their income caused a slight frown to darken her brow, but then

172

she banished the thought from her mind in favor of the more enjoyable consideration of the Winters' rout.

Daphne sighed with satisfaction as she recalled the apricot gown she was having made from a delicate silk fabric with tiny cream flowers dotted across it. The style she had selected was a high-waisted sheath with a rounded neckline that scooped daringly low and had elbow-length sleeves buttoned *à l'anglaise.* The frothy skirt swept gracefully to just below her knees, and from there one frilly flounce fell to the floor. She smiled in contentment.

It was wonderful to have money, she decided with a happy sigh. The idea occurred to her that it would be nice to wear her lovely new gown where Lord Stranham might see her.

She straightened in the chair. Now, whatever had brought that absurdity into her mind? There was no earthly reason why she should wish to deck herself out to attract the marquis's attention. She had neither seen nor heard from him since the evening of Lady Drayton's ball, and it was quite likely she never would again. That, she told herself as she rose abruptly, was exactly how she wished it.

CHAPTER 19

After Cedric's visit Lord Stranham had given some thought to the situation of the Brown girls while he decided what course of action he intended to follow. If they were indeed penniless, as Cedric had indicated, then it would be most ungentlemanly of him to pursue an impoverished and unprotected woman with the intention of setting her up in keeping. But that was very much the goal he had in mind for Daphne. It was an object that he was loath to abandon, although he might have done so in the case of a great many other young women should such a situation as this have arisen. But he didn't wish to relinquish his plans for the violet-eyed nymph who so occupied his thoughts of late. Of course, there was still much of the young lady's behavior that was not above question. For one thing, why had she come to London in such straited financial conditions if not to find a man to take care of her?

Added to that, he had been about the world long enough to know when a woman was attracted to him, and he was well aware that Miss Brown had more than a passing interest in him. Oh, her manner had not always been all that was inviting, but there was frequently a certain soft expression in her eyes when she looked at him, which he knew to be the unmistakable sign of an intrigued lady.

The thought of marrying Daphne, fascinated though he was by her, was totally inconceivable. Only yesterday he had spent some time trying to convince Robert that the girls were not in their class. The baronet, he was forced to conclude, really was in love with Joanna Brown. He had never seen his friend so overwrought as he had become upon hearing the marquis's advice that he have nothing further to do with the girl. Lord Stranham only hoped he had made his point with the young fool. It would not do at all for the baronet to marry beneath his station.

As far as the matter of his matrimony stood, he intended to offer for Lady Diedre shortly. Why he had not yet paid his addresses to her was difficult to explain, but he would do so within the next week. In the meantime, he considered, he would pay a call on Miss Daphne Brown. In a very short time, he felt sure, he would be able to do much more than merely sit in her parlor and exchange commonplaces, but it would do for a start.

He ordered his curricle brought round, and a few minutes later he was tooling the ribbons smartly, giving the horses their heads as he proceeded north to Upper Wimpole Street.

From the front parlor window Daphne saw the marquis's curricle pull up before the house. "Oh, dear," she said aloud, dropping the dust cloth to the floor as she hastily straightened her yellow cotton day dress. She had not seen Lord Stranham since the ball, and they had parted in less than congenial humor. Still, if he was calling at her house, she must be gracious. After all, he *had* obtained the invitations to Lady Drayton's party for her.

The knocker sounded and then sounded again. "Where is Cedric?" she asked aloud, and then realized the futility of the question, since he was undoubtedly at the cockfights. She proceeded reluctantly into the hall and opened the door.

"Good day, Miss Brown," the marquis greeted her with a bow.

"My lord, won't you come in?" she said cordially.

He obliged, handing her his cane and tall-crowned beaver hat as he did so. Daphne stood holding them uncertainly. "I beg your pardon," he said as he retrieved them with alacrity. "I did not think."

"That's quite all right," she said with a wintry smile. "I'm certain most of the houses you visit have a butler to receive your hat. Ours," she added loftily, "is out at the moment."

"I see."

"This way, my lord." She led him into the parlor and motioned to the sagging wing chair. As he lowed his tall frame into the chair, she stealthily kicked the dusting rag under the settee. "Would you like tea?"

"Yes, tea would be nice."

She pulled the bell rope and then stopped, turning a flustered face to him. "I fear we may not have tea," she apologized. "Rose, the housekeeper, is out and, as I have said, Cedric has also been called away."

But Cedric very shortly proved that statement wrong by appearing in the black tricorne he always wore to the cockfights. He inquired with elaborate formality, "You rang, Miss Daffy?" The stiffness of his bearing and the proud tilt of his head were somewhat marred by the hiccough that escaped unstifled before he could raise a belated hand to his mouth.

"Tea," she commanded, and turned back to the marquis as Cedric exited unsteadily. "Lovely day, is it not?" she asked brightly.

"That fellow has been in his cups again," Lord Stranham said shortly, disregarding her pleasantry.

"That, my lord, is none of your affair," she retorted.

"Quite right," Cedric agreed, thrusting his head back in the door in a shameless manner that indicated he had never removed himself far from the room.

"You were directed to leave," the marquis commanded sternly.

Cedric favored his lordship with a haughty look before disappearing through the door.

"How dare you order my servant about!" Daphne kindled angrily.

"I don't care whose servant he is, he has no right to listen at the door."

"Cedric," she said with frosty hauteur, "*never* listens at doors."

The full import of those words was considerably lessened by the sound of a hiccough coming from right outside the room. Daphne blushed furiously as an amused grin spread slowly across the marquis's handsome face. His enjoyment at her expense was humiliating, she thought angrily.

Actually, could she have but known it, quite another thought was passing through Lord Stranham's mind. A glance at his watch, which was attached to a gold fob chain, showed him he had already been there five minutes. Far from wishing to take his leave, as he frequently did after five minutes spent at Lady Diedre's house, he found he very much wanted to stay. This was the most diverting scene he had witnessed in some time.

Daphne, however, saw the furtive look at his watch and put quite a different interpretation on that action. The man was counting the minutes until he could leave! Why had he called to begin with? she wondered indignantly.

The knocker sounded again, and Daphne excused herself to answer it. She discovered Mr. Peter Morne standing in the doorway with a bouquet of jonquils in his hand. Daphne's smile of welcome widened as she regarded him. Mr. Morne had called only once, and then he had not brought flowers. This, she decided gleefully, was definitely a strong show of interest—the very thing needed to draw Joanna's attention away from thoughts of Sir Robert.

In her excitement Daphne forgot her sense of decorum so far as to whisper, "I am so glad you have come. Do step in and I shall tell my sister you are here." She stood aside for him to enter and then turned and walked up the steps to knock on Joanna's door. She pushed it open without waiting for a reply. "Joanna," she called softly, "you have company." She sped back down the steps and relayed to Peter, "My sister will be down shortly."

A moment later Joanna appeared at the top of the stairs, smiling radiantly downward. Her smile faded perceptibly upon seeing their guest. He was obviously not the visitor she had been hoping to find. Daphne directed a hasty glance at Mr. Morne to see if he had detected Joanna's lack of warmth, starting as she realized his eyes were not focused on her sister. They were, instead, directed at her in a wistful, almost longing gaze. He had come to see her, not Joanna, Daphne realized dazedly.

She was dragged back to reality upon hearing her sister say politely, "Won't you come into the parlor, Mr. Morne?"

The three of them entered that room, where Lord Stranham stood courteously while Daphne introduced the two men. The chemist acknowledged the introduction with the proper words, but Daphne noted that his eyes never left her face for long. She ventured a furtive look at the marquis to see if he was also aware of that fact. Judging from the expression on Lord Stranham's face, he was well aware that she had made a conquest, for he sharply scrutinized the newcomer as they sat down. No doubt, Daphne thought irritably, the marquis considered Mr. Morne a perfect fool to display any interest in her.

Talk was interrupted when Cedric entered with tea. As he sailed across the room, the young people held their breaths listening to the cups clatter ominously and the liquid slosh inside the teapot. Setting the tray down with careless abandon, he announced, "Tea is served."

"Thank you, Cedric," Daphne said swiftly.

The butler, however, did not take the hint of dismissal so readily. He turned to the marquis and smiled crookedly. "Howareye today, your lerdship?"

179

Lord Stranham gave the red-faced, inebriated man a quick perusal. "I go on well," he replied curtly.

"That's good," Cedric noted, still making no move to depart.

Daphne stirred restlessly on the settee. She very much wished her servant would leave before Peter realized how far past sobriety he was.

Lord Stranham must have read her mute appeal, for he stood up and put an arm about the old man's stooping shoulder, leading him from the parlor and back to the kitchen.

Inside that room, Cedric closed the door. "Did you talk to the cent per center?" he asked as he seated himself comfortably on a settee by the hearth and began to pick his teeth.

"I did," Lord Stranham replied, and turned to leave.

"How much did you have to pay 'im?" Cedric asked with casual interest.

"Two thousand. I believe that was the original amount you borrowed?"

" 'Twas, but 'e told me two thousand wouldn't pay it back without interest," Cedric related.

"Quite right," the marquis said dryly. "I was one of those two thousand who would not pay him the exorbitant interest."

Cedric continued hopefully: "Since we got that 'un paid fer, why not let's us, you and me, that is, combine our money and bet on the red that will be fighting tonight."

"What would your contribution to the bet be?" Lord Stranham asked with restrained amusement.

"I would pay at such time as I win," Cedric explained. "My finansheal situation is such at present that I could not contriboot—"

The kitchen door swung open and Daphne entered. "Whatever are you doing?" she demanded ungraciously of the marquis.

180

"Me and 'im's talking business," Cedric said with a pointed look at Daphne that indicated she was not welcome to stay.

Ignoring that hint, she turned back to Lord Stranham, her lips pursed. "It is customary for a guest to sit in the parlor and visit with the family rather than attend to some sort of questionable business dealings with a servant. I should think," she added with hauteur, "that you would have the decency not to embroil Cedric in any of your schemes. He hardly has the money to be engaging in dealings with you." No doubt the two had struck up quite a friendship when Lord Stranham had returned Cedric from the cockfights. She would not allow her servant to become a betting partner with Lord Stranham.

"I shall not involve him in any wild schemes," the marquis told her with the maddening hint of a smile.

No doubt, Daphne fumed, the marquis thought it a subject of great jest that her servant was something of a gambler and a drinker. But that was no reason for him to encourage Cedric in such low pastimes. "I do not find the conversation at all amusing," she informed her guest coldly.

"Do you not? You are perfectly correct, of course. I was, unforgivably, discussing plans to gamble with Cedric, and you are quite right to say that we must on no account undertake such plans." He turned to Cedric and spread his hands in resignation. "I fear we have been uncovered and must abandon our scheme." The marquis bowed politely. "I shall take my leave now," he told Daphne as they started down the hall. He would come back another time when she did not have company and when her temper was improved.

Daphne had no intention of allowing him to leave so blithely. First she intended to tell him exactly how she felt about his plottings with poor misguided Cedric. As they reached the front door she spoke in a low but deadly tone:

"If I discover that Cedric is engaged in betting on the cocks with you, I shall hold you personally responsible for any money he loses."

"Indeed?" he asked with a sardonic laugh.

"Yes," she hissed.

"I see. Then you would not," he asked wickedly, "be a party to such bets, and you would not wish your servant to?"

Daphne looked at him warily. It was true that she *was* a party to betting on the cockfights, but that was for entirely different motives—certainly not for sport. Besides, the marquis had no way of knowing that her family was forced to meet its bills in such an unconventional way. She tossed her head proudly. "I would never be engaged in any activities that were not proper. Certainly I would never attend a cockfight." Her words were, strictly speaking, true.

She did not actually engage in an improper activity, since she did not *place* the bets. Cedric was her businessman, and it was not for anyone to question how he invested her money.

"I see," the marquis returned with a final sardonic laugh before putting on his hat and opening the front door.

His good humor did nothing to improve Daphne's own spirits, and she returned to the parlor with a growing sense of chagrin. Lord Stranham, for all his lofty words about preserving the dignity of his position, was totally without principle. It was just as well that he did not think her a suitable wife, for she would not have him. She definitely would not have him, she repeated to herself as she fluttered her eyes provocatively at Mr. Morne and rewarded him with her most encouraging smile.

CHAPTER 20

At the same time that Lord Stranham was tumbling into bed late that night, Daphne was rising from her own cozy bed. The gentle splashes of rain that had started some hours earlier as a polite patter against her window had become steadily more insistent. From somewhere within the house she could hear loud plunks of water dropping onto the bare wooden floor.

She sighed and rose, throwing an old peignoir over her shift before lighting the candle beside her bed. Venturing into the darkened hall, she felt a splatter of water fall heavily on her head. The cool wetness beneath her toes was also water. Judging from the feel of it on the hem of the faded green dressing gown, there was a considerable amount collecting in the shallow depression of the floor at the head of the stairs. She stepped onto the carpeted steps and continued down to the first floor, feeling the water squish uncomfortably through her toes.

Tomorrow, she thought wearily, something must be done to the roof. In the meantime she would have Cedric put some pans under the worst part of the leak and she would mop up what she could of the water.

The clock striking in the parlor informed her it was three in the morning. For a moment she considered the appealing thought of remounting the steps to her warm bed. No, she told herself firmly, there would be time enough for sleep later. For the present she needed to attend to the flood in the hall before it worsened.

Daphne stepped off the bottom step, proceeded down the hall to Cedric's small bedroom, and tapped quietly on the door. No answer. She rapped louder. Still no answer. Cedric was a heavy sleeper, and since she hadn't heard him come in that night, he had doubtless been out until late and was now sleeping soundly. She pushed open the door and started across the room to his bed.

From the wavering glow of her candle, it was immediately obvious that, although Cedric was thin, he was not slight enough to be occupying the bed. No form showed beneath the covers. In fact, the bed had not been slept in at all.

Daphne sat down on the narrow bed in confusion. Three in the morning. Where could Cedric be? But even as that question flitted through her mind, she knew the answer. What had undoubtedly happened was that he had collapsed drunk somewhere; it had happened a time or two before.

A loud clap of thunder caused Daphne to jump in surprise. Poor Cedric. He would be dreadfully drenched and might catch a terrible chill. She paced to the front parlor in agitation, pulling back the curtain to look out the window.

Outside she could discern only utter darkness. But as she looked through the pane, a flash of lightning lit up the sky, revealing a shadowy figure lying across the street a few houses down. Then all was blackness again. Daphne peered intently outward, trying to make out the shape again, but the inky darkness of the night prevented her from doing so. It was several minutes before another wild flash of lightning lit the streets, and she saw that there was indeed someone slumped against the house. Who else would be out at this hour and in this weather? It could only be Cedric.

The poor dear, he had come so close to attaining the house. He must be very soaked, and he was so thin and frail he could easily catch a chill. Moved by that thought, she made her resolution: She must go and get him.

184

Turning, Daphne mounted the steps to her sister's room and roused Joanna. "Cedric has not returned home, but there is a man who has fallen across the street and I am certain it is he," she informed the sleepy girl. "I will awaken Rose while you dress. We must go rescue him."

Five minutes later, dressed in old clothes and with dark, hooded cloaks thrown over their shoulders, all three women plodded out into the storm in the direction Daphne indicated. The lantern they carried was extinguished almost as soon as they stepped outside the door when a strong wind blew into the glass chimney. In the darkness they could barely see each other.

"Shouldn't we go back in for another light?" Joanna asked.

"I fear it would be to no avail," Daphne replied. "It's very dark, but he isn't far away. If we all take each other's hands, we are in no danger of being separated and we will be all right."

They linked hands, and Daphne started forward again, moving slowly against the strong wind of the storm. When she reached the dark form after several minutes of stumbling around near him, Daphne bent to shake him gently. "Cedric, you must wake up. You are only a short distance from the house and we will help you home—" She broke off in a lusty scream.

The man who was rising was not Cedric. All three women began to run wildly back to the house as the man lunged toward them. Daphne raced as hard as she could, taking long, slogging steps in the rain and trying to keep pace with the fleeter-footed Joanna and Rose, who were already lost in the black night.

"Stop!" a voice behind her ordered.

She continued, unheeding. She must be almost to the house, she thought desperately.

"Stop!" the voice cried again, closer this time.

Holding up the bulk of her sodden cloak as best she

185

could, Daphne tried to flee. But not for long; her arm was grasped firmly and she was whirled around by a man's firm grip.

"I'm taking you to Bow Street," the man growled.

"Bow Street?" she repeated with blank fear.

"Yes. You can explain to the magistrate why you were trying to outdistance a runner."

"Thank heaven!" she exclaimed, weak with relief. "You see, my home isn't far from here and—"

The man didn't give Daphne a chance to finish her explanation. With a yank of her arm he started her walking in the direction he had come from.

"But you do not understand in the least. I live near here. You have only to knock on the door." When he made no reply, she tried again. "Sir, perhaps you were not attending. I live close by."

"Tell the magistrate," he said in a bored voice.

Daphne's renewed arguments went unheeded, although she continued them valiantly all the way to Bow Street. There, she was thrust inside a depressing little room lit by garish sconces that dotted the dirty wall. The long wooden benches, which composed the sole furnishings of the room, were full of drabs and thieves. The runner pushed Daphne toward a vacant space, and she sat down unceremoniously.

Beside her, a toothless hag carefully scrutinized her before initiating a conversation. "Yeh shot the cat?"

"No, of course not. I never drink!" she denied vehemently.

"'Ave yeh been 'ere 'fore?" the crone asked.

"Certainly not," Daphne declared with feeling. "I should not be here now were it not for a misunderstanding. As soon as I have explained that to the magistrate, I shall be leaving."

"Cheer ap, yeh'll get uset t' being brang in 'ere once yeh been in the bus'ness fer a time."

"Been in what business?" Daphne demanded indignantly.

The old crone cackled. "Nothin' ta be 'shamed of, luv. 'Tis tha owldest profession in the world."

Daphne's eyes widened in shock. "I am a lady. I am not a streetwalker!"

" 'Course y'ar a laidie. I'm too. I jest sells flawhrs like a pore re'pectable gel, 'n the runners keep brangin' me in 'ere time after time. Kin I 'elp it if men find me 'tractive?" she asked virtuously.

Their conversation was interrupted when the door opened again. The tall old man who was half dragged, half carried into the room was protesting loudly.

"We's business 'sociates, is what we is. That's 'ow I come to be at 'is house."

The runner gave a short, nasty laugh. "When the likes of you is a business associate with the marquis of Stranham, I'll eat my boots. He wouldn't even let you wipe *his* boots. Business associates!" he snorted, and then pushed Cedric toward a seat and marched out, closing the door behind him.

"Cedric!" Daphne cried.

" 'Ow noice fer yeh," the crone commented pleasantly. "I meets friends 'ere too, I do."

Daphne ignored her, starting up out of her seat as Cedric lurched over to her. "Are you all right?" she demanded with concern.

Cedric evinced no surprise at seeing his sedate mistress among a roomful of criminals and vagabonds. He merely dropped down on the bench, squeezing in between the bawd and a ragged man whose head lolled sleepily on his chest. Daphne continued to stand, wringing her hands in agitation.

"Course I'm all right," he snapped. "Some runner found me outside 'is lordship's house and got some maggot in 'is 'ead that I was going to try to break in the 'ouse.

187

I tried to get him to knock on the door so's Lord Stranham could explain what I was doing there, but 'e wouldn't 'ear of it. No, sir, 'e says, 'e ain't going to disturb his lordship."

Daphne, who was finding few things to be thankful for that night, was at least grateful that Lord Stranham had not been summoned.

"What'd yeh say yeh got pinched fer?" the old woman asked Cedric.

He surveyed her suspiciously while the bawd took his measure.

"Yeh don't 'ave ter tell me if yeu don't wan' teh. I thought it might 'ave somethin' ter do with yer odd clothes."

He looked down at his half-century-old faded blue livery and then turned affronted eyes back to the woman. "This is the costume of a respectable butler," he pronounced.

"Oi, is it? I ain't niver seed a bloke wear teh loikes of that."

"I am not surprised," Cedric returned with lofty dignity. "You would not be admitted to houses with butlers as grand as myself."

The door opened again, and several uniformed men entered and began to circle about the room, talking to some of the people. They allowed a few to leave and led others away. Finally one of the runners approached Daphne and Cedric.

"You the one that was caught trying to break into Lord Stranham's house?" he demanded.

" 'E's a bu'ler, 'e says, but I ain't niver seed such clothes," the old woman replied at the same time that Cedric declared with asperity, "Summon 'is lordship at once and 'e will explain the whole of the matter."

"No, don't," Daphne interjected.

Unfortunately her words came too late. The door opened again and the marquis strode into the room, looking elegant and well turned out for one recently roused from his bed. His black many-caped driving coat billowed behind him as he stalked commandingly toward their little group.

"What is amiss here?" he demanded of the runner.

"We found this man outside your house, your lordship. He was trying to break in."

"Fustian!" the marquis pronounced. "He had been standing about singing indelicate ballads for a quarter of an hour before you arrived and making no attempt to enter the house. Obviously the man is foxed. He should have tired of his opera after a time and taken himself home. Release him."

"Yes, my lord." The runner acquiesced swiftly, and Cedric was led from the room.

"And what," Lord Stranham asked as he turned toward Daphne and gave her a frosty perusal, "have we here?"

"Oi," the crone said loudly, " 'e's a bang-up gen'leman, 'e is! Air yeh 'is fancy piece?" she asked Daphne with a new reverence.

"She's just some woman of easy virtue cleared off the street, my lord," the runner replied as Daphne flushed hotly.

"I most certainly am not!" she denied vehemently.

"We found you running down the street," the runner countered. "And you're talking with Carrotty Moll, the most notorious woman of the night in London."

"I sell flawhrs," the old woman informed him pertly. "Kin I 'elp it if a gen'leman tries to steal my virtue now and agin?"

"Your virtue is long gone," the runner retorted. "You sold it more years ago than you can remember."

"I am not interested in the good woman's concerns," the marquis snapped. "I wish to know about this young lady." He indicated Daphne with a curt nod of his head.

"Like I said, your lordship, we found her running through the streets."

"No doubt she was out for a stroll," Lord Stranham said with sardonic casualness. "Why have you not taken off your sopping cloak, Miss Brown, and made yourself at home here?"

Daphne pulled the wet garment tighter around her and stared with a freezing hauteur back into the marquis's face. "I wish to leave," Daphne said stiffly.

"Of course you do," the runner mocked. "No doubt you're losing business with every hour spent here."

"I cannot think why I am being held against my express wishes and forced to listen to such shocking accusations." Her words were brave, but the hands hidden inside her cloak were trembling.

Lord Stranham regarded her with a speculative, suspicious look. "What exactly *were* you doing walking the streets in the dead of night, Miss Brown?" he asked with awful formality.

She bristled. "I am not obliged to explain my actions to you."

"*Were* you perhaps out for a stroll?" he pursued sarcastically.

Daphne turned blazing violet eyes at the marquis's taunting face. "If it pleases you to think me a fool, I give you leave to do so. I am quite obviously that, else I should not be here. However, if you think my actions bespeak that I am less than a lady, you are fair and far out in your assumptions." She finished with a defiant upward tilt of her small chin.

"If she ain't 'terested in yeh, yeh lordship, yeh could come 'round teh m' place at the Fryin' Pan in Brick Lane. Name's Carrotty Moll. I sell flawhrs, I do. I'm re'pectable."

Ignoring her offer, the marquis turned to Daphne with a cold gleam in his eye that did not soften as he took her hand roughly. "I shall see the lady home," he told the runner authoritatively. He pressed a coin into the old woman's hand before drawing Daphne toward the door.

"Oi, thank yeh, milord. I won't forgit yeh. Yeh can come 'round anytime yeh needs some . . ." She paused, then added flirtatiously, ". . . flawhrs."

Daphne allowed herself to be led out to the marquis's closed carriage and handed inside. In the concealing darkness she relaxed back against the squabs and closed her eyes as Lord Stranham gave his driver directions to her house.

Her blissful rest was short-lived, however, as he settled himself in the seat beside her and demanded brusquely, "Now, Miss Brown, would you be so good as to explain yourself?"

"I was looking for Cedric," she lashed out scathingly.

There was a short silence in the darkened carriage before the marquis said in a reflective voice, "I see. Alone?" The last word was almost a challenge.

"No, not alone. I was with a legion of men, trysting with first one and then the other." Sarcasm weighted her voice.

"Miss Brown, do not try my patience," he warned harshly.

"Of course I was not alone," she snapped. "I was with Joanna and Rose."

"I see. It must have been an interesting sight, the three of you running down the darkened streets looking for your servant."

"We were not running," she corrected coldly.

"The Bow Street runner said you were."

"Well, we were when he saw us, because someone jumped out at us and we were naturally frightened. But until then we had been walking along calmly enough."

"I can quite imagine how sedately the three of you were walking along in the pouring rain through the black streets poking your heads in every alley to discover if your

191

butler was passed out in a drunken stupor," he said caustically.

Daphne made no reply. He was twisting everything she had done to make her appear ludicrous. She would not give him the satisfaction of relating more details of the evening. No doubt the mention of how her flooded house had sent her off looking for Cedric in the first place would send him into whoops of laughter.

Beside her, Lord Stranham was more than a little irritated. He had been moving slowly in his attention to Daphne in order not to alarm her. While he was trying to approach her in a way that would not offend her sensibilities, she was out in the dead of night wandering the streets. The thought of her actions angered him. Who was she meeting at such a time? *He* was the one who had been paying her way; if she wished to pass her late-night hours with anyone, it should be with him.

With a rough, deliberate movement he reached a strong hand up under her chin and turned her to face him. In the interior of the carriage he could not see her, but his lips did not err when they bent to touch hers. Then his mouth closed completely over hers, smothering her startled gasp as he took full possession of her lips. She brought small hands up to beat against his wide chest, but he caught them easily and held them firmly. Token resistance was all very well, but he knew it for what it was.

For her part, Daphne was more stunned than outraged, although she was not a little of that. The marquis's strong grip on her hands, cutting into the soft flesh of her wrists and creating bruises, made her realize how powerful he was. It was useless to fight him. Not that she meant to submit; she certainly did not! But she allowed him to embrace her while she tried feverishly to think of some way to extricate herself from this coil.

Lord Stranham pulled back slightly. "Your lips are very

192

sweet, my pet, but there is no passion in your kiss. I will teach you."

"How d-dare you!" she sputtered.

"It would be my pleasure." He laughed as he pressed his lips to hers again. The kiss that ensued was lengthy and masterful. It became considerably more possessive when she struggled against him. When he finally released her, she was breathing hoarsely and her anger was even more heightened than before.

"You are loathsome," she said in shaken accents.

The carriage drew up in front of the house, and the marquis moved to help her alight. "I—I don't want your assistance," she said brokenly. She was unable to keep the quiver from her voice and, worse, to stifle the sobs of anger and humiliation that escaped.

"Miss Brown. I'm sorry, I thought—"

He got no further. The door slammed in his face, and a moment later he heard the door to her house close firmly. As the vehicle started slowly forward Lord Stranham sat motionless.

CHAPTER 21

The next morning Lord Stranham sat for some time in the crewel Chippendale chair in his spacious bedroom staring fixedly into the unlit fireplace. He was seeing nothing of the cold ashes that lay within the grate; the picture firmly imprinted in his mind's eye was that of a lovely woebegone girl sitting in a room full of cutthroats and thieves, waiting for someone to come to her assistance.

When he had entered the room last night and seen Daphne sitting there, looking fragile and lost, he had felt a curious emotion in his breast. For an instant he had a strong desire to stride across the room and encircle her protectively in his arms. The feeling had passed quickly and had been replaced by the more common emotion of anger. What the hell was the chit doing in a place like that?

Daphne Brown, it appeared to him, had a very nasty habit of involving herself in the most questionable situations. Even in his anger he did not try to deceive himself that that penchant quenched the interest he had in her. Stretching out a long booted foot, he kicked the lifeless embers. Had he wronged Daphne in his estimation of her? And if he had and she was a pure and innocent woman, then shouldn't he offer her marriage to make up for his abominable actions of last night?

He banished that thought with an angry scowl as he rose and paced to the window. Of course he shouldn't consider wedding her. His advances in the carriage might have been a bit hasty, but there was no call to think of anything so drastic as offering for her. His marriage to

Lady Diedre was almost a *fait accompli*. She, he told himself firmly, was the sensible choice for a wife. She was a biddable and agreeable women with a title, a dowry, and the virtue of accepting a man's judgment without question. Miss Brown had none of those attributes. But at the thought of Daphne he remembered her anguished sob before she had quitted the carriage. Something inside went cold at the recollection.

"Bah!" he said testily as he stalked back to the fireplace.

Charles, neatly laying out the marquis's evening clothes, looked up. "You spoke?" he asked.

"If you had the choice of marrying an agreeable chit with good breeding, money, and a tractable disposition or a veritable harridan of a woman with no money and very little to say for herself except a rather pretty face, which lady would you choose?"

Thus put, the question seemed rather straightforward to Charles. "I should marry the paragon, of course, my lord."

"Good," the marquis grunted. "Then that's just what I shall do." He walked from the room with a determined look on his face, leaving his valet staring after him puzzled.

Lord Stranham took his tall-crowned beaver hat and ebony walking stick on the way out the door and proceeded briskly to Bond Street. He needed nothing there, but he hoped the outing would divert his mind from the image of Daphne.

It *was* shortly diverted when he chanced upon his mother on the street. "Ah," she greeted him with an elegant gloved hand. "I should have taken to the streets sooner in the hope of seeing my beloved son. I had far better opportunity of seeing you here than awaiting your call at my home."

"I beg you will forgive me, my lady mother, but I have

196

had a number of matters to attend to. I should have called on you today at any rate."

"Why so?" she asked with her customary bluntness.

"I have some news of interest. I am going to set up my nursery."

"You shall, I trust, marry first," she commented. "I believe it is considered proper."

"I shall observe all of the amenities," he assured her dryly.

"Excellent. I thought the moment I spied the blond-haired chit that *she* would leg-shackle you. She had the look of a future duchess about her."

"Miss Brown is not to be my wife," her son corrected sharply. "I intend to wed Lady Diedre. Miss Brown has no connections and is wholly beneath the interest of our circle," he added coolly.

"Rather harsh words, my son," his mother reproved him.

"Damnably true," he grated.

The duchess gave him a shrewd perusal. "*I* shan't make a push for you to offer for any girl you find totally unacceptable," she said soothingly. "I can see that you have taken Miss Brown in the greatest aversion, and I should be the last person to attempt anything so foolhardy as trying to change your mind. In any event, Margaret and I had a lovely coze the other day, and she told me she had no objections whatsoever to Robert courting the younger Brown girl. Of course," she added as she looked casually up and down the street, "since their father was an earl, the girls do have something to recommend them, even if they have not had the advantages of wealth and a come out into society."

"Their father was what?" the marquis asked in stunned disbelief.

"An earl," she repeated with another assessing look at him. "Unfortunately, he was disinherited; that is why

Miss Daphne Brown and her sister were forced to come to London to look for positions as governesses or companions."

"Positions as *what?*" he demanded.

"Dear me, Mark, you cannot be attending me at all. Why else would you keep asking questions about something I have just explained? At any rate, this is hardly the place to pursue such a discussion. Why do we not repair back to my house and we can talk about the matter?"

Lord Stranham acquiesced in his mother's suggestion, helping her into her carriage and boarding behind her with an absence of mind that was peculiar to him. In truth, he was shocked by the knowledge his mother had imparted. Good God, Daphne Brown was of the nobility and he had made some most improper advances toward her. Small wonder she had been hurt and outraged. At the recollection of her tears the marquis felt a sudden constriction in his throat and pulled at his starched cravat to ease the pressure.

"Are you feeling quite the thing, Mark?" Lady Cochmeer asked as she peered at him from the carriage seat across from him.

"Indeed, I thank you for inquiring," he replied tonelessly.

Moments later they were inside her grace's spacious gold saloon. The comfort of her brocade chairs had been the source of many compliments to her ladyship in the past, but today she noted her son was unable to remain seated in one of them for long before springing up to pace the room.

He looked out the window for a few minutes before he asked, "How long have you known they were Quality?"

"The Brown girls, you mean?" her grace asked with feigned innocence.

"You know perfectly well I mean them," he barked.

Lady Cochmeer took little note of her son's lack of

198

civility; she merely smiled blandly at him. "Why, I believe I have known for better than a week, ever since the elder Miss Brown asked me to assist them in finding situations."

"Why did you not inform me of this fact as soon as you learned it?" He turned to glare at her.

"I had no idea it would be of any interest to you," she remarked calmly. "Although I did take the liberty of mentioning it to Robert when he stopped by yesterday on his way home from your house. You had managed to put him in quite a taking by telling him Miss Joanna was totally beneath him. I," she informed her son brightly, "was able to lay his mind at rest. I told him he could offer for the young lady, should he so desire, without fear of besmirching his family. I had thought," she continued, "that Robert's interest in the younger girl was merely a passing whim, but I no longer account it as such. He was mortified that he had not defended her honor in some earlier instance involving some words Mr. Atrium spoke. Robert was not very clear in the telling of the tale, but I apprehend he feared it reflected badly on his character and made him unworthy of Miss Joanna Brown. I assured him he was in every way an acceptable husband for the girl."

Lord Stranham heard but few of his mother's words. While she spoke, his mind moved rapidly. The conclusion he reached was that he must call on Daphne immediately and beg her forgiveness for his actions of last night. After that, he would court her in an entirely proper manner before making an offer. It was the gentlemanly thing to do.

At that very moment a disgruntled Daphne was giving some very direct reprimands to a certain butler in the house on Upper Wimpole Street. Daphne had spent the better part of the night lying awake staring at the ceiling, determining what she would say to the marquis, Cedric, Joanna, and Rose when next she saw them. She had an equally biting sermon rehearsed for each of them. Right now she had her first victim trapped in the front parlor. Cedric was seated on the settee as Daphne paced in front of him and delivered a blistering speech.

In truth, the full moral brunt of her lecture was somewhat lost on Cedric as he listened meekly. His head lolled sleepily against his chest, and most of her words were jumbled in his foggy mind. Only when she raised her voice to make a particular point did Cedric wince in discomfort, the volume causing an unpleasant throb in his head. He had, he lamented, drunk rather more than was good for him last night. He couldn't recollect anything about the events of the past evening, but Miss Daphne must have needed him at some time in the course of the night, for she seemed to be in a taking that he had not been in his room when she looked for him. Beyond that he took little notice of her words, wishing only that she would cease speaking so that he might retire to his room and nurse his hurting head.

Fortunately, Joanna appeared at that moment, and Cedric made his escape when Daphne turned on her younger sister. "I hope you slept well last night," Daphne greeted her sarcastically.

"Yes," Joanna answered blankly. "Are you overset about something?" she ventured, her violet eyes questioning and her delicate face quizzical.

"Overset?" Daphne shouted. "Whyever should I be? Merely because I was hauled to Bow Street like a common criminal and forced to listen to insults from a runner and Lord Stranham is nothing to be overset about. And when I returned home, everyone had retired blissfully to bed without a thought for my safety."

"Of course we were concerned for your safety," Joanna remonstrated, "but the runner who brought Cedric home said you would be here shortly and that there was no cause for alarm."

"And you didn't even sit up to see how I was?" Daphne demanded frostily.

"We *were* waiting up for you, but when I saw the marquis's carriage, I put out the candle, and Rose and I discreetly retired to bed. I knew you were safe, and I thought you might want some time alone with him. Did he say anything in particular to you? Anything of a personal nature?" Joanna's eager face reflected her hope that a romance was in the offing.

"He most certainly did," Daphne retorted. "He said several very particular things to me, all of a personal nature."

"Famous," Joanna enthused. "Perhaps he will develop a *tendre* for you, and you can marry him and I can marry Sir Robert. I think he is a very nice man, and you would probably deal much better with him than with Mr. Morne."

Daphne gave her such a chilling look that Joanna faltered in her enthusiastic plans.

She was prevented from replying to her sister's words when the knocker sounded. Daphne flung the door open to discover Lord Stranham standing on the threshold regarding her with a pained expression. As she noted his look a little of her anger died. Suddenly, irrelevantly, she was glad she had donned her pink muslin morning dress with an oval neckline adorned with gauze frill. Vertical lines of striped gold gallon decorated the bodice; it was one of her loveliest gowns.

"Good morning," he greeted her politely. "I trust you are well."

"I am, my lord," she replied stiffly.

"Miss Brown, I wish to speak with you concerning—"

"Why, Mr. Morne," Daphne interrupted him, and flashed a brilliant smile at the young man coming up the walk. He was bearing flowers and looked quite gallant as he presented them to her. Daphne thanked him prettily and favored him with another dazzling smile. "Do come in, sir," she invited the newcomer. Turning to Lord Stranham, she extended a chilled invitation, "My lord, will you sit with us?"

"I thank you, no; I have a pressing engagement." The marquis took his leave with a curt bow and one final glance at Peter Morne.

CHAPTER 22

"Ah," the duchess said to Robert as her son stepped into the lavish green and gold library of his house, "our host has arrived."

Lord Stranham looked from his mother to Robert. Both were seated on the emerald brocade camel-backed sofa sipping tea from delicate porcelain cups.

"How long have you been here?" he asked as he strode across the room to the liquor cabinet. He unstoppered a decanter of claret, poured a drink into a crystal goblet, and swallowed it in one gulp.

Her grace turned to Robert. "Does he not have the enviable manner of a very gracious host?" she asked. "A host who must, I am persuaded, be the delight of his friends and a source of high praise in polite society?"

"Would either of you care for a drink?" Lord Stranham asked, holding the decanter up for inspection before pouring himself another drink, which rapidly followed the first one down his throat.

"Before you drink yourself insensible, Mark, why don't you sit down and at least make the customary attempt at polite conversation concerning the deplorable state of politics and the wonderful weather," his mother suggested dryly.

He obliged her by walking over to an Irish Chippendale armchair covered in ivory linen. He leaned on the back of it as he addressed himself to his guests: "Lovely weather, is it not?" he asked perfunctorily.

"It is," Robert agreed uncertainly.

"I regret that I was not here to greet you. My lamenta-

203

ble memory, you know. But I did not recollect that either of you were engaged to call."

"We were not," his mother replied casually, arranging the iris-blue folds of her silk gown.

Robert was not quite so unperturbed as he watched his friend in fascination before blurting out tactlessly, "I say, Mark, I ain't never seen you look so put about. Why, you look as if you've scratched your new curricle or had to have one of your chestnuts shot."

"Nothing of the sort," his mother protested with a wise, assessing look at her offspring. "What he resembles more than anything is a man top over tail in love and making precious little progress in his suit."

The marquis gazed levelly at his mother before rising straight from the chair and stalking back to the liquor cabinet. Uncapping the decanter, he said, "Let me drink to your insight, Mother. It has never been better."

"I thank you for the toast," she responded tartly, "but if you were to contrive to put that bottle down, I believe we could make further progress in this discussion."

Robert watched the exchange between Lord Stranham and his mother with an open mouth. "Do you mean," he demanded, "that *you* have formed an attachment?"

"Yes," Lord Stranham's mother replied for him.

"By all that's wonderful," Robert exclaimed happily, jumping up and going across to pump the marquis's arm. "That's the very thing I'm here to talk to you about. I'm on the point of offering for Miss Joanna, and if you were to offer for Lady Diedre, we could have a large double wedding. What say you?"

"He says," the duchess interjected knowingly, "that if he is forced to have the shrewish Lady Diedre, he shall drink himself speechless and remain that way until such time as he finds himself either a grieving widower or the grieved deceased. Do sit down, Robert, and stop talking fustian. My son is not going to offer for Lady Diedre."

Robert looked suitably abashed at this piece of plain speaking, although he still ventured a question to Lord Stranham. "You ain't going to leg-shackle yourself to her?"

"No," the marquis assured him, realizing that fact for the first time as he said the word.

"Then who are you offering for?" Robert persisted.

"I am not offering for anyone," Lord Stranham responded moodily. "As I recall, I was on my way into the room to regale myself with a leisurely drink when the pair of you hatched this dull-witted idea that I was to wed."

Her grace deemed it necessary to explain to a puzzled-looking Robert: "He was on his way into the room to drink himself into an absolute stupor because all is not well with the woman of his choice. Am I correct, Mark?" she asked with a challenging look at the marquis.

He gave a mirthless laugh and walked over to stand in front of the sofa. Taking one of her small beringed hands in his own large palm, he bowed over it. "You, my lovely Mama, are as astute as ever."

"Quite so," she agreed with no pretense at modesty. "But let us not talk about my merits at this moment. What needs to be discussed is your lack of sense in the art of courting. Has the girl rejected you?"

Robert sat bolt upright and gave an astounded look to the small woman beside him. "Of course she ain't," he declared firmly. "There's not a chit in polite society who hasn't thrown her cap at Mark." Suddenly recalling to whom he was speaking, Robert paled slightly and added hastily, "I beg your pardon, your grace. I meant no offense."

Her grace, however, was undisposed to take offense at that moment, for she continued amiably. "A very good observation, Robert—any chit in polite society would have him. Which leads us to our next question. Is the beloved not a member of the *ton?*"

"My dear lady mother," Lord Stranham interrupted, dropping into a chair with carved cabrioles and crossing his legs carelessly, "you will forgive me if I do not care to discuss my personal affairs. Let us hear the good news that Sir Robert brings, as I am sure I am in need of some good news."

"Well," Robert began, "I haven't asked Miss Joanna yet, but I don't doubt that she will have me. Her eighteenth birthday is coming up shortly, and I thought to ask her then. Come to think on it, perhaps she and I could have a double wedding with Miss Daphne and Peter Morne. I called at their house only yesterday, and he was there again. He was paying marked attention to her."

Lord Stranham sprang from the chair and paced to the fireplace, where he kicked at the embers with the tip of a glossy boot. "You are intolerably anxious to be married along with someone else," he observed harshly.

"Is that not proper?" Robert asked uncertainly. "I only thought that since both girls would be married, we might as well have the ceremonies at the same time. That'll save me from being so conspicuous at the reception. Although," he said with a fresh burst of imagination, "if you give both girls away, that would save me from being the center of attention, as you're always the one noticed by the ladies wherever you go."

At the suggestion that he present Daphne in marriage, Lord Stranham muttered a low oath into the fireplace and kicked so viciously at the embers that he completely smothered the small fire.

"I do not think my son cares to give the brides away," the duchess noted mildly.

"No?" Robert asked hesitantly. "It was just a thought. I had best take my leave," he announced cheerily as he stood and bowed to the duchess before strolling from the room.

* * *

The lady under discussion was at that moment sitting in her front parlor sipping tea and noting ruefully that there was a tiny chip in her cup. Joanna sat beside her on the settee listening dutifully to Mrs. Winter wax eloquent about her upcoming rout.

"It will be the social event of the season. Mrs. Burns shall simply expire from envy." Mrs. Winter uttered her prediction cheerfully. "I trust you have ordered your gowns?"

"Yes," Joanna replied readily.

"Excellent. Everyone knows you are coming, and they can hardly contain themselves to meet such girls as you. I have, of course, told them you move in the highest circles. I have also noted on my invitations to the duchess of Cochmeer and the marquis of Stranham that you shall be present. They might not remember me, but of a certainty they will know you two," she said merrily.

"Yes," Daphne agreed with a sinking feeling as she shifted on the worn velvet settee. Upon receiving a card from such an obvious social climber as Mrs. Winter, the duchess would doubtless make short work of burning it. She must receive dozens of such invitations daily, Daphne thought with a mixture of humiliation and resignation. And Lord Stranham would not come either.

"Is Sir Robert invited also?" Joanna asked hopefully.

"Oh, indeed he is," Mrs. Winter acknowledged with a fond look at the younger girl. "Could you have thought otherwise?" She transferred a conspiratorial look to Daphne. "Mr. Morne shall be there also. I do not doubt that both of you girls shall leave my rout engaged."

Joanna smiled her excitement, and Daphne murmured a faint "Indeed."

"Yes, I do," Mrs. Winter reaffirmed staunchly. "Has not Peter been paying you marked attention? He wants only a suitable setting in which to make his declaration. And you cannot conceive how romantic my rout will be.

It's to be a surprise, but I will tell you that the decorations will surpass anything you have ever seen. They're in the oriental motif," she confided, "and most extravagantly done."

Daphne could well imagine the extravagance, not to say gaudiness, that Mrs. Winter would create as a setting for her rout. The prince regent had made bad taste and over-decoration the rage, and Daphne did not doubt that Mrs. Winter would carry it to a new high—or low—at her party.

"Now," their guest declared as she set down her cup and patted her coal-black hair, "I must be going." She bustled over to give each girl a light peck on the cheek; then, smiling gleefully to herself, she left.

Joanna turned to Daphne. "Won't it be fun?" she asked in happy anticipation.

"No," Daphne replied dampingly.

"Oh," Joanna said in confusion. "But Peter will be there, and if he proposes to you, that will make it an evening to stand out above all others."

"I do not doubt it will be a night to be long remembered," Daphne remarked dryly. "I suspect when I am one and eighty I shall see quite vividly the brightly colored dragons that will adorn every wall in the house."

Intent on bolstering Daphne's spirits, Joanna added further words of encouragement. "It will be nearly as exciting as Lady Drayton's ball, since the duchess will be there as well as Lord Stranham."

"Joanna," Daphne replied impatiently, "there is absolutely no reason why they should come to such an event. The duchess and her son move in the highest circles of the *ton*. I can think of no reason why they should demean themselves by appearing at such an insignificant social function as this."

CHAPTER 23

"You are not ready," the duchess accused as she stepped into the ornate red dining room and looked down the long formal table, past the silver epergne and fifteen vacant chairs, to where the marquis sat eating a solitary meal.

He looked up in surprise. "Oh, but I am quite ready. In fact, I was very nearly famished by the time the food was served."

"Your disposition seems much improved," her grace noted as she walked the length of the damask-covered table to stand before him. "But you have not addressed yourself to my question. Why are you not dressed for Mrs. Winter's rout?"

Her son looked up in genuine astonishment. "You are seriously considering going to that woman's party? You intend to bask in her crocodile smiles for the whole of the evening and listen to her bore her fellow peasants with details of her wonderful success at Lady Drayton's ball?"

"Yes," she answered calmly, transferring her mink-lined wheat-gold pelisse from her arm to the back of a Queen Anne walnut chair before seating herself beside him.

"Why?" he demanded.

"Because a certain lady of interest to you will be there. I should have thought it would have been noted on your invitation as it was on mine."

With a sudden and perceptible waning of his appetite, Lord Stranham laid down his fork. "So, my dear mother, will the inestimable Peter Morne."

"That is all the more reason why you should go," she declared quietly.

"You are fair and far out, dear mother. That is the very reason why I am not going to go. Miss Brown has no interest in me and I do not care to compete with some bloodletter for her attentions."

"He is a doctor?" Lady Cochmeer asked.

"Chemist," he replied shortly.

"If you are persuaded that he is the more attractive man," his mother said as she rose and picked up her pelisse, "then I consider it very handsome of you to admit defeat. It is important to know when one has met his match, I think," she said. "Enjoy your meal, my son," she adjured him, and swept from the room.

It was a request with which he could not comply. What had only moments before tasted like pheasant done to perfection in a rare wine sauce and garnished liberally with watercress now had the unpleasant, tasteless feel of mush slushing about in his mouth.

What fustian for his mother to tell him it was well to know when he had been bested. He could have any chit in London by crooking his little finger. Pushing back his chair, he paced from the room and up the curving staircase to his bedroom. Bested indeed.

"Charles!" His valet appeared and was given curt directions to prepare the marquis's evening clothes.

An hour later Lord Stranham looked suitably bored but exceedingly well turned out in a square cutaway claret-red coat with double-breasted front and long lapels and a pearl-gray underwaistcoat. His velvety-looking white moleskin unmentionables were molded to his leg with no crease in sight, and his shirt points were high starched wonders. Cane and hat in hand, he was shown into the Winters' house by an obviously awed servant.

Conversation died in the long narrow room as all eyes turned to him. Mrs. Winter bustled forward with an incredulous smile of welcome on her face while the marquis's mother gave him a veiled smirk from the depths of a huge armchair where she was holding court with a dozen fascinated women.

The room, he noted with distaste, was adorned in a cheap fashion that was obviously meant to imitate the opulent, full-blown garishness of Brighton Pavilion. Firebreathing animals made of paper lined the walls of the room, and little square paper lanterns hung from the ceiling.

He looked past the decorations to the people present—tradesmen and shopkeepers. He smiled faintly at them as Mrs. Winter drew him through the room. The wonder-struck stares of those present told him they would bore their friends past all bearing by recounting again and again his words and actions this night.

But he was there and, he noted with a pleased look about the room, Miss Daphne Brown was also there. Peter Morne was not.

After a few minutes' discourse with a fat man who believed the marquis should immediately exercise his influence in the House of Lords to have the man's taxes lowered, Lord Stranham worked his way around to where Daphne was sitting alone. Robert, he noted, was ensconced in a corner with Joanna, and both seemed oblivious of the fact that Daphne was seated by herself and looking more than a little forlorn.

"You have been forsaken," the marquis remarked as he sat down beside her.

She answered with a wan smile, "I have indeed, my lord. My sister and Sir Robert have forgotten there is anyone else in the world, let alone in this room, and I very much feared I should sit here by myself for the whole of the evening."

Although she felt uncomfortable in Lord Stranham's company, she was nevertheless glad to talk with him. She had behaved rudely when he had come to the house two weeks ago; he had obviously meant to apologize for his actions in the carriage, and she was inclined to forgive him. She had not thought he would come tonight, but since he had, she was glad she was dressed in her finest clothes, much nicer than the ones he had seen her wearing thus far. Her underdress was of sky-blue satin edged with fringes of gold thread, and over it was a delicate gauze overdress of winter white with a high waist and décolletage. Small blue feathers, which matched her little feather fan, clustered in the blond curls atop her head. She noted his look of approval before demurely dropping her eyes.

"Where is Peter Morne?" the marquis asked.

Daphne carefully opened her fan and waved it idly in front of her face before replying: "He was called to attend a sick person. I doubt he will return."

"I see," he said shortly. "I cannot stay above a minute or so more myself. I have a pressing engagement that I don't wish to miss."

"You cannot leave so quickly," Daphne said hastily.

"Why is that?" he asked with a casual glance at her earnest face.

"Because Mrs. Winter is inordinately glad that you have come, and if you take your leave immediately, she will think I have said something which caused you to depart."

"I little care what Mrs. Winter thinks," he said gruffly, a contempt for Mrs. Winter, her party, and her guests reflected in his tone.

Daphne bristled at his arrogance. "I do not doubt it," she flashed, then stopped in horror. Her words had been spoken loudly enough to draw the attention of several people seated near them. She nervously brushed a stray ringlet back from her face as she attempted to compose herself.

The marquis also noted the looks from those about

them. He stood abruptly and stretched his hand out to her. "Come, Miss Brown. We must take a turn about the garden," he said.

His pleasant tone, Daphne realized, as she stood and linked her arm in the marquis's, was belied by the steel in his gray eyes. Together they walked wordlessly out into the hall and started down the narrow hallway toward the back of the house.

"I doubt," she said frostily, "that they even have a garden."

"It doesn't matter whether they do or not," he rasped. "I wish to speak with you, and I could scarcely do so with those people watching us."

She removed her arm from his as he held the back door open for her. They stepped out into a tiny yard surrounded with high hedges. " 'Those people' you speak of with such condescension are very agreeable men and women," Daphne snapped. More so than he, she fumed, as she walked toward a bench in the corner without a backward glance at her companion.

"There's no need to fly up into the boughs, Miss Brown."

"I have not," she retorted. Goaded by his manner, she pursued, "I am surprised you came to a gathering such as this. I did not think mingling with commoners was your usual style."

"It is not," he replied evenly.

She stiffened as she seated herself on the cold stone bench and he sat down beside her. "You do us a great honor," she said caustically.

"Thank you," he responded with equal sarcasm. He recovered himself with a start. What was he doing sitting here bandying words with her? he asked himself. He should be asking her forgiveness for acting a coxcomb when he escorted her home from Bow Street.

"Miss Brown, I am deeply sensible of the pain I inflicted

by forcing my unwanted attentions on you. I can offer no excuse for my actions; I know they were reprehensible, and I can only beg you will forgive me for them."

Daphne studied her hands in the dim light from the moon before murmuring softly, "It was not so much your actions, my lord, as the regard in which you held me, which I objected to."

"Miss Brown—Daphne, look at me." With a gentle hand he lifted her face to his. "I am excessively glad to hear it was not my kiss which you found so offensive. I am sorry if my conduct that night was intolerable; I have since learned much that has changed my attitude greatly."

Looking down at her and seeing her eyes shining in the pale light, Lord Stranham was sorely tempted to repeat the offense for which he now begged her pardon. But that would not do at all. He looked away sharply.

"Have I said something wrong?" she asked quickly. "You have only to tell me if there is something in my manner which oversets you."

He looked slowly back at her. "There is nothing in you that I find unpleasant except that I wish to kiss you and dare not."

"Oh," she said faintly.

Daphne remained motionless beside him, still gazing up into his face. With one arm he drew her closer to him, carefully lowering his face to hers, allowing her time to protest should she wish to. Daphne did not object. Indeed, her long lashes fluttered closed and her lips parted expectantly. He kissed her carefully, as if she were fine porcelain and he didn't wish to crush her; but he kissed her thoroughly, and she emerged from his embrace with her eyes aglow as she looked breathlessly up at him.

Gratified by her response, he pulled her back into his arms and brought his lips down on hers forcefully. His mouth burned hers with a branding kiss, and his hands moved seductively up her back.

She wrenched herself free and jumped up. "How dare you!"

"Don't be coy, Daphne," he said brusquely, and moved toward her again.

Outraged by his words, she said, "You dragged me to this forsaken garden and forced me to submit to your embraces! I shall scream the house down if you touch me again. What do you think of that?" she challenged, her small hands curling into fists as she shouted wrathfully into his calm face.

"I think you have a fine disregard for the truth, Miss Brown," he said in tones that brooked no quarrel. "You enjoyed my kisses every bit as much as I did."

"I did not!" she denied vehemently.

"Daphne," he said with unloverlike brusqueness as he attempted to grasp her hand, "I—"

"Don't touch me! I am betrothed to Peter and I would not have you were you to beg me." The words were not true, but she didn't care; she was lashing out at him with every weapon she could find. Employing his vast libertine experience, he had put some sort of spell on her to make her respond to his advances. She flushed hotly as she recalled her humiliating response to him.

"Are you engaged to Peter?" he asked with a dangerous quietness. "My congratulations. Before tomorrow is half over, I shall be betrothed to Lady Diedre, so it appears we are to wish each other happiness, does it not, Miss Brown?" Without waiting for her reply, he took her arm, drew her from the bench, and led her wordlessly back into the house. There he thanked his hostess graciously and took his leave. With a sinking heart, Daphne watched him go.

CHAPTER 24

"Where have you been all night?" Robert asked curiously as he roused himself from the comfortable chaise in Lord Stranham's library and looked at the marquis.

The marquis, entering the room wearing the same clothes he had worn to Mrs. Winter's party the previous evening, looked as if it had not been a peaceful night. His handsome face showed lines of wear, and he stalked into the room like a prowling lion.

But Robert noticed nothing of his friend's manner as he stretched languidly and sat up on the chaise. "I came here last night after the rout to tell you about my betrothal, and when you weren't here, I thought I'd wait for you. What time is it?"

"Six in the morning," his host snapped rudely.

"Did your doxy throw you out this early in the morning?" Robert asked innocently.

Lord Stranham fixed his guest with an unwelcoming glare, his lips tightly compressed.

Sensing that the marquis was not in a mood to jest or exchange light banter, Robert returned the conversation to his original news. "I have asked Joanna to marry me and she has agreed," he stated.

The marquis pulled a chair to the unlit fireplace and gazed into it unseeingly.

"I think it is customary to offer your congratulations," Robert prompted helpfully.

"And her sister?" Lord Stranham asked tonelessly.

"Yes, she offered her congratulations," Robert affirmed.

"Have your wits gone begging, Robert?" the marquis demanded irritably, his first show of spirit since entering the room. "I don't give a damn if she felicitated you or not. I want to know if she's engaged."

"Oh, yes, she is," Robert said hastily, baffled by the marquis's black humor.

His lordship uttered a succinct oath into the fireplace before turning back to Robert. "When is she to be married?"

"I don't know, but she was so awfully glad to get engaged—you know she's almost one and twenty, so she's a bit on the shelf, anyway. As I was saying, she was so happy to become betrothed that she just kept crying into poor Peter's coat, and he never could get her to set a date. I collect he's going to call round at her house today to do so."

Lord Stranham made no response.

"She said you told her you are to marry too," Robert ventured. The marquis seemed terribly uncommunicative this morning. Obviously, if he was back at his house at this hour, all had not gone well with his light-skirt, and Robert knew from experience that that didn't tend to improve one's spirits.

"I am engaged," Lord Stranham said with unnecessary volume as he rose from his chair. "I am engaged in playing the part of the greatest fool in London. Did you know that, Robert? I am the dullest-witted man alive in all of England. What say you to that?" He directed a challenging look at the baronet. He had spent the whole night walking the streets contemplating last night's scene without coming to a clear resolution of his emotions. He knew only that he was miserable.

"The doxy must have led you a merry chase last night," Robert pronounced.

"Doxy! Ah, now there's a thought. I should have set the

218

chit up in keeping the moment I spied her. That, Robert, is how women need to be treated."

"Light o'loves, perhaps—although those days are behind me," Robert informed him virtuously. "But ladies, of course, are an altogether different matter."

"Ladies should be hidden away in some rural retreat where they can delight their lord with their feminine charms and then be bundled off to a remote sitting room to churn out samplers. A man must be brutal with a woman," he finished savagely.

"Well," Robert objected meekly, "I rather think women prefer men who are strong but have a touch of gentleness in them and a bit of romance."

The marquis whirled from his pacing. "Get out of here, Robert," he directed uncivilly.

The younger man wisely retreated. "I shall come later to give you more details about both weddings," he volunteered before the marquis slammed the front door shut in his face.

Tempers were more equable in Upper Wimpole Street at that moment, although it, too, was filled with unwelcome talk of marriage. Daphne, listening for the fourth time to Joanna's description of how Sir Robert had proposed to her, thought she would scream from vexation.

"He was so poetic," Joanna murmured dreamily, leaning back on her sister's bed and looking at the canopy.

"Humph."

"Aren't you interested?" Joanna asked, lifting herself on her elbow to look at her sister.

"I have heard the story before, and I know the ending," Daphne said shortly.

"Oh, then perhaps you would like to tell about Peter's proposal," Joanna suggested pleasantly.

"No!"

Joanna rose from the bed and walked to the door. "Why

219

don't you just go back to sleep for a time?" she suggested. "I didn't mean to wake you, but I thought since it was seven in the morning, you would be awake anyway, planning the details of your own wedding." Joanna closed the door and left Daphne staring after her.

Her own wedding! What had she meant by telling Peter she would marry him? She had done so only because she was angry with Lord Stranham. She didn't even love Peter. In that joyful frame of mind the newly affianced mistress of the house pulled herself from her chair. Wrapping her faded peignoir more tightly about her, she went through the house looking for Cedric.

He appeared in the hall, still in his long nightshirt and striped cap, rubbing the sleep from his eyes.

"You had better go out and win a deal of money," she told him crisply, "since we are to be paying for two weddings."

Cedric looked considerably startled, all traces of sleep instantly banished from his face. "Married?" he asked vaguely, looking closely at her through squinted eyes.

"Yes," she replied in tones of resignation that one might use to announce they were about to be sent to Newgate prison.

"To who?" he demanded.

"Joanna is marrying Sir Robert, and I am marrying Mr. Morne."

"Ye'd best apply to the gentlemen to pay the cost," he suggested, and turned to leave.

"Cedric," she snapped, continuing irritably as he turned back to her in surprise, "gentlemen do not pay the cost of weddings. I might also add that if it is possible to win some dowries, that would be very helpful, and save us some embarrassment as well."

Cedric looked discomfited. Lord Stranham, he reasoned, had laid out the blunt for the girls when they were penniless and unprotected. But Cedric had a strong suspicion that his lordship would not wish to set them up in style as brides for other men. It had, in fact, more than once entered his mind that the marquis might be partial to Daphne. Nothing serious, of course, but partial enough so that he wouldn't relish the thought of paying for her to marry someone else.

"Well," Daphne demanded imperiously, "how much do you think you can win?"

"The cocks ain't been very good lately. They ain't predictable, you know what I mean. I don't think this is a good time to be betting on them."

"You're wrong, Cedric," she contradicted. "There has never been a better time to bet on them. Now we need the money more than ever to put on a grand wedding in a style that will make Lord Stranham sit up and take note of us."

Cedric choked on the words he had been about to speak. Had it not been so preposterous, he might have seen humor in the fact that Miss Daphne was asking him to get money from Lord Stranham so that she could put on a wedding to impress that same man. However, just now his thoughts were not running along the lines of humor.

"I shall give you half of our money, and don't come home until you have made six times that amount," she ordered. She stalked off and returned to press a fistful of coins into his reluctant hand. Cedric stared down at the money as Daphne turned to walk away.

Cedric called after her, recalling his manners, "My congratulations on your betrothal."

Daphne whirled and gave him a withering look, then turned to stomp up the steps.

"She's a bit churlish this mor'ing," he observed to himself as he returned to his room to dress.

An hour later Cedric was in the book-lined study at Lord Stranham's house, standing before a huge cherry desk regarding the marquis. The old man shifted uncomfortably as he tightened his grasp on the hat he clasped before him. The reception he was receiving from the marquis was a dauntingly chilly one. Added to that, his request for ten thousand pounds did not seem to be meeting at all with Lord Stranham's approval.

"What for?" his lordship demanded harshly. "The chits can't eat that much, and at this point I am only concerned with their basic needs."

Cedric turned to leave in defeat. He did not think his lordship was doltish enough to contribute to another man's wedding. The firm line of the marquis's mouth did not encourage him to confide about the grand wedding Daphne envisioned.

"What do they want the money for?" Lord Stranham asked again, iron in his voice.

"Wed'ings," Cedric mumbled, folding his hat nervously and fixing the oriental carpet with a steady stare.

"What?" Lord Stranham demanded incredulously.

"Yes. Miss Daphne 'ad a notion for a nice wedding and mebbe a dowry."

"Had she a notion for such a wedding?" the marquis asked caustically. "Then perhaps she should marry someone who can afford her tastes."

"I'm sure I wasn't consulted on that," Cedric returned with dignity.

"Why is she marrying him?" Lord Stranham barked.

"I don't know." Cedric shrugged. "You never know about women. One minute you think you've got them figured out and the next you know you ain't."

"Yes," Lord Stranham agreed, sighing as he leaned back in his leather chair.

"Like one morning last week Miss Daphne was asking me all sorts of questions about you and this morning she's wanting to throw a wedding that will make you sit up and take notice. It's like she don't like you and wants to show you something."

"She what?" The marquis's words carried through the air like the crack of a whip.

"I said she wants a nice wedding."

But Lord Stranham was no longer listening. Instead he had thrown his head back and was laughing heartily. "The little firebrand. Wants to make me jealous, does she?" he asked, now chuckling as he spoke.

"Begging your pardon," Cedric interjected hopefully, "does that mean you will give the money?"

"Decidedly not," Lord Stranham returned firmly, but his face was still relaxed in a smile, his fine gray eyes radiating inner amusement.

"I thought since you 'ave so much money and you seemed to be in a tolerably better mood, you might have changed your mind. I 'ate to go 'ome without the blunt. Miss Daphne was in such a terrible bad temper when she sent me out to win it."

"Was she? A strange mood for a newly betrothed young lady," the marquis commented mildly. "No, I have not changed my mind. I may be in a more amiable mood, but I am not a candidate for Bedlam. I am keeping my money for the future Lady Stranham, and so you may tell her."

"I don't know how I'll explain it to 'er." A worried Cedric twisted his hat mercilessly in his bony hands.

"Let her sulk," the marquis advised cheerfully. "I think she will shortly determine for herself that no marriage at all is preferable to one with someone she does not love. I believe I can safely predict she will be courted by another eligible man when that event occurs."

"You think she will become betrothed to someone else?" Cedric asked, puzzled.

"I do," he responded. "I do," he repeated with a chuckle. "Aren't those the words from some sort of ceremony?"

CHAPTER 25

The marquis's good humor was not shared by everyone in London that day. In fact, Daphne was in a mood that Joanna described as unfriendly and Rose called downright surly. As Daphne waited for Cedric to return from his trip to the cockfights, her temper was not improving.

It was past eleven o'clock at night, and Cedric had been gone all day. The cockfights, she was certain, were not what was now detaining him. He had undoubtably been at some low gin shop for most of the day, and she little doubted his arrival would be unsober and unsteady.

She was proven right when Cedric weaved in the back door a few minutes later. He was holding a bottle to his heart affectionately and repeating disjointed snatches of a nursery rhyme: "Oranges and lemons,/Say the bells of St. Clement's . . ."

"It is appropriate you should speak of churches," she commented acidly from the darkened end of the hall outside the front parlor as he stumbled into the hall.

After his first startled look at her he relaxed and leaned against the wall, putting a grimy hand to his spinning head.

"Did you get the money?" Daphne demanded crossly.

"Money?" he repeated, and then set the word to a little homemade melody: *"Mon-ney, mon-ney, brings us hon-ney."* He smiled at the rhyme. "I made that up," he informed her with a childlike pride.

"The money, Cedric," she repeated coldly, her hand outstretched imperiously.

"What money? I don't think we 'ave much." He tilted

225

his head in silent thought. "No, we don't," he decided, and smiled at her crookedly.

"That is correct. But you were to go to the cockfights to win some," she explained with strained patience. "Did you do so, or have you spent the afternoon sprawled out in a disgraceful heap in some alehouse?"

"I went to the cockfights," he informed her, his pride wounded.

"Did you win?"

He scratched his head in thought. "I remember talking to Sammy and Lardy."

"Cedric, I am not interested in your reminiscences. Did you get the money?"

"Let's see. Before that I talked with the markey and I don't recollect everyone after that. But 'e wouldn't give me no money, the markey wouldn't."

"Markey?" she repeated in confusion.

"Lerd Strangleham."

Daphne drew herself up proudly. "I should not expect him to give me money," she said severely. "I would never accept such a thing from him."

"Just as well," Cedric observed affably, " 'cause 'e said 'e weren't paying for another man's wedding. I didn't think 'e would—man can't be 'pected to provide for you now. Your 'usband will 'af to now," he slurred.

Through the incoherent and broken words Daphne had the uncomfortable feeling there was a message she had not quite grasped. Although her present mood was not conducive to engaging Cedric in a lengthy chat, she stopped him as he began to slide down the hall toward his room.

"Cedric, forgive me, but I wasn't attending you very carefully. What did you say about the marquis giving us money?"

"He won't," Cedric informed her with finality.

"Yes, I realize you said he won't, but what did you say

about his paying for another man's wedding and providing money before?"

"You really ought to invite 'im to the wed'ng because I think 'e likes you," Cedric suggested with a coy lopsided grin.

"I shall invite him," she said wearily. There seemed little point in talking with a man too drunk to comprehend her words. She turned and mounted the steps to her bedroom.

Half an hour later she was still lying wide-eyed in her bed. Cedric's words were tumbling about in her head. What had he meant about money? She flung the covers back and padded down the steps in her bare feet. Her white muslin chemise billowed as she marched into Cedric's room and shook him awake.

He opened his eyes and blinked as she lit a candle. "Let me hear this one more time—with clarity—Cedric. Then I shall go away and leave you alone."

"What?" he asked dazedly.

"Did Lord Stranham ever give you money for us?"

Cedric, who had a drunkenly hazy notion he was not supposed to be telling that, was equally vague on what he *was* supposed to divulge. He tried to sort out his thoughts aloud. "I think I won the money at the fights, isn't that what the markey said to tell you? Yes, it were. 'E gave me the blunt and tole me not to tell where it came from."

"Lord Stranham has been providing us with money all along?" Daphne asked in horror.

"I can't tell," Cedric told her conscientiously. " 'E tole me not to."

"For how long?"

"I don't think 'e ever means for me to tell you 'e's been giving you the blunt." Cedric decided after a moment's reflection.

"For how long has he been giving us the money?" she repeated. "Did you win *any* at the cockfights?"

"No," Cedric admitted dejectedly, remembering something about a black rooster with a perky little comb that had not been the winner Cedric had at first thought him to be. "The black one weren't the fighter I thought 'e would be," he apologized.

Daphne nodded dumbly as Cedric continued in his explanation of the undependability of the cocks, but her mind was elsewhere.

Lord Stranham had been providing money for the household, the food, even her clothes for the past month! No wonder he thought he could take liberties with her! He considered that he owned her!

Daphne rose and, as if in a trance, walked out into the darkened hall and down to the front parlor, dropping into the wing chair and staring unseeingly out into the moonlit night. Her hands were shaking as the cool night air stirred her thin gown, but it was not the cold that made her tremble.

What sort of web had Lord Stranham woven about her? It was obvious that he had expected some sort of repayment all along. He had given money, planning to collect on his investment someday. His actions in the carriage and in the Winters' garden had undoubtedly been prompted by his impatience to obtain his payment as swiftly as possible.

As those thoughts raced through her mind her anger rose slowly and steadily, replacing the numbed feeling she had experienced upon hearing Cedric's words. Yes, she owed Lord Stranham a debt and she intended to pay! She would go to his house in the morning and tell him what she knew. It would be up to him to name the price he wanted.

Tomorrow morning seemed a lifetime away. In the meantime all she could do was worry. And for what? The marquis intended to demand *her* in payment. Hadn't his actions implied as much already?

He had ruined them. Once Lord Stranham learned of

Sir Robert's engagement to Joanna, he would tell the whole story to the baronet, and the marriage plans would be at an end. Her sister's happiness would mean nothing to the marquis. He didn't care how many people he harmed as long as he obtained what he wanted in the end. Her mind completed the dismal circle back to the starting point—he wanted her.

There was little way she and Joanna could ever repay the money they owed, especially now. Mr. Morne would surely cry off when he learned she was deeply in debt. In fact, it would be her duty to terminate her betrothal to him. Sir Robert could hardly be expected to wed a girl whose sister Lord Stranham wished to make his fancy piece. A furious blush rose to Daphne's cheeks at the thought. But she might as well call a spade a spade. That was quite obviously what he had wanted.

In the back of her mind an idea was slowly forming. There was little to be salvaged from this affair for her, but perhaps something could be saved for Joanna. After all, Daphne considered, Lord Stranham might be willing to make some concessions if she went to him freely and offered herself. She might be able to pay the debt to his satisfaction and persuade him to say nothing to Sir Robert. At the unbearable thought of how Joanna's heart would be broken if her engagement were ended, Daphne made her resolution. She would go to the marquis; it was the only way she could hope to ensure Joanna's happiness.

She pushed herself out of the chair and rushed back to Cedric's room. Her decision was made in haste, and she wished to carry it through as quickly as possible before her fears dissuaded her.

"Cedric." She shook the snoring man. "Get up!"

"What?" he mumbled.

"Get up. You must take me to Lord Stranham's!"

"Later." He waved her aside impatiently and closed his eyes.

"Now," she returned loudly, accompanying her request with a sharp jolt of the mattress.

Cedric sat up in bed and looked at her unkindly. "What do you want?" he asked sourly.

"Put the horses to immediately. I want you to take me to the marquis's house."

"Ain't it late to be calling?" he asked uncertainly.

"It is the perfect time for what he has in mind," she replied grimly.

Still clad in his rumpled clothes, Cedric put one foot over the bed, stood up in resignation, and stumbled toward the back door. Daphne grabbed her dark cloak and followed a moment later, holding the bemused horses while Cedric hitched them to the landaulet.

As they drove toward St. James's Square Cedric said doubtfully, "I don't think you should be calling on a gentleman at this hour of the night. It is night, ain't it? It's still dark, leastways."

"It's night," she agreed tersely, wrapping her cloak closer around her and feeling the clammy cold of her own skin as one of her hands brushed against her arm.

"I don't much like getting out at this hour," Cedric complained.

"I shall take a hackney cab the next time I decide to go sight-seeing at such an hour," she said with spirit.

Cedric lapsed back into silence and did not speak again until they pulled up below the hazy glow of a gaslight in front of the marquis's house.

"There is no need to wait," she said firmly as she slipped down to the cobblestone street. On an impulse she turned back to Cedric. "Do you have a flask of something with you?"

"Yes," he admitted reluctantly, "but it's my last and—"

"Give it to me," she ordered.

The authority of her tone brought a sigh of exasperation

from Cedric, but he handed her the flask, which held his last few precious drops of gin.

"You can go now," she directed.

As Cedric drove off into the blackness, Daphne brought the flask to her lips and drank some of the fiery liquid. She didn't mind the choking it occasioned. That, she reasoned, was a small price to pay for some of Cedric's enviable dullness rather than her own alert wariness. She took another drink and then mounted the steps to the darkened house.

CHAPTER 26

Daphne reached the top step and wavered for several minutes. The thoughts that ran through her mind alarmed her considerably, and more than once she determined to leave. But she didn't. She would not go craven now.

She banged the knocker before her shaky resolve collapsed. It was some moments before the door opened. Bosley looked at her with butlerlike propriety, although he was wearing a brightly colored robe and his hair was disheveled. "I have come to see Lord Stranham," she announced in a quavering voice.

"He is not at home," Bosley answered promptly.

"Nonsense," she said with more spirit than she felt. "He's expecting me."

Bosley looked momentarily stunned by her lie. He had never seen this woman before, but she didn't look like the type of woman his master would have come to the house at this hour—or any hour. In point of fact, the master took his pleasures out and had never before had a lady come to his home. Still, he thought hesitantly, if she had indeed been invited, he would look excessively foolish shutting her out.

While he vacillated she stepped inside the door. "Where is the marquis?" she demanded, looking around the huge entry foyer lit only by the butler's wavering candle.

"Begging your pardon, ma'am, but he has retired for the evening. If you leave your name, I'll tell him in the morning that you called," he said helpfully.

"I shall see him now," she insisted. "Where is his room?"

233

Bosley looked indecisive. He thought he had caught the whiff of gin on her breath, and he was rapidly reaching the conclusion that he had erred in admitting her.

"Lord Stranham is expecting me," Daphne repeated resolutely. "I will show myself up to his room. Which one is it?"

The stern delivery of this question, as well as the level gaze the young lady turned on him, gave him pause. She was a pretty piece with those sparkling violet eyes and dainty features, and it would be easy to see how the master could be taken with her. Although it was highly irregular to direct a young lady to the marquis's bedroom, his lordship was the best judge of whom he wanted in his bed and whom he did not. Bosley, for one, wouldn't have objected in the slightest to finding such a chit as this in his bed.

"Where is it?" she asked testily.

"First one on the right at the top of the stairs."

"Thank you." She started toward the massive oak staircase and stopped. "You may retire now," she directed in a low voice, not turning to look at the butler.

"Yes, ma'am," he replied before hastening back to his bedroom to regale his wife with the story of the scandalous events taking place, or about to take place, abovestairs.

Daphne was unaware of the belowstairs chatter as she forced one foot in front of the other on the long, long flight up to the second floor. She reached the landing and paused to gather her courage, fighting back the desire to rush back to her house on Upper Wimpole Street, dive into the bed beneath the covers, and forget all of the night's events. That thought was exerting such a peculiarly attractive appeal that she was forced to tell herself sternly that nothing would be served by such flight.

She walked to the first door and pushed it open. The room was dark, the drapes preventing even a shaft of moonlight from penetrating the inky blackness. It was some seconds before her eyes adjusted themselves enough to discern the darker shape of a large canopied bed. She edged toward it. As she reached the bed she saw that the curtains had been left open, and she could hear the steady breathing of the marquis as he slept peacefully.

"Your lordship," she whispered, bending toward him.

No answer.

"Lord Stranham," she said in a louder voice.

Still no answer.

She reached out to shake the still form but drew her hand back as if she had touched a live coal, as she realized she had touched his bare skin. What if he wasn't wearing any clothes at all?

Still he slept.

"Lord Stranham," she said desperately, "please wake up."

"Why?" an amused voice asked. It was not the voice of a man who had recently awakened.

"You weren't asleep," she accused.

"I confess I was not. However, I think before we thoroughly investigate the depravity of my pretensions, we might explore what *you* are doing here. I am not ordinarily a stickler for details, but I do not recall hearing the butler announce you."

"Oh . . ." She faltered before continuing in a rush: "I talked to Cedric tonight and he told me that I never won any money at the cockfights and all the money he gave me came from you, so I—" She caught her teeth in her lower lip and stopped.

"So you what?" he prodded.

"Well, I realize I owe you a sum of money, so I have come to pay you."

"Lay it on the bureau," he said disinterestedly.

This was not proving to be easy. "I don't have any money," she finally managed to whisper.

"Then how do you intend to pay me?" he asked bluntly.

"I thought, well, I—" She tried again. "You see, your lordship, I—"

"How do you intend to pay me?" he asked again, making all her politely turned phrases seem inappropriate answers to his direct question.

She took a deep breath. "With myself."

"I see. You expect me to take the payment out in trade."

She gasped. "That's a rather indelicate way of phrasing it," she sputtered.

"If you'll pardon my saying so, it's a rather indelicate offer, Miss Brown. I have had few females offer to settle their debts by arriving in my bedroom in the middle of the night."

She could not read his voice, but it carried a tight, vibrant note that she had never heard before.

"Well," he said with a lazy drawl, "get in." She could hear the rustle of covers as he laid them back for her.

She gasped again. "But you have no clothes on!" she objected as she backed away a step.

He greeted that piece of prudery with a hearty laugh. "And what if I haven't? It can scarcely matter to an adventuress like yourself, Miss Brown."

Her resolve deserted her like a faithless rat leaping from a sinking ship. Her courage was gone in an instant, leaving her alarmed and shamed. "I can't," she said weakly.

"Then I suggest you do not come to gentlemen's bedrooms acting as if you not only can but will. However, if it makes you any easier, I do have clothes on the lower half of my body."

"Oh." She could feel her face growing hot.

"Now don't go shy," he said smoothly as he reached for her and put both his strong arms around her to lift her into the bed.

"No!" she cried, attempting to draw back.

"Miss Brown," Lord Stranham said patiently, "you have come to pay a debt, have you not?"

236

"Y-y-yes."

"I like the way you said that," he commented approvingly. "It has such a ring of confidence."

"Please, I've made a dreadful mistake!"

"Really? How can that be? You have been here ten minutes and we have done nothing."

"But I don't want to do anything!"

His hands still rested on her waist. "Changed your mind, have you?" he asked sympathetically.

"Yes. Oh, yes!"

"Now that," he observed, "has a more positive sound to it."

"There must be a thousand ways I can pay the money back! I could clean your house or I could mend your clothes or—" She broke off in a panic.

"It was a great deal of money," he commented, his hands never loosening their hold. "It is doubtful you could pay me back by acting as a servant."

"Then how?" she demanded, and swiftly added, "Besides t-this?"

"It will come to this eventually, I think," he said calmly. "I have a great interest in sharing my bed with you. I think we could remove to the country and share a very rewarding alliance."

She stiffened and suppressed a cry.

"There now, don't put yourself in a fret," he advised kindly, releasing his hold on her. "As you don't seem inclined to do so tonight, then we can wait until the morning and talk about it with a clear head. From the smell on your delicate lips, you have fortified yourself with some rather strong spirits to get yourself here. In the morning, as I mentioned, when you are sober, we can talk the whole affair over rationally. I daresay some sort of agreement can be reached."

As he spoke the marquis rose from the bed and walked to a dark corner of the room, continuing to talk as she

237

heard the rustle of his clothes as he pulled them on. "I shall call on you early tomorrow and we can discuss this more fully." He emerged from the corner and came toward her. "And now, my nightingale, I shall escort you home." He chuckled softly and nuzzled his face against her neck. "I shouldn't want anyone to, er, harm you. I want my merchandise unsullied."

She yanked herself away from him. "You are an animal."

"Quite," he agreed amiably.

He took her arm and led her through the house and out the back door to the stables, cheerfully hitching his horses to the phaeton as he whistled a song. When he finished, he helped her up into it and they left, driving through the night streets.

As they passed the murky glow of an oil lamp, Daphne ventured a look up into the marquis's face. At the same moment he looked down at her and grinned mischievously. "Ah, my dear, you were so anxious for me that you tracked me to my bedroom. I shall remember that in the days ahead when you are shy with me, for I shall know that underneath you are on fire for me."

She turned her head to stare stonily ahead.

They pulled up in front of her house, and he came around to help her alight, lifting her easily down and retaining his hold on her small waist as he looked down on her. She could just make out his features. They were wolfish in the obscure light, and she could see a glint in his eye.

"Daphne," he said softly, "you have played into my hand, you know. But I won't make life miserable for you. In fact, my love, I shall do everything possible to make it very enjoyable." He bent and kissed her as she stood rigidly. "Good night," he whispered, and released her, watching her as she fled into the house.

CHAPTER 27

That night sleep did not come easily. Daphne tossed and turned restlessly and finally abandoned the attempt altogether at five in the morning. She dressed carelessly in the flickering light of a single candle, pulling a gray poplin gown over her head before twisting her hair back into a chignon. Then she walked woodenly down to the front parlor and sat in the dark room. Slowly the morning street noises began to sound, and finally the sun peeped uncertainly through the window.

In the first light of dawn Daphne roused herself to ascend to her room and pen a letter to Mrs. Winter begging for her assistance to help them obtain positions immediately. Lady Cochmeer had not done so and she would obviously not do so now.

Writing in a hand that shook, Daphne told Mrs. Winter they were desperately in want of money and beseeched the older woman to help them. She closed with an apology for deceiving Mrs. Winter, however inadvertently, by leading her to believe they moved in high circles. Then she awoke Cedric and sent him off to deliver the message while she returned to the parlor.

She was not quite certain what she would say to Lord Stranham when he came this morning, but one thing was positive. She would not become his fancy piece. She had been willing to offer herself last night if it would have saved Joanna from losing Sir Robert, but she was not going to give her life over to the marquis. Nothing would be gained from it; the baronet would not marry the sister of his friend's mistress.

239

A tear drifted slowly down Daphne's cheek as she thought of the marquis. The terrible thing was that she loved him. This man who sought to use her and who wanted her only for her body was the man to whom she had given her heart. How it had happened, she could not entirely say. Her meetings with him had often been fraught with unpleasantness, and even now he was seeking to use her abominably, and still she loved him. No matter how desperately she adored him, she would not put herself in his power. She would find a job and pay the money back to him as she was able; she would explain all that to him when he came.

She was still sitting in the parlor when she heard a vehicle draw up in front of the house. Boots thudded on the cobblestone street, the sound changing to that of a determined stride as someone walked up to the door. Her quickened breathing was the only outward sign of nervousness Daphne betrayed, but her thoughts were whirling like dervishes.

The knocker sounded, and she started to rise, then sank back into the chair as she heard someone open the door.

"I wish to see Miss Brown," Lord Stranham announced confidently and cheerfully.

"She ain't 'ome," Cedric replied in a decidedly nasty tone.

"Stand aside my good man."

"No!" the servant retorted unequivocally.

"Don't be an ass, Cedric. I've come to see your mistress."

"She ain't 'ome," he barked, none of Lord Stranham's cheerfulness contained in his reply.

"Yes, I am, Cedric," Daphne called. She did not rise from the chair, although her grip on its arms had tightened considerably.

"I'll keep the scoundrel out!" Cedric called to her gallantly.

"I really don't think you can, Cedric," Lord Stranham said affably.

A moment later he showed himself into the front parlor, smiling happily. He came toward Daphne holding out a small nosegay of daisies.

She looked at him glacially, making no attempt to accept the flowers.

Lord Stranham appeared undaunted, however, as he strolled to the mantel and deposited the flowers in an empty vase. "You'll want to remember to water them," he cautioned. "Now then," he continued briskly as he returned to stand in front of her, "where was I? Ah, yes . . ."

He continued speaking, but Daphne did not hear his words. Her eyes were fixed behind him where she could see Cedric sneaking through the door in his stocking feet, stealthily creeping toward the unsuspecting marquis. Both of Cedric's hands were drawn up over his head clutching the largest frying pan their kitchen boasted.

"No!" she shrieked just as Cedric moved to bring the weapon down on his lordship's head.

The marquis whirled to face his attacker. "I say, Cedric, there's really no need for such harsh actions," he drawled.

"Ain't they?" Cedric demanded ferociously. "Where was this gel last night?"

"At my house."

"Don't lie to me!" Cedric roared, paying no heed to his antagonist's words. "I 'appen to know she was at your 'ouse."

"I believe I said she was there," Lord Stranham commented mildly, a faint touch of amusement on his face.

"What 'ave you to say for yourself before I crack your 'ead open?"

"I'd like to say that I wish you would not," Lord Stranham observed calmly.

"Well, if that is your last wish, it ain't a very good one,"

Cedric snarled as he stepped forward, making swishing circles with the pan while Daphne watched in horrified fascination.

"Cedric," the marquis said reasonably, "I should hate to hurt you."

"Fine words for someone who ain't in much place to do me any 'arm."

But as Daphne watched, Cedric's words were swiftly proven wrong, and the situation was reversed. One minute Cedric was waving the skillet menacingly and the next minute the marquis drove a lightning-quick hand underneath Cedric's flying arm, catching it in a viselike grip and twisting it until Cedric let the pan fall with a clatter. As Cedric rubbed his injured limb Lord Stranham turned back to Daphne. "Your pardon, but I wish to have a word with your butler, Miss Brown. I shall attend you in a moment."

"Don't hurt him," Daphne cried, springing up from the chair and starting forward as Lord Stranham ushered Cedric from the room.

He slammed the door unceremoniously in her face and locked it from the outside. "You wretch!" she screamed, banging both fists on the door so loudly that she could barely hear the voices of the two men in the hall.

In a few moments their voices ceased and the door opened. The marquis entered and pulled the door closed behind him. "Where were we?" he asked politely.

"What did you do to Cedric?" she demanded wrathfully.

"Do? Why I applied to him for permission to pay my addresses to you."

"That's outrageous!"

"It is a bit irregular," he conceded, "but since you have no family and it didn't appear I could ask for your hand until I had quieted him, it seemed the only sensible thing to do." He bent his head toward her and said solicitously,

242

"You don't look quite the thing, my dear. You're not feeling the effects of your drinking bout last night, are you?"

"No!"

"Good. I hate to criticize you, but I shouldn't like my wife to drink overmuch. Lord, I especially don't want her to drink just to gather her courage to get herself in bed with me. Actually, I had thought I should insist on sharing a bedroom."

"No!" she cried.

"No? I don't see why not. We shall, of course, have separate dressing rooms."

"I am not going to marry you." She dropped her eyes to the floor and added in a low voice, "You don't really wish me to."

"You're wrong on both counts," he contradicted smoothly. "You are going to marry me, and I very much wish you to."

Her eyes flew up to stare into the gray ones watching her intently. "That's preposterous! Only last night you spoke of setting me up in keeping."

"I never spoke of such a thing. If you misunderstood my innocent words, then I can only believe it is because you were so caught up in the role of being a fallen woman that you let your mind wander. Now," he continued, "I believe we should plan the wedding immediately, since I intend to be married by special license within the next three days."

Daphne stared at the marquis with disbelieving eyes. He was really asking her to marry him. Obviously he felt honor-bound to do so because of her indiscretion last night. It was equally her duty to refuse him; she could not let him sacrifice himself for her. But she found she could not frame the words of a refusal. She would marry him, she thought wildly, and be such a good and biddable wife that he would come to love her in time. He *must* come to love her in time, she thought passionately, because she loved him desperately and couldn't bear to think of living without him. Not now, not after he had offered for her.

"My—my lord," she stammered, "you do me a great honor, but men in your position do not marry dowerless girls such as me." She was not actually refusing him, but she felt she must tell him, remind him more fully, of the grave error he would be making in marrying her.

"It is true that men in my position frequently marry wealthy ladies, but I am not constrained to do so. And why should I? I am not in love with one; I am in love with you."

Had the marquis told Daphne that London had fallen into the Thames, he could scarcely have received more of a reaction. She gazed at him with an arrested expression, leaning slightly forward, her head tilted curiously as if to hear again the startling words he had just uttered. "W-what did you say?" she finally managed to whisper.

"I said that I wish to marry you because I am top over tail in love with you."

The words penetrated slowly. *Love,* he had said *love.* "But you are only offering for me because I have compromised myself and you feel duty-bound to marry me now," she argued.

"Were I to marry every chit I had compromised," the marquis said bluntly, "I should have been leg-shackled long since."

"Then you aren't offering for me because of last night?" Daphne pressed, still struggling to comprehend the full import of his words.

The marquis had had quite enough of talk. He pulled her impatiently from the chair and wrapped his arms firmly about her. "Daphne, you shall marry me and I shall not accept no for an answer," he began imperiously before breaking off in surprise. "Why are you crying?"

Daphne's lips were trembling violently, and tears slid

down both cheeks as she stared fixedly into his cravat, struggling to regain her composure. He really wanted to marry her! He loved her! In the emotion of the moment her tears were unstoppable. They continued to roll down her cheeks as she stood encircled in his arms.

"Don't cry. I shan't bully you into marrying me," he offered with an uncertain look at her. "If you don't wish to, then of course I shall accept no for an answer."

"Iwanto."

"What?"

"I w-want t-to," she managed to repeat, and then dissolved in another flood of tears.

The marquis pressed a clean handkerchief into her clutched fist. When she proceeded merely to wring the handkerchief in one hand as she cried into her other hand, he deemed it best to take matters in line. Pulling her against his chest, he murmured soothing words until she emerged from the soaking fabric of his waistcoat to look up at him with a face that was beautiful even with lashes rimmed with tears and a nose wet and red from the crying bout.

"See here, Daphne, I have seen you in any number of circumstances and I have never known you to let anything so overset you as my declaration has. You're a veritable cloudburst."

"I'm sorry." She sighed as she wiped her face with his handkerchief and tried to regain her dignity. She gave him a wan smile and looked back fixedly into his lapels.

But the smile had had its effect, for Lord Stranham tilted her chin back up to meet his gaze, and his lips came down slowly on hers. As Daphne responded to his kiss she was certain music was playing nearby—she could hear it. And it must be terribly light outside, for there was a series of vivid colors playing through her head as she felt the soft possessiveness of his lingering lips. She put her arms about his neck, and he pulled her closer to him as their kisses became more ardent. She realized dazedly that she must be spending a most improper amount of time alone with his lordship, but she didn't care.

Someone knocked on the outside door, and she pulled herself reluctantly back from his embrace. "We have company," she murmured.

"Tell Cedric to send them about their business," he replied, his eyes resting on her face as he took in the blush on her cheeks, the sparkle in her eyes, and the tantalizing quiver of her lips.

"Yes," she answered, pursing her lips in invitation.

Neither one looked up from their caress a moment later when the door to the front parlor opened. "I thought you were engaged to Peter Morne?" Robert Drayton asked in obvious confusion.

"She is," the marquis remarked as he pulled back slightly from Daphne, his eyes never leaving her face.

"Oh." Robert paused uncertainly before continuing: "As today is Joanna's eighteenth birthday, I have come to ask for consent to pay my formal addresses."

"Yes, a marriage would be lovely," Daphne said dreamily, her eyes focused on the marquis.

"Hold one minute," Lord Stranham said, releasing Daphne as Robert turned to go in search of his beloved. "I believe you should ask me for permission to pay your addresses and then you and I shall review your prospects."

"What?" Robert cried, turning back in surprise.

"It is only proper. In three days' time I shall be Joanna's brother, and I demand to know by what right you present yourself as her suitor. What have you to offer? In point of fact, I think you're a bit of an odd fellow, coming at this ridiculous hour of the morning to pay your addresses," Lord Stranham lectured. "Have you even thought to bring the chit any flowers?"

"Well, no," Robert was forced to admit.

"Take these," the marquis said magnanimously as he

walked to the mantel and extracted his own nosegay from the vase and crossed to thrust it into a stunned Robert's hands.

"What about your prospects?" Lord Stranham repeated.

"Well, I'm the only heir and I—" Robert broke off in confusion and then seemed to regain his footing. "Now see here, Mark, you know my prospects as well as you know your own. I may not be as rich as you, but I'm quite well to pass and I fancy I can support Joanna in fine style." He added defiantly, "And I don't care a fig if you refuse me permission to pay my addresses because I'm going to marry her. With every day that passes I realize how miserable I would be without her."

"What do you think, my love?" Lord Stranham asked, deferring to his betrothed. "Do you want that madcap for a brother, or should we wait for someone better to present himself?"

Daphne looked at Sir Robert. "I believe Joanna is somewhat partial to Sir Robert, so perhaps we should take him."

With a sulky look at the pair the baronet left the room to continue in search of his intended.

He was followed almost immediately by Mrs. Winter, who strode into the room and looked around with an air of self-righteous indignation. "There you are." She addressed Daphne accusingly, wagging a long finger at her.

"Mrs. Winter, what a surprise. I did not expect to see you so early in the morning."

"I should not be out of bed yet had not my maid brought me your singularly dull-witted note." Noticing the marquis for the first time, she stretched a thin smile across her face. "I see that you too were duped by the pair of them. Imagine, imposing on my good nature to help them obtain situations! I don't doubt they also took advantage of you shamelessly. I shall not have the first thing to do with either of them ever again. Certainly I will not aid them by doing anything so lowering as seeking employment for them. And I shall, of course, inform Mr. Morne that a marriage with *her* would be wholly unsuitable."

"I quite agree," Lord Stranham said, stilling Daphne's words with a raised hand. "It won't serve at all for her to marry Peter Morne. I am persuaded you are doing the entirely correct thing to cut them from your acquaintance."

Mrs. Winter nodded in satisfaction and turned a reproachful glare back at Daphne. "You are a shameless baggage looking only to improve your station."

"She is," Lord Stranham agreed with deceptive blandness before his voice took on a hard inflection, "improving her position somewhat. She will shortly be elevated from the daughter of an earl to the wife of a marquis. And upon the death of my father she will become a duchess."

"A duchess," Mrs. Winter repeated faintly. "You are going to marry h-her?"

"That is correct. Her sister, when she weds Sir Robert, will not gain such a lofty title, but I fancy she will be well respected."

"My dear," Mrs. Winter cried in delight, "you did not tell me! Only conceive what Mrs. Burns will say when I am received at your house!"

"I shouldn't think she would say anything because you will never be welcomed into our home." Lord Stranham looked at Daphne and asked in a soft voice, "I trust I speak for my future wife?"

She nodded.

"Then there is nothing more to be said." He walked to the door and held it for Mrs. Winter. "I suggest you take your leave, madam."

She stepped through the door, protesting, "My lord, you have misunderstood me entirely. Why, I—"

Slamming the door, Lord Stranham turned back to Daphne. "Insolent woman," he muttered.

"Are you offering for me because my father was an earl?" she asked quietly; her eyes never left his face.

He ran a hand through his hair before replying unsteadily, "I can't say exactly why I want to marry you. Part of the reason is because you have lovely soft curls and partly because you have struggled so hard to make your own way in the world and mainly because I would be miserable without you whether you were the daughter of an earl or a peasant. I've been terribly arrogant, my love. I thought only positions and breeding were necessary in a wife. My choice, a beautiful woman with a heart of ice, had all those attributes and would have made me miserable for the rest of my life. Somewhere in the course of my courting of Lady Diedre, my damnable pride gave way to the more natural emotion of love. I knew then that I would have to have you as my wife." He bowed his head and added in a regretful voice, "At first I did not understand the depth of my feelings for you and I sought to make you my mistress. Can you ever forgive me for that?"

"If you have made mistakes in your judgment of me, it is not more than I have done with you. From the beginning I was attracted to you, and I fought my inclination so hard that I tried to convince myself I disliked you intensely. I never did," she finished simply. "Now," she continued with a small smile, "wouldn't you like to kiss me again?"

As he moved toward her she backed around to the other side of the wing chair and regarded him playfully. "I wonder," she mused, "if I am doing the right thing by marrying you. Did you not mention that you wished to live in the country?"

"I did."

"Perhaps after the dazzling social life of Upper Wimpole Street I shall be bored there."

"You won't be bored. I shall see to that," he told her as he edged around the chair toward her.

"What shall we do for amusement?" she asked provocatively.

"I intend to show you that in due time," he murmured as he caught her in his arms.

From the bestselling author of
Loving, The Promise, and Palomino

The RING

Danielle Steel

A DELL BOOK
$3.50 (17386-8)

A magnificent novel that spans this century's most
dramatic years, *The Ring* is the unforgettable story
of families driven apart by passion—and brought
together by enduring compassion and love.

**Breathtaking sagas
of adventure
and
romance**

VALERIE
VAYLE

From the author of *Evergreen*

RANDOM WINDS

by
BELVA PLAIN

From a quiet village in upstate New York to elegant house
parties in the English countryside…from the bedsides of the
rural poor to the frenetic emergency room of a Manhattan
hospital…from war-torn London to luxurious lovers' hide-
aways on the Riviera, here is the unforgettable story of three
generations of doctors—and of a love no human force could
surpress.

A Dell Book $3.50   (17158-X)

"THE MOST ROMANTIC NOVEL SINCE LOVE STORY."
—Good Housekeeping

Change of Heart

SALLY MANDEL

Once in a long while, a story is so bursting with tenderness that its charm is irresistible.

That story is Sharlie and Brian's story, *Change of Heart*— a love story for a lifetime.

A Dell Book $2.95 (11355-5)